JACKDAW

DANIEL COLE

Ebook ISBN: 978-1-80508-273-6
Paperback ISBN: 978-1-80508-275-0

Cover design: Henry Steadman
Cover images: Henry Steadman

Published by Storm Publishing.
For further information, visit:
www.stormpublishing.co

ALSO BY DANIEL COLE

Ragdoll Series

Ragdoll

Hangman

Endgame

Mimic

Pornographic content: remove.

Hate preaching... Remove.

Far from feeling as though he were doing some good to make the digital landscape a more pleasant place to while away one's life, Matt felt dirty, part of the problem, no more than a minion employed to sweep the true state of the nation under the carpet to save anybody facing up to some harsh realities.

The truth was: it was all just an arse-covering exercise to document that 'appropriate steps had been taken' should an eleven-year-old wind up dead in his room, and far simpler than wasting resources on ensuring he receives the support he needs. But hate sells, and people far more likely to engage with their product when outraged or provoked – the foundation upon which all such companies are unashamedly built. After all, beneath every desperate plea for recognition sent out into the world, a *dislike* button waits expectantly – its sole purpose: to encourage discourse.

With a yawn, Matt moved on...

'*Jesus Christ!*' he gasped, falling from his chair in his haste to put some distance between him and what had just appeared on his screen. 'Justin!' he yelled without taking his eyes off it, his colleagues watching in alarm as he scrambled to his feet and sprinted the length of the office towards an empty glass room. '... Where is he?!' he demanded of his boss's prickly assistant.

'Conference suite... But you can't go in there!' she called after him as he tore down the corridor and burst into a meeting where the man he required was addressing a number of their most influential backers.

'Matt!' his boss blurted in surprise before quickly regaining his composure. 'Everyone, this is Matthew Lewis – one of our best and brightest. Matt, what can I do for you?'

'Sorry for the intrusion, but I need you... *now.*'

Without asking him to elaborate any further, the CEO turned back to his audience. 'Ladies and gentlemen, I'm afraid

PROLOGUE

There have to be worse jobs out there, Matt Lewis assured himself; although none immediately sprung to mind.

An offensive and inappropriate content officer at a global social-networking company, he was well into his third consecutive hour of wading through the bombardment of hatred, cruelty and perversions that inundated their systems on a daily basis.

Feet. He nodded, removing an abhorrently racist post flagged-up on a charity page dedicated to raising funds for a little girl with leukaemia. *He hated feet. Chiropodist, pedicurist... shoe salesman: he simply wouldn't be able to do it.*

He moved onto a far less public account, an eleven-year-old boy with just eight followers including his grandmother, and the message that had been festering there for over a week now informing him that he was 'an ugly piece of shit' before going on to advise he 'do everyone a favour' and just kill himself.

Remove.

Teeth! He couldn't physically bring himself to stare into people's revolting mouths all day long, not for all the money in the world.

you're going to have to excuse me for just a few minutes.' And with that, he calmly followed his subordinate out, the two men breaking into a sprint the moment they were clear of the doorway.

'Show me,' said Justin, tinting the windows of his office with the touch of a button as Matt brought the distressing post up on the wall-mounted screen, gagging when the familiar images returned. The first: lying on a dove-grey carpet, a beautiful woman wore a glittering golden dress, the silk scarf used to crush her airway still wrapped tightly around her neck. Her famous green eyes were bulging and red where the tiny blood vessels had taken it in turns to burst, and her ever-flawless skin was now decorated with five deep scratches, as if someone had dragged their fingernails across her face as a final insult.

But it was the second image Matt knew was going to haunt him...

2.1 million reposts and counting.

Heaving, he pulled the waste-paper bin towards him. 'Shall I block it?' he asked between steadying breaths, already reaching for the mouse; however, his boss appeared not to have heard him as he watched the numbers climb while the world shared news of the D-list celebrity's coronation into pop-culture royalty. '... Shall I block it?'

2.2 million... 2.3 million.

'Wait for it,' replied the man sporting flip-flops with a smart suit. He held his hand out as though it were poised over an imaginary button.

...2.4 million...

'...Wait...'

'For Christ's sake, Justin!'

'...OK... Now!'

The grotesque images were immediately replaced with a generic message to inform that the post had been removed for breaching the terms and conditions of the site, the counter below frozen at a little over 2.5 million. With a sigh of relief, Matt returned to the floor and the bin he suspected he might still be requiring, as his CEO took out his phone and found the details for the National Cyber Crime Unit, with whom he was in regrettably regular contact.

'...Hi, Karen? It's Justin Strong here at... Yes, that's right... Not exactly. I thought you'd want to be the first to know...' He paused, just to really sell his insincere distress. 'There's been another one.'

ONE

THE PRETTY LITTLE RICH GIRL WHO
INEVITABLY LOST HER HEAD

The metal doors parted.

...Silence.

A web of hazy sunshine spanned the entrance hall, dust particles roaming threads of light as she stepped into the capacious Knightsbridge penthouse.

'Hello?' called Detective Constable Scarlett Delaney, her voice carrying effortlessly, sounding like it belonged to somebody else: fuller, more assertive, the sparse room's acoustics stopping just shy of an outright echo.

...Silence.

Drawn toward the vista beyond the double-height windows, she made her way across the expanse of wooden floor to gaze out over mid-morning London, deceptively calm from the roof of the city – the skewed perspective that just eight to ten million pounds could buy you.

When the sun retreated behind a cloud, a ghostly reflection appeared in the glass, Scarlett surprising herself with the pang of sadness she felt on seeing just how out of place she looked amid such lavish surroundings. Her beat-up pair of Converse

All-Stars were doing little to smarten the ensemble of ripped jeans and a grey hoody. Feeling a little self-conscious, she quickly tied her hair up in the makeshift mirror – deep red smouldering against fair skin as she twisted the band into place.

'Scarlett?' a voice boomed from across the apartment. '...In here.'

'Coming!' she called back, giving herself one final look before heading over.

Evidence of a sophisticated party was strewn neatly across the living area as she passed beneath a glass staircase that seemed to defy the laws of physics where it zigzagged up to a stunning mezzanine kitchen. Empty champagne flutes assumed the role of crystal decorations upon the fireplace while a Steinway piano had been reduced to a serving table for finger food, most of which she couldn't even identify. Removing a pair of disposable gloves from her pocket, she followed the flash of the crime scene photographer's camera into the master bedroom.

'Sorry to call you in on your day off,' rasped Detective Sergeant Frank Ash, with his back to her.

'It's fine,' replied Scarlett, snapping a glove over her hand and then walking around the bed to regard the inevitable horror on the other side.

She froze, the scene that awaited her stealing her breath away... but she didn't let it show.

'Oh, brace yourself by the way,' Frank told her, only five seconds too late, as he regarded her inappropriate work attire. 'You look... *comfortable*,' he commented, a smile combined with a fondness of sunny holidays spent reading by the pool making his leathery face crease up to match his linen trousers.

'Am thanks,' she replied tartly, although only playing along with the man who'd had her back all throughout her fledgling career... and for a good long while before that as well.

'It's definitely them again,' he concluded, stepping aside to allow Scarlett a closer look, the sun streaming through the windows bathing her in light as she stared down at this latest, yet eerily familiar, scene. 'Number three. Same as always: strangled with a silk scarf, five scratches across the face. And I don't know if you'd noticed but she's been decapitated – the body inexplicably vanished.'

They both flinched when the photographer took another painstakingly structured shot of a decidedly unstructured bloodstain: '...Sorry,' apologised the man, moving away from them.

'...Inexplicably?' Scarlett prompted Frank.

'Two photographs were uploaded simultaneously onto social media with her own phone. The first, presumably taken in the moments following the strangulation, of the victim's body still intact to show the world what they'd done. The second, taken later, her decapitated corpse lying *right here* at sunrise.'

'OK.'

'The only window was double-locked from the inside.'

'OK?'

'The boyfriend was asleep in *that* bed there.'

'O... K.'

'And three friends who never left after the party were up all night sitting right outside that door.'

'Oh.'

'Yeah... "*Oh.*"'

'Do we know what they took yet?' asked Scarlett.

Frank removed his phone and jabbed at the screen with clumsy fingers, eventually finding a copy of the deleted social-media post. He passed it over to her. 'Spot the difference.'

'You mean aside from the fact that—'

'Yes, aside from the decapitation and missing body.'

She nodded as if to say 'just checking' and then, careful not to touch the discarded pair of jeans strewn across the floor, crouched down to take a closer look at the remaining head atop the blood-soaked carpet. She zoomed in on the digital pictures. '...Her earrings?'

'Bingo!' said Frank as Scarlett handed him back his phone. 'The Jackdaw strikes again.'

She frowned disapprovingly at him using the press-given nickname – uncomfortable with their shameless attempts to mythicise a dangerous and disturbed individual, turning the pain and suffering of real-life victims into entertainment for the masses – but the killer's ability to vanish into thin air and penchant for taking shiny trinkets as trophies was, unsurprisingly, too tempting to resist.

'Those were the pictures uploaded onto social media?' she asked him.

'Yep.'

'Anyone see it?'

'Only one or two...' he answered, Scarlett nodding in relief, '...million.'

'*Jesus*... Who is she?'

'You don't know?' Frank sounded surprised. 'Even *I* know this one, and I've got almost twenty years on you: Francesca Labelle.'

Scarlett looked none the wiser.

'*Officially*, she's a fashion... narista.'

'Fashionista,' the photographer corrected him, something in his tone suggesting that in an ideal world he'd be taking pictures of glamorous women rather than the blood spatters they left behind.

Frank nodded and pointed in his direction animatedly. 'Yeah. What *he* said. She was on that celebrity dating show where she got together with that guy with the beard from that band.' Scarlett shrugged. '...You know. With the video... with the emus in.' She looked over at the photographer for help. But then, shuffling self-consciously, Frank cleared his throat and began to sing a tuneless melody: "'I didn't do it... *No. No. No.* I didn't do-*ooo* it.'"

'Well, that's very fitting,' deadpanned a voice, seemingly from nowhere.

In confusion, Scarlett stood on her tiptoes, now spotting the pair of legs sticking out from beneath the bed.

'Forensic examiner,' explained Frank when she looked at him enquiringly.

'...And *unofficially?*' she asked before anyone else could jump out at her or break into song.

'She's just the spoilt rich daughter of—'

Raised voices reverberated out in the main room, followed by the sound of footsteps approaching.

'...Speak of the devil,' muttered Frank, hurrying out to intercept and pulling the door closed behind him.

Although only able to decipher occasional words of the heated discussion taking place out in the corridor, the anguish of a grieving parent was unmistakable, Scarlett listening closely as the aggression subsided and voices faded away.

'Edgar Crews,' the forensic examiner finished on Frank's behalf, resurfacing from behind the bed to bag a bloody swab.

'I thought her name was Labelle?' said Scarlett, her dislike for the little man she recalled all too vividly from a previous encounter giving way to curiosity.

Disinterested, he simply shrugged in response, the sunlight reflecting off his shiny head scattering stars before her eyes. Keen for any excuse to end their short exchange, she decided to take an intense interest in the piles of loose photographs littering the dressing table: their victim surrounded by a crowd of equally beautiful people, posing in a variety of designer outfits, holiday snaps featuring turquoise waters and a yacht approximately five times the size of her own modest townhouse.

She took particular note of the few images deemed worthy

of an actual frame: an especially scruffy-looking Border Collie, a young Francesca with her arms around an elderly woman and a yellowed photograph of her younger still – laughing as her father gave her a piggyback ride.

Heavy footsteps built to a crescendo as Frank reappeared in the doorway. 'I need you to take Mr Crews home,' he told Scarlett, checking that the billionaire was out of earshot before continuing. 'He's a state, but find out what you can. Might be the worst possible time to speak to him—'

'Or might be the best,' she nodded, reciting just one of the hundreds of similar pearls of wisdom he had bestowed upon her over the years.

'Precisely. Call me when—'

They were all blinded yet again in time to the snap of the photographer's camera, Frank glaring over at him in irritation. 'Seriously?!' he scolded the man, rubbing his eyes and turning back to Scarlett. 'Call me when you're on your way back.'

'Will do.'

As Frank focussed his attention back on the crime scene, squatting down beside the decapitation with an old-man groan, Scarlett made her way out, pulling the door closed behind her.

'...That was Deranged Delaney,' she overheard the obnoxious forensic examiner say as she loitered out in the hallway.

'*Detective Constable* Delaney to you,' Frank replied pointedly, making her smile.

She pressed an ear to the door.

'And you're... Well, you're *you*.'

'Last time I checked.'

'So, isn't that kind of... *awkward*?'

'We're fine.'

'But weren't you the one who—'

'I said we're fine!' snapped Frank, the uncomfortable silence from the other room palpable.

Scarlett remained where she was, however, continuing to listen in as the repellent little man presumably retreated back to the safety of his bodiless victim, eventually working up the nerve to mutter under his breath: '...*Clearly*.'

TWO

THE CHARM OFFENSIVE

Dressed in a classic Savile Row three-piece, tan Oxfords that resembled polished wood, and wearing his dark hair swept back off his face bar a few boyish strands, Henry looked the epitome of the English gentleman as he passed through the doors of Mayfair's famous Erstwhile House restaurant.

'Good afternoon, Mr Fairchild,' chimed the immaculate woman on reception as she got up to take his briefcase.

'Afternoon, Jennifer,' he smiled back, making her blush by remembering her name. 'You know, I *think* I'm going to hold onto this today,' he told her, rapping his fingers against the leather as he leaned in close and lowered his voice. 'I've tucked a cheeky little nine-millimetre into the inside pocket should this meeting take a turn for the worse.'

Laughing hysterically at the joke, which had really only been average at best, she then asked him: '...That's a gun, right?'

'It is,' he nodded, only setting her off again. '...I can show myself in.'

He walked through into the sumptuous dining hall, where little lights twinkled like stars from within the leaf-lined canopy and the sound of a jazz quartet carried unobtrusively from across the room. As always, he scanned the rows of tables in interest: for every lunchtime, without fail, they would accommodate a who's-who of the country's most powerful one per cent. Gorging themselves on the most pretentious of foods and finest of wines, they converged like this daily to discuss matters affecting the lives of millions, guffawing and slopping their drinks as they did so like plump little gods.

'*Ah*, Mr Lampert!' a red-faced diner greeted him as he passed.

'Mr Peterson. You're looking very well,' replied Henry, shaking the man's hand and moving on but only managing another ten steps before being stopped again, this time by the restaurant's eccentric hands-on owner. With an endearingly stained apron strapped like a bullet-proof vest over his white shirt, he was the very picture of a man torn between his business and his passion.

'Monsieur Chavasse!' he called with a thick French accent despite being born and bred in Burton-upon-Trent. Rushing over with a steaming bowl of orange liquid, he excitedly demanded that Henry 'Try! Try!'

Obligingly taking the spoon, he placed it in his mouth, closing his eyes to give the man's creation his undivided attention. After a moment, he nodded. 'Jacques, no word of a lie: that is *perfect*.'

'Not more pepper?'

'Definitely not.'

'More coriander?'

'No! Don't touch it. Don't even look at it for too long. It's absolutely perfect as it is.'

Delighted, the man slapped him affectionately on the back and then hurried off towards the kitchens.

Suspecting it might be time to find a new meeting place,

Henry made his way over to a private corner of the room where a stocky man with a well-weathered face was occupying himself on his phone as he waited.

Approaching the table, Henry cleared his throat. 'Mr Pavlov, I presume?' he said, extending a hand.

'Dmitry,' the man replied, still focussing intently on a life-time-best effort on *Candy Crush*. Dying only moments later, he swore aggressively in Russian and then put the phone down on the table to regard his well-dressed guest. 'And you must be Mr Devlin?'

'Henry,' he smiled, giving the other man a firm handshake and taking a seat.

'You drink with me,' said the Russian, making it sound more like an order than an invitation.

'Alright,' he replied, more than happy to oblige. 'A double Scotch on the—'

'You!...You!' the man called, clicking his fingers obnoxiously as if summoning a dog while Henry struggled to hide the look of contempt on his face.

'Yes, *sir*,' replied the waiter, clearly unaccustomed to being bellowed at from across the room.

'Another of these,' said the Russian, gesturing to his empty glass, 'for me and my friend here.'

'Of course, sir.'

But as the young man went to walk away, he reached out and grabbed his arm. 'Actually, why not just bring the bottle?' With a curt nod, the waiter left them to speak in private, the Russian turning back to Henry. 'The best vodka in the world. From my home country,' he explained proudly, thumping his fist on his chest like a gorilla. 'A hundred pounds a glass!'

Henry raised his eyebrows in an attempt to look politely impressed.

Several moments passed in which the man just stared at him without saying a word. Neither rising to nor submitting to the common intimidation technique, Henry simply waited, holding the Russian's gaze until their waiter returned to pour them out a measure each before placing the bottle on the table.

Simultaneously, the two men raised their glasses in toast and knocked their drinks back, Henry again having to stop his true feelings from materialising on his face.

'You are not what I was expecting,' the Russian told him, pouring out another two shots of liquid misery.

Leaning back in his chair, Henry waited for him to elaborate.

'Most men in our line of business...' He trailed off with a dismissive shrug, face decorated in old scars, hands blue with even older tattoos. 'But you – you're prettier than my prettiest mistress's stuck-up prettier sister.'

Needing a moment to follow the man's roundabout way of delivering an accusatory compliment, Henry smiled modestly. 'Well, I do like to take care of myself. Just one of the benefits of doing what we do... of making the lucrative *deals* that we do,' he said pointedly, forcing the conversation back on track.

The Russian glared at him, apparently debating whether or not he was insulted. 'You're right! Enough chitchat,' he said, slamming his fist against the table. 'I have thirty-seven girls on a cargo ship on their way over to you now... Good-quality girls,' he added lecherously.

'Our deal was for thirty-eight.'

The man chuckled. 'Breakage during transport. These things happen. You won't be charged,' he said, pouring himself another glass.

'Nationality?'

The Russian looked blank.

'...Of the girl who didn't make it,' Henry pushed him.

The other man frowned at the question, not seeing why it mattered. 'Polish. I think.'

Henry nodded, apparently satisfied.

'...And the payment?'

Reaching under the table, Henry retrieved his briefcase. Flicking the catches, he was careful to keep its tan leather back facing his associate as he opened it up. He glanced at the handle of the nine-millimetre revolver protruding from the inside pocket, removing a thick brown postage bag instead, which he placed on the table in front of him.

'Half now, half on delivery, as agreed,' he said, sliding it over.

'You couldn't just've given me the case?' asked the Russian as he peered into the bag.

'It's my favourite,' replied Henry. 'Matches my shoes.'

'Then why not bring a *different* case?'

'Because... then it wouldn't match my shoes, would it?'

Clearly at an impasse, the Russian decided to move on. '... We make delivery at eight-thirty tomorrow night... give or take,' he said, gesturing for the bill.

'Eight-thirty it is... How does the bar at Park Chinois sound?'

'Like *you* chose it... The Mendeleev?'

'Beautiful,' smiled Henry amicably as the Russian leaned in close.

'You might look respectable and proper, and you might talk like the Queen, but when it comes down to it, you're just as much of an evil piece of shit as I am,' he chuckled. 'Never can tell, can you?'

'Never can tell,' agreed Henry, ever the gentleman – getting to his feet to shake hands with his departing guest.

'Tomorrow night then, Mr Devlin,' said the Russian, downing one last drink before swaggering out.

Sitting back down, Henry wiped his hands on a napkin and removed his phone from his pocket, a red light flashing as it continued to record background noise – the incriminating sound file resembling a digital mountain range of peaks and troughs.

'Sir,' said the disgruntled waiter, dropping the unpaid bill beside the inexplicably expensive bottle of vodka.

Throwing the napkin down on the table, Henry begrudgingly reached for his wallet. 'Son of a *bitch*.'

THREE

CROCODILE TEARS

Scarlett was beginning to feel a little inadequate as she drove her Fiat 500 through the gates of Edgar Crews' expansive Surrey estate. On either side of the narrow lane, the trees bowed in on themselves as if in reverence of the returning lord of the manor, forming a sun-dappled tunnel that led all the way up to the house.

She pulled up and gazed out at a stately home plucked straight from a fairy tale: alive with tangled roses and beanstalk ivies that choked every last inch of the brickwork. Remaining staunchly professional, she made no comment when two peacocks strutted across the driveway in front of them – the rat she'd lost a shoe to the only thing roaming around outside her house.

She glanced over at Crews in the passenger seat. Despite only wearing a polo shirt and pair of chinos, he somehow looked as though he belonged surrounded by such extravagance in a way that Scarlett knew she never could – something in the way that he carried himself, the way he walked, projecting an utter self-assurance even in his current state. He didn't appear to have noticed they'd stopped as he stared down at his hands, lost in the company of his thoughts.

'Mr Crews?... Mr Crews?!'

Clearing his throat, he wiped his eyes and sat up straight, running his hands through his salt-and-pepper hair before turning to her. 'Yes. Sorry. Thank you.'

'There are some questions we're going to need to go over at some point,' Scarlett told him softly. She hadn't managed to get a thing out of him during their fifty-minute drive out of the city.

'Of course,' he replied, voice cracking.

'Will you be home tomorrow morning?' Crews nodded in reply. 'I'll come back then.'

A polite smile later, he climbed out and started making his way up the steps to the grand front door.

Having had an utterly wasted journey, Scarlett double-checked and then checked again that there wasn't a fluorescent bird under the wheels before putting the car in gear, the deep gravel sounding like a landslide beneath her. Rolling towards the turning circle, she spotted two members of staff talking over by the garages. With a glance in her rear-view mirror to ensure Crews had made it inside, she parked up alongside them and got out.

Wearing a maid's uniform, the woman in her late fifties had clearly been crying, while her grubby co-worker had to be a groundsman based on the amount of dirt outlining his well-chewed nails. Like guilty teenagers behind a bike shed, both quickly hid their cigarettes as she approached.

'Mind if I join you?' asked Scarlett, rubbing her forehead in a way that suggested it had already been 'one of those days'. The scruffy man hesitated but then offered her the packet and a light. 'Thanks. I needed this,' she told them, leaning against the wall as she inhaled a satisfying breath. 'Sorry. I'm being rude. I haven't introduced myself. I'm Detective Constable Delaney... Scarlett,' she added with a smile.

'Detective?' the older woman asked eagerly, as if she'd been hoping a police officer might wander between the woodstore and the garage at some point.

'*Annette*,' her gruff colleague warned her.

'But she's seen her!' the woman argued back, turning to Scarlett. 'That's right, isn't it? You've seen her?'

'Don't do it to yourself,' he told her knowingly. 'She can't tell us anything anyway, can you?' he said, also turning to face her.

Scarlett shook her head regretfully. 'I'm sorry.'

'See.'

Disappointed, the woman returned her gaze to the ground.

'I was just bringing Mr Crews back home,' she explained, the despondent maid scoffing on mere mention of his name. '... Not a fan of the boss then? Been *there*.'

'I'm not a fan of *any* parent who can turn their back on their own child like that man did.'

'It's not the time, Annette,' mumbled the groundsman.

'And when will it be?!'

'You're talking about Francesca?' Scarlett asked her.

'Eighteen months, at least, we haven't seen her... Isn't it?'

With an exasperated huff, her colleague nodded. 'Yeah. I'd say it's about that.'

'We basically raised that girl,' the woman continued. 'Not just us... everyone here. God knows her father never lifted a finger to help. And then, just like that, he tells her she's not welcome in her own home anymore. None of us saw her again... or ever will now,' she finished, bursting into tears.

'What about her mother?' Scarlett asked, stamping the cigarette butt into dozens of others on the ground.

'She died...When Francesca was just a girl. Car accident.'

Although there could be no doubt that Francesca's murder was the distinctive work of their serial killer, Scarlett was intrigued – primarily because she prided herself on her ability to read people and considered Edgar Crews' restrained grief as genuine as any she'd ever encountered. 'What did they fall out about?'

'Everything,' replied the groundsman.

The older woman shrugged. 'She was young – a teenager who was thrown into the limelight.'

'And who *repeatedly* went *out of her way* to sabotage her father's businesses while still expecting to be kept in the lap of luxury.'

The man clearly had a chip on his shoulder, although Scarlett was really struggling to pin down what it was: rich people in general? Entitled children not making their own way in the world? Failing to respect one's elders – even if said elder happened to be rich and entitled – by standing up to them and in doing so, to some degree, trying to make their own way in the world? She wasn't convinced he knew himself.

'She was idealistic,' argued the maid.

'And every new cause she decided to back *just so happened* to directly target his companies?' he fired back sceptically. 'Give me a break.' He turned to address Scarlett. 'She liked to think of herself as an "activist",' he chuckled, folding his mud-caked arms, 'but believe me, whatever people, trees or seas she was campaigning on behalf of were the very *last* thing on her mind.'

'That's an awful thing to say!' the woman scolded him. 'She didn't agree with a lot of the things she saw her father doing, so those were the things she tried to put right. Who can blame her for that?'

It was clear the surly man was growing tired of the conversation, Scarlett using the natural pause to enjoy the warm sunshine on her face, closing her eyes when a pleasant breeze laced with freshly cut grass blew across the grounds. She could have stayed in that spot all day and suddenly realised why: it was completely silent bar the sound of sheep in the adjoining field, a sensation she'd forgotten even existed having lived in the capital for so long.

'So, you think those are crocodile tears then?' Scarlett finally asked him.

'Now, I wouldn't go as far as to say that,' the groundsman clarified. 'The man's just lost his daughter after all. But if Mr Crews is the crocodile in this scenario then someone just sank the hunting boat for him... Excuse me,' he said, flicking the remainder of his cigarette away before disappearing round the back of the garages.

FOUR

STINK BREATH KENNY

'I'm stepping out for a bit,' announced Frank, needing a few minutes' reprieve from the severed head's watchful gaze. Knees clicking as he got back up, he headed into Francesca Labelle's sun-drenched living room and slumped against the wall. With his palm pressed firmly against his temple, he closed his eyes, willing the headache to pass. He'd been getting them more and more frequently of late.

'Detective Ash?' someone asked in concern from the balcony. He hadn't noticed them out there. Immediately straightening up, Frank pretended to yawn and shot the young officer an unconvincing smile. '...Is everything alright, sir?'

'Fine. What is it?'

'The boyfriend's lawyer is en route to Hyde Corner and asking for an ETA.'

'*Uh huh*,' replied Frank, disinterested.

'And the friends from the party – the ones who found the bod— ... the victim in that state are still across the road in the coffee shop.'

The word *coffee* the only thing he'd really taken from that sentence, Frank made a decision. 'OK. I'll go talk to them now. I'm on my phone if anyone needs me.'

On entering the café, Frank immediately spotted the table of dishevelled witnesses. Having been up all night drinking, the group had crashed out in a booth in the far corner. One of the women's dark make-up was smudged down her face like war paint from where she'd been crying, while another sat barefoot, having abandoned a perilous pair of heels on the table. Across from them, sprawled beneath a leather-jacket duvet and Ray-Ban eye mask, a third person appeared to have passed out.

Head still splitting, Frank decided to visit the counter first, stomach grumbling on regarding the assorted offerings behind the glass. 'Could I get a bacon roll and a—'

'*Errrr*, we're a *vegan* café,' interrupted the man at the till, who looked at Frank as though he'd just defecated in the middle of his store.

'Oh. Right... Egg then?' he tried.

'For the *second* time: we're a *vegan* café... *sir*.'

With a huff, Frank returned to the glass window to pick out the most appetising thing he could amid the elaborate display. 'What's that one... at the back?'

'That would be our famous chickpea, lentil and hummus rye bread,' the man informed him proudly.

'*Jesus!*' blurted Frank, pulling a revolted face. 'Forget it. Just a cappuccino then.'

'Suit yourself,' the server replied tartly. 'Is that with soy, almond or coconut?'

Frank just stared at him: '...Soy?' he answered unsurely.

'That'll be five pounds.'

'Of course it will,' he nodded, pressing his card to the reader. 'Don't suppose you have any aspirin or paracetamol back there do you?'

The man's mouth fell open as coffee sprayed out over the floor.

'...Tested on animals?' guessed Frank. 'Just give me the *bloody* coffee.' The appalled man pretty much threw it at him. 'Thanks. And the very best of luck with your... *business venture*,' he called back insincerely, making his way over to the washed-out assemblage in the corner. 'Afternoon,' he greeted them, placing his drink down beside the shoes in order to check his notebook. 'Lilliana, Coco and... Howard?' he double-checked, a bored pair of eyes peering at him over dark sunglasses.

'Howie.'

'Sorry to have kept you all waiting so long. I'm Detective Inspector Ash... Frank,' he added with a smile to make him seem more relatable, a trick he'd passed down to Scarlett on day one. 'May I?'

The group made a meal out of shuffling up to make room for him, Howie having to go through the inconvenience of sitting like a grown-up as Frank took them through a predictable set of questions:

Did you see anything unusual? – No.

Was there anybody there you didn't recognise? – Yes, a few people.

How did Francesca seem to you? – Fine.

And so on...

'...Stoner Pete, Big Al, Little Al...' the barefooted girl reeled off as Frank compiled a list of party guests. 'Oh, Stink Breath Kenny!...We call him that because—'

'He has stink breath?' Frank finished on her behalf.

'*Errr*, yeah!...You know him?' she asked in surprise.

'...Sure,' he told her, rapidly losing the will to live. He placed his pen down on the table. 'You don't happen to know any of these people's *actual* names, do you?'

Blank faces all round.

'...Their contact details then?' he tried, scribbling down phone numbers, Instagram accounts and Twitter handles alongside his collection of thirty names.

'And then there were the others,' Smudge Eyes told him. 'Friends of friends, you know? Like...' She paused mid-sentence to poke and flick at her phone, bringing up a photograph of an overweight man lying unconscious in a bathtub while dressed in a pink tutu.

Hedging his bets this wasn't their killer, Frank just added him to the list:

Passed-out Bathtub Tutu Man

It did, however, bring him rather neatly onto his next question: 'Do you have any other photos from last night?' he asked the black-eyed girl.

'Some,' she said, again jabbing away at her phone. 'Like... sixty.'

Frank almost choked on his horrible coffee. 'Sixty?!'

She nodded.

'You have sixty photos just from last night?' She nodded again, at a loss as to what the old man was finding so difficult to comprehend. 'The last photo I took was of a butterfly in my rosebush about two months ago,' he told her with a disbelieving shake of his head.

'That's... *nice*?' she said, looking to her friends for help.

'Would've been,' agreed Frank, '...had I not had my finger over the lens. What about you?' he asked No Shoes. 'Photos?'

'Yeah. I've got ...forty-two.'

'And you?'

Howie huffed, picked up his phone, possibly sent a text or

two and then answered: 'Only twenty-eight. *Sorry*,' he said, tossing it back onto the table.

'OK,' said Frank. 'Here's what we're going to do: those photographs are now evidence in a murder investigation.'

'Murder?!' gasped No Shoes, even her friends shooting her a look this time; it seeming highly unlikely that Francesca had cut off her own head, and damned-right improbable that she'd then gone to the trouble of removing her own body from the scene.

Ignoring her, Frank continued. 'You're not to delete *any* of them. Understand?'

They nodded unsurely.

'I mean it,' he said. 'I'm going to count them in, and I expect sixty... forty-two and twenty-eight,' he told them in turn. 'You'll be contacted later today by someone who'll give you instructions on where to up-and-or-down-load them. OK?... OK. You're free to go.'

The moment they'd cleared out, Frank closed his eyes and rested his head on the table, reaching out blindly to hold up the absurdly high pair of heels when the slap of bare feet came running back over.

'Thank you!'

'You're welcome.'

FIVE
OXBLOOD OR CHERRY VELVET?

Scarlett's phone went off the moment she stepped out of the lift and back into Francesca Labelle's apartment.

Mark (boyfriend)
Calling...
Accept Decline

Her thumb hovered indecisively over the screen for a moment but then she hurried across the living area, hitting *accept* on reaching the balcony. 'Hey.'

'Hey yourself. I've been trying to call you.'

'Yeah. Sorry. I was driving. What's up?'

'Nothing. Just wanted to see how your day's going.'

'Fine. Yours?' she asked, foot tapping impatiently.

'Good... Good. Got home about half an hour ago. Just got out the shower.'

She frowned. 'You're not doing that thing where you tie the towel around your head like a girl again, are you?'

A telling pause: '...No.'

'I *hate* it when you do that.'

'I have incredibly thick hair! Would you prefer I just shave it all off?'

'Sure,' she shrugged, nonplussed.

'...Well, I'm not going to.' A gust of wind blew the few loose strands of Scarlett's own hair across her face. 'So, where are you?' he asked her.

'Knightsbridge.'

'Very nice. Enjoying your day off?'

'*Uh huh*,' she replied noncommittally. 'I'm at a... social event... with a friend.'

She'd never been any good at lying.

'That "friend" happen to be Frank, by any chance?'

'...Yes.'

'And the "social event" you're so enjoying?'

'...A beheading.'

'You promised!'

'Hey, by all means print off a copy of my rota to hand to The Jackdaw should the two of you ever bump into one another.'

'Whatever.'

'Don't sulk.'

'I'm not. Can I at least cook for you tonight?'

'That would be lovely, but I've got to go now.'

'OK. Love you!'

'Yeah... OK. Yeah,' she replied, hanging up and slipping the phone back into her pocket.

'Not still doing that towel turban thing is he?' asked Frank from the doorway.

Scarlett smirked. 'How long have you been standing there?'

He joined her to look out over the city. 'So, any good come from dropping Crews home?'

'Saved a billionaire an Uber fare.'

'Hmm.'

'I'm going back tomorrow... But I did have an interesting conversation with a couple of members of staff...'

Five minutes later they were still standing out on the balcony, Scarlett having passed on what she had learned about Edgar Crews and his late daughter's strained relationship, Frank explaining his plan to obtain photos from every guest at the party in order to build a visual record of the evening.

For a few moments after, neither of them spoke as they watched the tiny insignificant people carrying out their tiny insignificant lives, but then Frank clicked his back and stretched as if preparing to do something energetic. 'Ready to go over the timeline?' he asked.

'Sure,' replied Scarlett half-heartedly, knowing from the previous murders that by doing so they were likely to create far more questions than they would answer.

'Come on then,' he said, leading the way back inside, where he took out his notebook and pushed his reading glasses up onto his nose. 'Right...The party started at around 8 p.m. and was mainly contained to the living area, kitchen and balcony. We've got a list of thirty-two names who were here over the course of the evening with a handful of others we hope to identify through the photographs. Francesca seemed happy playing hostess like usual until just before 1 a.m. when she complained of feeling unwell and headed to bed while the party continued out here.'

They walked through into the bedroom, the thick grey carpet rising like a flood around their shoes. Thankfully, both the severed head and their assorted colleagues were gone, only the dark bloodstain remaining behind as a reminder.

'At about 4 a.m. the beardy boyfriend stumbles through and falls into bed.'

'With Francesca?' asked Scarlett.

'He's... "eighty-six per cent sure",' read Frank. 'I'm not positive how he arrived at that number but he says, and I quote: "It was dark wo'nt it? And yea, I was buzzin', but not so buzzin' I don't notice my girl lying there on the flo." ...Make of that what you will. Either way, the party is winding down by this point but a small group continue drinking on the sofas just on the other side of that door.

'Now, here's where it becomes mildly vexing. At 7:37 a.m. the photographs of Francesca's dead body are uploaded onto social media with her own phone. One of which clearly shows her headless corpse lying right here,' – he gestured to the conspicuous bloodstain – 'in this very room at sunrise.'

'With the boyfriend still asleep in the bed?' Scarlett asked him, desperately trying to keep up.

'He's not in the shot but presumably so. *And* the all-nighters still drinking just ten metres away out there. It takes a little while for the post to start circulating. And then at 8:33 a.m. one of the friends out in the living room sees it and comes running in to find Francesca's decapitated head, the body gone.'

Scarlett opened her mouth to say something.

'And the window double-locked from the inside,' Frank reminded her, pre-empting the question.

'I mean, that's impossible.'

'No more so than the other murders,' he replied, looking at a loss at where to begin.

'Can I see the pictures again?' she asked, Frank taking out his phone, finding the email from the Cybercrime team and handing it over. 'So, we're thinking the *only* possible way that this series of events could've unfolded is if the boyfriend was in on it... right?'

'And he's lawyered up accordingly over at Lavender Hill,' shrugged Frank. 'But do you *really* see the lead singer of The Antidote teaming up with The Jackdaw? And then thinking he'll get away with it by going back to bed in the middle of the crime scene?'

'...No.'

'No.'

'So, what do we do now?' she asked him.

'*We* don't do anything. *I'm* going to head back to base, carry on chasing up party guests and more than likely get roped into helping the chief prepare a statement for the press. *You* go home. It's your day off, after all.'

'But—'

'Speak to Crews in the morning like you've already arranged. Now go home! That's an order.'

'Only if you send me a copy of these photos,' she said, looking down at them. '...Deal?'

Frank sighed heavily. 'Deal.'

Later that evening, Scarlett and Mark were relaxing on the sofa, the remnants of their favourite Jamie Oliver recipe crimson smears on plates that were yet to make it out to the kitchen. With her feet resting on his lap, Alkie the cat fast asleep on hers, they were each engrossed in their phones as the television entertained itself. While Mark deliberated over new curtains for the second bedroom, Scarlett gazed into the eyes of a dead girl, drinking in every last detail of the deleted social-media post and the few snaps Frank had let her take at the scene, magnifying various sections until they exploded into an incoherent mess of pixels.

'I can't decide: Oxblood or Cherry Velvet?' blurted Mark, holding out his phone to show her the two identical blocks of colour. '*Ooo!* Which have you found?' he asked, gesturing to the perfect shade filling Scarlett's screen.

'Decapitation red.'

'Oh... *Oh*,' he said, pulling the exact same face as Frank when confronted with the prospect of a vegan sandwich. '... What are your thoughts on blue?'

'Blue's good.'

'Blue it is.'

SIX

HALOS AND TARGETS

Scarlett rolled onto her side, looking at her phone just as the neon numbers rearranged themselves:

6:00 am

Careful not to disturb Mark, she slid out of bed, managing to avoid treading on Alkie en route to the bathroom.

By 6:19 a.m. she was showered, dressed, and pouring out a bowl of Rice Krispies while the kettle boiled. And by 6:31 a.m. she was outside in the dark, crawling about on the tarmac, checking under the wheels of the car before setting off into the city.

The sky above Knightsbridge was a calming inky blue by the time she showed herself back into Francesca Labelle's crime-scene apartment. Knowing she had only minutes, if that, Scarlett hurried through to the bedroom, referring to the deleted social-media post so to position herself precisely where their elusive killer had been standing only twenty-four hours earlier.

She wanted to see the room *exactly* as The Jackdaw had.

Question everything, Frank had always taught her. *So, why take the second picture at sunrise? Why take it at all, for that matter? Why from that particular spot? Why leave the removed head out of the photograph? And why frame it in such a way that the sunlit panes of glass demanded as much of the composition as the killer's macabre trophy?*

Lining up the edge of the bed with the three picture frames on the dressing table and discarded pair of jeans on the floor, Scarlett readied the camera app on her phone, recreating the killer's photograph with victim removed, watching the glowing patch of sky in anticipation.

All of a sudden, orange light spilled over the roof of the building opposite, reaching across the expanse of plush carpet as she took several pictures in quick succession, breathing colour into the dark bloodstain before washing over her feet. She closed her eyes to focus, asking herself *why now?* Listening for movement within the building, any vehicles outside, anything...

'Knew you'd be here.'

'*Jesus!*' she complained, holding her hand over her heart.

She turned to see Frank standing in the doorway, a take-away coffee in each hand. He was wearing the same clothes as the previous day, although that wasn't unusual in itself. His all-encompassing mantra of *if it didn't come out of someone, it's not dirty* must have saved him countless loads of washing over the years.

'What are you up to?'

'Questioning everything,' replied Scarlett.

'Good girl. Find anything?' He offered her one of the card-board cups.

'Just recreating the scene like you taught me,' she told him, slipping her phone back into her pocket to take the coffee from him.

'Send me a copy?'

'Of course.'

'Spoke to twenty-two of the party guests yesterday, got a few more to add to the list, and already over three hundred photos to go through with a fine-tooth comb.' He left an expectant pause before continuing. 'Yeah, it's *a lot* of work... Got to identify *every single person* in *every single picture.*'

'*Uh huh.*'

'This is the part where you jump in and offer to help.'

'Can't,' she shrugged. 'Need to be in Surrey with Edgar Crews at ten. Plus, no offence, but it sounds *really* boring.'

'Wonder if I should have a run at Crews this time?' Frank pondered aloud. 'He might open up to me, you know, man to man.'

'*Huh.* Interesting... Interesting,' said Scarlett, rubbing her chin as if actually considering it. 'Thing is, I feel I've already established a rapport with him, plus the house staff know me now and might want to follow up on our conversation yesterday. I'd hate for us to miss out on a possible lead because I wasn't there.'

Frank looked unimpressed. 'Know what your problem is?'

'What?'

'I taught you *too* well.' Scarlett smirked. '...Fine. I'm off to the office then for a day of hell,' he announced. 'You staying here for a bit?'

'Might as well.'

'And hey,' added Frank, pausing on his way out. 'If you're hungry, I'd recommend a bacon roll from that café across the road. Best I've ever tasted... *ever.*'

She was quite tempted. 'I might just do that.'

And with that, Frank showed himself out, chuckling to himself as he went – for revenge is a dish best served cold... and sandwiched between two pieces of rye bread.

. . .

Scarlett entered the living room. With almost an hour to spare before she needed to set off for her meeting with Edgar Crews, she thought it an ideal time to get to know their victim a little better in preparation. A set of shelves climbed the tall walls, displaying an eclectic collection of awards and achievements from all aspects of Francesca's life, two in particular catching her eye:

THE DONALD HOPE AWARD 2019
has been presented to *FRANCESCA LABELLE*
for her tireless work in helping families
of those communities displaced by major industry

W.A.W.I. Spokesperson of the Year
2021 – 2022
FRANCESCA LABELLE
In recognition of her continued efforts towards
equality in the workplace and a fairer world for all

Scarlett moved over to a console table and the piles of post that the recipient would now never have to sort. Knowing that Frank and their colleagues would have already flagged anything of significance, she started flicking through, finding five almost identical letters from various charities, all wanting to bring Francesca's attention to their well-meaning causes.

Although she'd only dipped a toe into the most superficial aspects of the dead girl's life, Scarlett was already getting the impression that everybody had wanted a piece of her – that the halo she was so desperately striving for looked more like a target to some.

Feeling a little sullied by the whole thing, she moved on, going through into a breath-taking bathroom fashioned out of bamboo and natural stone. As if chiselled from a mountain in the heart of the capital, a crude set of steps led up to a raised

platform where a free-standing bath was romantically positioned below a cluster of skylights. She turned her attention to a
large mirror surrounded by rock, tangles of fairy lights twisting
around the artificial flowers that 'grew' there. Unable to resist,
she walked over to it and flicked the switch, a thousand tiny
bulbs framing her in light.

Scarlett stared at herself for a moment, for once thinking
that she looked quite pretty as she tied her long hair to the side
in loose curls. Expensive make-up was littered all over the shelf,
presumably from where drunken friends had helped themselves, and the number of glasses balanced precariously around
the room suggested some had spent most of their night in there.

She checked both the other bedrooms, finding little more
than forgotten drinks and slept-in bedding, and then returned to
the master, hopping over the bloodstain on the floor to open up
the wardrobes. Scarlett felt her heart beating faster on seeing
the incredible collection of clothing inside: Versace... Gucci...
Vivienne Westwood, running her fingers down a stunning
emerald Victor & Rolf evening dress that seemed to ignite her
hair just for being near it – it was even in her size.

A fond memory returned to her: a perfect, sunny weekend
her younger self had been looking forward to for months, her
foster parents at the time allowing Frank and Eleanor to have
her at theirs for the entire bank holiday. While Frank tended to
the garden, she and Eleanor had whiled away the hours flicking
through dog-eared copies of *Vogue* and *Cosmo*, picking out all
the outfits they were going to buy 'one day': one day – when
life's fickle scales balanced out in their favour.

The lift made a mechanical whirr.

Letting go of the dress, Scarlett quickly closed the wardrobe
back up and headed out into the main room, listening as the
voices disappeared into one of the apartments below. Knowing
she needed to focus on the job at hand, Scarlett unlocked the
front door and stepped out into a soulless corridor lined with

maintenance cupboards, walking the length of it to reach another door at the far end. Noting the absence of any security cameras, she tried the handle and entered an industrial stairwell, all breezeblock and metal, that jarred with the rest of the luxurious building. She peered down at the concrete floor below but then followed the steps upwards instead.

'Please don't have an alarm... Please don't have an alarm... Please don't—' She shoved the bar to the emergency exit, relieved when it swung open without evacuating the entire building, and stepped back out into the chilly morning as the heavy door slammed shut behind her.

'Oh, shit!' she whispered, grasping the metal doorknob, which resolutely refused to budge. '*Shit! Shit! Shit!*' she hissed, shaking it in frustration. 'Nice one, Delaney,' she scolded herself, buttoning up her jacket as she turned her attention to the decked roof garden.

Candles lined the walls like colourful shrubs, trails of hardened wax snaking their twisted roots down the brickwork. Strings of dulled lights crisscrossed overhead while a Swedish-style hot tub occupied the far corner. As the breeze played with the discarded bottles and empty glasses, she unenthusiastically approached the edge of the building... and peered over, unsure herself whether she was relieved or distraught to see the metal fire escape that tumbled clumsily down the outer wall towards the alleyway below.

'OK. You got this,' she lied to herself. No fan of heights, Scarlett tentatively straddled the wall, giving the rusted stairway a few distrustful kicks before committing her entire weight to it. Slowly, she started to descend, pausing at the familiar bedroom window to confirm that there was no visible damage and no possible way of opening it from the outside. She then continued down, peering through the darkened window of the vacant apartment below: a pristine white carpet awaited the next aristocratic owners, along with a stripped bed and a few other items of furniture that the previous occupants had apparently deemed disposable.

On reaching the alleyway floor, Scarlett found just one security camera, which was directed at the entrance to the underground carpark a little further along. A set of commercial bins were propped up on tiny wheels: one general waste, one recyclables and one, inexplicably, for garden waste, should anyone decide to cut down the last remaining tree on the street. She lifted the lids in turn to find them all but empty, the few stray pieces of rubbish on the ground suggesting they'd been collected recently.

...But then she spotted something: a set of deep marks etched into the concrete, only noticing them because they'd reminded her of The Jackdaw's calling-card facial scratches. She crouched down, running the tips of her fingers over them. Uniform in colour and absent of any moss, they appeared fresh and could only have been made by something substantial – heavy enough to chew up the street like that.

A shadow flashed past the window above her head, which belonged to the flat on the ground floor.

Checking the time, Scarlett got back up and rounded the corner, the handful of eager reporters outside failing to notice her until she was already walking into the building's lobby. With a nod to the bemused concierge, who'd now seen her enter twice that morning without leaving, she knocked on the door to Apartment 1.

Several seconds passed and then Scarlett's eyes were assaulted with an epileptic's nightmare – a barrage of clashing colours – hot-pink walls lined with lime-green sofas.

'Yes, dear?' smiled a woman in her seventies dressed from head to toe in tight animal print and with more lipstick on her front teeth than even came in a regular-sized tube.

'Hi, I'm Detec—'

'Haven't you got such beautiful hair?' the woman interrupted her, surprising Scarlett by revealing that she actually *could* see.

'Thank you. I'm Detective Constable Delaney... Scarlett,' she added pleasantly.

'Oh, come in. Come in,' the woman insisted, stepping aside to allow her into her psychedelic lair. 'Absolutely terrible what happened... Terrible. That poor girl.'

'I won't take up much of your time. I just wanted to ask—'

'Someone already spoke to me yesterday,' the woman interrupted again. 'And I told them: I'm sorry, but I didn't see or hear a thing. I didn't even know she was having a party up there.'

'*Actually,*' said Scarlett, a little tersely, 'I wanted to ask you about the alleyway outside your window.'

'Oh,' said the woman, clearly a little disappointed. 'Well, I only use that room for storage. No one wants to look out at a brick wall.'

'I noticed a mark on the ground suggesting that something big and heavy had been out there at some stage. I was just wondering if you knew what that might have been?'

'The bins,' she tried.

'I don't think it's from the bins... Something bigger.'

'Oh, the skip!'

'Skip?' asked Scarlett, interest piqued, it striking her that should one need to remove the body of an impossible target from an impossible situation, a skip was possibly a very good way of doing so.

'Yes. It was there all last week.'

'Do you know who requested it?'

She opened her mouth as if about to say something useful. '...No.'

'Anyone in the building renovating?'

'Not that I know of.'

'Any idea when it was collected?'

'I'm sorry, dear. I hardly use that room, look out of that

window even less, and don't find the comings and goings of skips particularly noteworthy.'

'No. I suppose not,' said Scarlett, sensing a dead end looming.

'I did naughtily toss my old toaster away in it though,' she admitted with a giggle.

Peering into the woman's garish kitchen, Scarlett had an idea. 'What colour was it?'

'The skip?'

'The toaster.'

'Oh, it was lovely: burnt orange to match the microwave.'

'And do you still have any paperwork for it? An instruction booklet or a warranty?'

'It was quite definitely broken, dear,' the woman assured her, as though she thought Scarlett was asking in order to track down a freebie.

'It's quite a distinctive toaster,' Scarlett explained patiently. 'If you've got a serial number on any of the paperwork, I can ring round all the local tips, ask them to check their electricals, and if we get a match, we'll know where that skipload ended up. From there, we might be able to work out who took it in.'

'You're a clever little thing, aren't you?' said the woman, impressed. 'I'll go and have a look. I bet I've still got something.'

Five minutes later Scarlett was back in the alley taking pictures of both the original scratch marks and a second set that she'd found six feet away. She knew it was probably nothing but *why have a skip when there was no sign of any recent building work? Why place it so close to the bottom of the fire escape – a clear breach of health and safety regulations? And why risk blocking the rubbish trucks from accessing the bins when they so easily could have placed it further along?*

Question everything.

SEVEN

WHITE CLIFFS/BLACK MARKETS

Parked alongside South Foreland Lighthouse, the white van looked much like any other vehicle in the Dover viewpoint carpark, its driver like anyone else out for a mid-morning stroll across the clifftop. Long coat billowing behind him like a sail, he stood fast against a bracing wind, watching the boats come in... waiting.

Right on schedule, one of the dark shapes on the horizon revealed itself to be a cargo ship. With hundreds of colourful containers stacked haphazardly on its deck, it looked playful, innocent even – as though a child had drawn a picture of a boat. But the reality was that it was anything but, and the fortified port below as plagued by secrets and corruptions as any other border crossing in the world.

Returning to the carpark, the figure checked he was alone and then opened up the back of the van. Removing his coat, he pulled a bullet-proof vest over his head in its place, tucking a pistol into the inbuilt holster before assembling the components of an AK-47 assault rifle. Closing the doors back up, he climbed into the cabin, wedging the weapon securely into the passenger footwell.

. . .

The engine started up, the white van wheel-spinning out of the parking area in a cloud of dust, taking a sharp left onto the main road and then tearing down the hill in the direction of the port...

EIGHT

AFFABLY ACCUSATORY

'Follow the road for... *Doh!*... then you have reached your destination.'

Thinking nothing of it, Scarlett glanced at the screen to find that she had just two miles of country lane left to go, Mark having set the voice on the satnav to Homer Simpson for a joke that had become rapidly less funny when he couldn't work out how to change it back again. Rather than waste eighty pounds on a new one, she had simply learned to live with it.

When she pulled in to allow someone to pass from the other direction, her phone started ringing. With Mark having managed to cods-up her in-car Bluetooth as well, she remained in the bush she was parked in to answer it. 'Frank?'

'You there yet?'

'Almost.'

'Just checking you knew that Crews made some very generous donations to a number of Francesca's charities this morning.'

'I did *not* know that.'

'Tread carefully. Remember this guy's a *billionaire*. If you piss him off, he could literally buy the entire police force and blast us all into space, should he so desire. Don't upset him.'

'Affably accusatory?' she suggested.

There was a thoughtful pause. 'More... casually curious. Whatever the situation between him and his daughter, don't lose sight of who the real villain is here, and that you're *only* speaking to *him* to help us find them.'

'Got it.'

'Don't upset him!'

'OK! I've got it.'

Glass of water in hand, Scarlett followed Edgar Crews around the ground floor of his expansive Surrey home. In contrast to the pampered aristocrat waited on hand and foot she'd presumed him to be, the man appeared physically incapable of sitting still, finding an apparently endless supply of odd jobs that required his immediate attention. Shadowing him into the vaulted orangery, she got the distinct impression that her visit was impeding on his day far more than grieving for his daughter was.

'I need to keep busy,' he explained, reading her mind. 'If I stop too long...' He trailed off.

'Can you think of anyone who'd want to harm Francesca?'

He seemed surprised by the question. 'Correct me if I'm wrong, but I was under the impression the police were treating this as the work of... you know – The Jackdaw.'

'Standard question,' she shrugged, being careful not to disclose any details of the investigation.

'But the papers—'

'*Regardless* of what the press say,' Scarlett cut him off. 'So... can you think of anyone who would want to harm Francesca?'

Crews frowned. 'Alright. Like anyone with a significant online following, she had her fair share of detractors and... *trolls*, do they call them? As well as catching the attention of a few less-than-savoury stalkery types. But, as far as I'm aware, that was all resolved. Do you want me to make some calls to—'

'We have the police reports,' Scarlett stopped him. 'What about anyone from within your companies? I understand Francesca's crusades have cost you millions of pounds over the years.'

Crews folded his arms defensively. 'She campaigned fiercely on behalf of a number of very good causes.'

'And how was your relationship with your daughter?'

'Fine... Good. She made me a better person. I think I'd lost sight of what was truly important. She showed me that,' was his politician's answer.

'So, you didn't kick her out of the house eighteen months ago and tell her never to come back?'

Crews looked taken aback and then, for the first time since her arrival, gave Scarlett his undivided attention. 'Why are you asking me these questions?' he asked challengingly. 'My little girl was killed by The Jackdaw!' he told her, voice rising, eyes welling up. 'Who took a picture of her dead body and uploaded it for the world to pass around like a *fucking* cat video before cutting off her... her...' He took a few moments to compose himself. 'I don't even have a body to bury. And you *dare* come into *my* home and talk to me like this! Get out!'

'I just have a couple more—'

'I said get out!'

Calmly, she set her glass down, nodded curtly and headed for the door.

Pulling in down the road over the bush she'd already flattened once already, Scarlett held her phone to her ear:

'Yeah, Frank? Just a heads-up... I think I upset him.'

NINE

THAT JUNCTION IN MAXTON WITH THE CHIP SHOP ON THE CORNER AND THE DEAD PIGEON THAT'S BEEN THERE FOR MONTHS

An endless procession of lorries thundered out of the gates, the sound like a freight train building momentum. Like a herd of animals they clustered together, moving as one, finding safety in numbers. But at every fork in the road, another handful would peel off, leaving the pack diminished, weakened – presenting any skulking predator with an opportunity.

When a lorry carrying a distinctive blue-and-orange cargo container pulled up at a junction, a tatty white van rolled to a stop beside it, its driver facing forward while waiting for the lights to change, showing no interest whatsoever in the hulking vehicle that was encroaching into their lane.

They were being watched, of course, by the armed mercenary sitting up in the truck's passenger seat, who'd made the run over a dozen times before and always dreaded the opening start/stop half hour before they hit the open motorway. As the crossing traffic ceased and the lights turned green, his associate crunched the lorry into gear, the watchful mercenary letting his grip on the weapon in his lap relax as he turned his attention back to the road ahead.

. . .

Pulling a balaclava down over their face, the driver of the white van kicked the door open and calmly stepped out into the queuing traffic. Aiming the assault rifle up at the cabin of the truck, they pulled back on the trigger. With every click, the weighty weapon tried to kick free, but they held it firmly, spraying the windshield with bullets, the two men inside convulsing as though they'd been electrocuted.

There were screams as people began to panic, the tightly packed vehicles colliding and scraping across one another in their desperation to get away. But amid the pandemonium, two custom-painted Mercedes remained conspicuously still.

The gunman approached them, raising their weapon again in anticipation as the matt-black doors swung open in unison. Showering the first vehicle with bullets, he took cover, three bodies dropping to the ground as his gun ran empty. Discarding it, he pulled the pistol from his vest, waiting patiently while the windows above his head were blown out one by one, raining glass over him.

'*Perhot'-podzalupnaya!*' someone shouted.

The gunman frowned, his Russian a little rusty.

'*Perhot'-podzalupnaya!*'

'*Huh,*' he said, affronted, definitely catching the sentiment the second time round.

Clearly a little unhinged, the woman who had him cornered roamed between the remaining vehicles, seemingly with no regard for her own safety. As she continued to scream hysterical insults at him, she fired again and again, the semi-automatic shotgun in her hands powerful but notoriously slow to reload. Growing weary of her, he counted her erratic rounds as the tyre beside him deflated like a punctured balloon, and then casually stood up, discharging a single bullet that struck her directly between the eyes.

Sprinting across open ground, he rolled beneath the lorry

itself, seeing only one pair of boots approaching, heading straight for the driver's-side door.

They were still trying to salvage the truck.

Unable to wait until he'd located the final mercenary, he closed one eye to focus his aim and fired, the front of the leather boot exploding as its owner landed heavily on the ground, a look of fear crossing the battle-worn face in the split second before the next round snapped his head back violently.

Cautiously scrambling out from beneath the truck, he heard the click from above too late, the force of the bullet spinning him round as he fired a desperate shot that struck the person atop the cargo container in the chest, throwing them fifteen feet down onto the concrete.

'*Shit...*' hissed the gunman in pain, making sure that the vest had caught it before walking round to where a man lay gasping in the road, a constant trickle of frothy blood escaping from the side of his mouth:

'Please,' he wheezed, raising a pathetic hand to shield himself. 'I have family.'

His executioner reloaded. 'I suspect they'll be better off without you,' he replied emotionlessly, pointing the gun at the incapacitated man's forehead and pulling the trigger.

Gritting his teeth, he struggled to pull the bullet-proof vest over his head and then rubbed his shoulder. 'Son of a bitch,' he complained, giving the dead mercenary at his feet a few solid kicks for good measure.

As the first sirens caught on the breeze, he struggled up onto the back of the lorry, pulling the lever to open the container's heavy doors. Even through the balaclava, the smell that greeted him was nauseating, the metal box flooding with light to reveal a crush of filthy faces – thirty-seven women caged up and living in their own waste for days. Some looked afraid of him while others regarded him with hope as he stepped carefully between them, making it almost halfway in before pausing to lift the chin of an unconscious girl. And then, without saying a word, he scooped her up in his arms and carried her out.

Still holding his shoulder in pain, he closed up the doors to the white van and staggered back over to the dead mercenary lying in the road to give the corpse a parting angry kick, just as a sea of blue lights rounded the corner.

'Oh, *shit*,' he whispered, hobbling back to the driver's door as quickly as he could and speeding away.

TEN

SILVER CHAINS AND YELLOW TAPE

'Who's this one?' yawned Scarlett, feet up on the desk, blouse covered in Wotsit dust as she helped catalogue the now three-hundred-and-eighty-seven photographs from the party.

Frank stopped dialling the number that 'definitely, maybe, might' belong to the elusive Stink Breath Kenny and peered over the top of his reading glasses. 'Oh, that's Passed-out Bathtub Tutu Man prior to getting in the bathtub, putting on a tutu or passing out.'

'Well, of course it is,' she huffed, making a note as she realised they'd been at it for over three hours. 'It would be helpful if they'd all stop changing their clothes.'

'Tell me about it,' said Frank, returning to his phone call. 'One of the girls actually decided to dye her hair a different colour sometime between arriving at the party and midnight. That's four hours of my life working *that* out I'm never getting back... Oh, hello. Is that Stink— Is that Kenny?'

Frank had eventually agreed to let Scarlett go so that she could follow up on her skip theory. Paper-thin as it was, she had contacted every tip within a twenty-mile radius and now found herself at the scene of a previous murder, scouring the tarmac for any markings similar to those in the alley.

The Old Playhouse was tucked away down a narrow walkway in the heart of the theatre district, its unassuming façade an almost magical deception – the Tardis-like interior wrapping around the surrounding buildings to create a venue that felt simultaneously secret and as grand as any in the capital. As such, it was sad to see the long-standing London institution looking so forlorn – doors sealed with silver chains and yellow tape, its box office shuttered, tactfully vague signs plastered over posters for cancelled shows – as if every soul on the planet hadn't heard about what had occurred there, and to the production's leading lady, only twelve days earlier...

A lacklustre applause signalled the welcome arrival of a twenty-minute intermission – the sort of begrudging etiquette-dictated formality that made one question whether the audience was clapping the first half of the play or the fact that someone had finally dropped a curtain over it.

The reviews had been scathing, the auditorium bleeding seats every subsequent night, the show a stain on the CVs of all involved, and everybody knew it, everybody but the star of the play herself: Dame Edith Donohue, who had written, directed and produced this car crash of a vanity project straight over a cliff.

Jodie Watson hurried down the tatty backstage corridors – obstacle courses of wood and tools framed in peeling paint that were making her ridiculous job even more difficult. Personal assistant to Ms Donohue, she struggled to balance the bouquet of freshly cut flowers, the tub of hot soup from the restaurant opposite, bottle of part-iced water and two mobile phones, as she used her elbow to open the door to the dressing room. She had barely set it all down on the table when the self-proclaimed national treasure entered the room.

'Another wonderful show, Ms Donohue,' smiled Jodie, genuinely wondering which of them was the better actor as she quickly rearranged the flowers, removed the lid from the soup and unscrewed the cap from the bottle.

'Thank you, dear,' the older woman replied in a deep husky voice, slopping water over the floor as she snatched it out of her minion's hand. As she chugged half the bottle without pausing for air, she regarded Jodie with her judgemental eyes. 'You must eat, sweetheart. Look at you – you're practically wasting away!'

'I will,' Jodie promised, keen to change the subject before they could get onto the well-trodden topic of her appearance, having so far been informed that she looked like *Harry Potter with boobs, C-3PO... with hair and boobs, and that thing from the television with the bowl cut and the nice boobs... but without the boobs.* 'They're a little light on the ground again this evening, so I'll come and get you myself in precisely...' – she checked her watch – 'thirteen-and-a-half minutes.'

'*Uh huh,*' nodded the actor, pulling a face when she felt the temperature of the soup container.

'Oh, and your husband called... Twice.'

'Not his lawyer?'

'No. It was Peter.'

Dame Donohue huffed. 'What on earth does that vultureous hyena of a man want this time?' Unsure whether or not the question was rhetorical, Jodie remained silent. 'Very well. Go on then. Go on,' she was told while being unceremoniously shooed from the room.

Seven minutes later, Jodie was back in the same depressing corridor. Unable to say *no*, she'd somehow inherited the job of Assistant Stage Manager for the night on top of carrying out all the absurd tasks her employer had set her. She went over the list again in her head:

Once she had dropped the replacement chair by the stage, she needed to run back to the crew room and take Edith's shoes out of the fridge – an idiosyncrasy that had never sat well with the rest of the staff whose sandwiches were packed around them. Then, if she had a spare twenty seconds, she would treat herself to a swig of water and a biscuit before heading back to give Edith her three-minute warning, at which point she would loiter outside the door like an idiot until the star decided to grace them with her presence.

But despite her rammed schedule, as she passed the dressing-room door Jodie paused, listening in as her boss argued with someone over the phone and showed no sign of letting up. Looking at her watch again, she swore under her breath, picked the heavy chair back up and hurried towards the stage.

Another six minutes later, Jodie stepped aside as a member of the crew sprinted past, no doubt dealing with one of the last-minute disasters that seemed to arise on a nightly basis. Refrigerated shoes in hand, she approached the dressing-room door, concerned to hear Edith still on the phone and sounding more worked up than ever. It was the very *last* thing they needed right now – tears holding her make-up to ransom, a poor performance at this stage certain to seal the dying play's fate once and for all.

She knocked loudly. 'Two-and-a-half minutes, Ms Donohue!' she called, stepping back against the wall as the star of the show continued with her impassioned tirade on the other side of the door, the tired walls alive with the sound of the audience returning to their seats.

The yelling had ceased over a minute earlier, but Jodie hadn't dared move, leaving it to the last possible moment before disturbing her employer again, knowing that the proud woman would only resent her for walking in on her while upset. One of the crew came round the corner, raising her arms in a 'where the hell is she?' gesture.

'She's coming! She's coming! Right now,' Jodie assured her,

taking a deep breath and rapping against the door. 'Ms Donohue? It's time!'

…Silence.

She knocked again. 'Ms Donohue? We've got to get you to the stage!… Edith?… I'm coming in!'

She slowly pushed the door open to find the dressing room empty, the en suite bathroom similarly so, while the security bars on the windows cast dark shadows against the frosted glass.

'Edith?!' Jodie called half-heartedly, wondering whether she was going mad. She was utterly exhausted: *perhaps she'd been hearing things or somehow missed her coming out.*

And then, in a rare moment of sympathy for her unsympathetic employer, she noticed the jewellery box out on the dressing table, the box in which, despite all of her ranting and raving, she kept her wedding ring. A felt-lined container of hurt and regret, which now stood empty, the phone call perhaps prompting her to put the ring back on… or throw it away once and for all. No stranger to the actor's dramatic gestures, Jodie decided she would root through the bin just in case when she had a moment.

Hurrying along the corridor, she snuck through a set of doors that led to the auditorium just as the house lights dimmed, the spotlight overhead blazing to life, burning expectantly into the red curtain as it started to rise…

Nobody reacted at first – the indifferent audience clearly thinking they'd missed something, bemused murmurs asking why there was a severed head sitting grotesquely atop a table centre stage. Still nobody reacted until Jodie let out a bloodcurdling scream worthy of a far better production that caught in the hall's acoustics, sending a wave of panic through the crowd as people abandoned their seats, pushing and shoving their way towards the exits.

And all the while, the leading lady watched from her place up on the boards, five vicious scratches torn across her face and yet the hint of a smile curling at the corners of her mouth as if she'd known that, finally, she'd delivered a performance that no one would ever forget.

ELEVEN

LOST LUGGAGE

Scarlett was on her second lap of the theatre and earning herself enquiring looks as she searched for scratch marks beneath parked vehicles, mountains of rubbish bags and an unusually bitey homeless man named King Gerry. Dirty, hot and tired, she wished she'd started on the other side of the road when a double-parked delivery van pulled away to reveal a rusted skip behind.

'*Typical,*' she muttered, wiping her hands on her trousers as she crossed the street to peer over its metal lip at the stained mattress, piles of clothes and sheet of tarpaulin inside. But then something small and shiny caught both the light and her attention.

With a never-more-heartfelt sigh, she pulled herself up onto the grimy edge, arm extended as she reached for the sparkle amid the detritus. Fingertips brushing smooth metal, she stretched further still... losing her balance and toppling head-first into the assorted unpleasantnesses – a frustrated scream reverberating around the metal walls.

'Are you alright in there?' enquired a voice from above, a figure silhouetted in the sun all she could make out from atop her soiled mattress. 'Come on. Take my hand,' she was instructed, the unfamiliar voice upper-class and calm – 'speaking the Queen's English' as her mother would say – Scarlett allowing the stranger to help her back out onto solid ground.

Brushing herself off and detaching a stray ice-cream wrapper, she finally regarded her rescuer, disappointed in herself for the sharp intake of breath she took on first laying eyes on him: dressed from head to toe in black, he looked like the Cadbury's Milk Tray man.

'You've still got a little...' The man winced as he picked a piece of lettuce out of her hair and dropped it into the skip.

'...Thanks,' said Scarlett in embarrassment.

'Did you... lose something?' he asked while gesturing to the pit of despair in which he'd found her.

'Yeah... Yes. I dropped my...' Opening her hand, Scarlett peered down at her recovered treasure, '...bottle top,' she finished despondently.

A moment's silence.

'Well, it's a good thing you got that back,' said the ridiculously attractive man as he gave her a strange look, turned on his heel and swiftly resumed his journey. 'I'd move on though,' he called back to her. 'That's King Gerry's house.'

Surprised, Scarlett blurted: 'You know King Gerry?!'

While he waited for the traffic lights to change, her blue-blooded rescuer lifted his sleeve to reveal an old scar. 'Well enough to know that he's a biter,' he told her with a chuckle... and then he was gone, swallowed up by the capital's relentless crowds.

Shaking her head at the surreal encounter, Scarlett reached for her phone, hand patting an empty pocket. And then, with a roll of her eyes, she peered back down into the filthy skip. '...Bollocks.'

· · ·

Another half hour later, and finally accepting that the endeavour had been a monumental waste of time, Scarlett was already walking away when she noticed light that hadn't been there earlier escaping the crime scene's frosted windows.

'For Christ's sake,' she complained, marching over to the stage door.

The Old Playhouse's maintenance staff had been permitted to stay on, using this first significant reprieve from performances since World War II to carry out some much-needed restoration work. They had all been explicitly instructed to steer clear of Edith Donohue's dressing room and from setting foot on the stage, which had both been cordoned off just to really hammer the point home.

The peeling door had no handle – a security feature – and a bell sprouting frayed wires that led nowhere – *just a bloody annoying feature* – Scarlett having to use her open palm to bang against the metal in order to be heard. Almost a minute passed before a sun-starved vampire of a man finally came to the door, physically recoiling when the sunlight struck his face – that, or he'd spotted the silver cross dangling around her neck.

Scarlett held up her ID in greeting, the man stepping aside as she marched past and headed up the stairs, surprised to find the door to the dressing room closed, the yellow tape still in place despite the puddle of light seeping out over the front of her shoes. She momentarily considered calling for backup but then quickly dismissed the thought, knowing she'd never live it down should she drag a team of her colleagues across the city to discover a lamp on a timer switch.

Removing her taser from its holster, she gently twisted the handle, long legs climbing through the web of police tape as she pushed the door open...

'Police! Show me your hands!' she ordered when confronted with a dark-haired man kneeling over a bag on the far side of the room, something vaguely familiar about him. He had his back to her, but she saw him reach for something inside. 'I wouldn't if I were you,' she warned him. 'I've got a loaded taser pointed right at your back.'

There was a moment of deliberation... before the man half-heartedly raised his arms.

'Get up,' she told him.

With an unsubtle check of his watch, he did as he was told.

'OK. Now, *very* slowly turn around,' Scarlett instructed him, eyes widening on realising that it was the same Good Samaritan from before, a look mirrored across his own chiselled features on seeing the bottle-top-collecting ghoul from the dumpster again.

She saw him look down into the bag at his feet.

'I want you to take three steps to your right,' she said firmly, the taser now pointed squarely at his chest.

'You're *quite* sure about that?' he asked her in his dulcet tones.

'Do it!' she told him.

With a shrug, he took two-and-a-half wide steps into the bathroom before looking down at the toilet with curiosity. 'Now... do you want me to climb up on top or shall I just place one foot in the bowl?'

Scarlett could feel herself going red. 'Now, take *six* steps to your left... which is *my* right.'

'Ah, I see,' he said, watching her closely as he moved across the room. He seemed to be rather enjoying himself. 'Look, if you'll just give me a chance to expl—'

'Who are you?' she cut him off.

'Henry Devlin,' he smiled pleasantly, force of habit dictating that he offer his hand. 'Oh... right,' he realised, raising it back in the air. 'The pleasure's all mine, Officer...?'

'*Detective Constable* Delaney,' she replied curtly. 'And what are you doing in here, Mr Devlin?'

'Investigating the murder of Francesca Labelle.' She must

have let the confusion show on her face because then he added, 'By looking into her killer's previous escapades.'

'You're police?' she asked dubiously.

'God, no,' he laughed, looking again at the bag just a few metres away. 'No. I'm a private investigator hired by Edgar Crews to track down and bring to justice the person responsible for his daughter's murder... the serial killer known as The Jackdaw.'

Scarlett's grip on the taser slackened ever so slightly. 'A private investigator? It's only been twenty-four hours,' she said, still watching his chin dimple even though he'd stopped talking.

'Has it though?' he asked in appropriately theatrical rumination. 'Because as I understand it, the first murder took place almost *two* weeks ago.' He gave her a boyish smile. 'It would seem Mr Crews didn't trust you to be any more successful now than you had on the previous murders... No offence.'

'But he trusts *you*?' Henry shrugged modestly, a floorboard creaking under his weight as a frown formed on Scarlett's face. *Crews certainly had the means to hire additional resources, and her disastrous meeting with him that morning would have done little to instil confidence.* 'Well, then it's a shame you're going to have to disappoint him too. This is an *active* crime scene and you are trespassing, which means you're...'

'Endearingly roguish?'

'...under arrest.'

'*Oh*. Detective... Delaney?' he double-checked. 'My phone is in my pocket,' he told her, already reaching for it. 'Just let me call Crews and—'

'Don't move!' Scarlett shouted, Henry returning his hands to the air as she produced a pair of handcuffs. 'Turn around. Hands behind your back.'

'Is this *really* necessary?' he asked, rolling his eyes as he faced the wall and brought his wrists together.

Taser still trained on him, Scarlett edged closer, a floorboard creaking as she placed her foot down.

Henry reacted on instinct, spinning round and pushing the weapon away as she pulled the trigger, the two barbs wasted into the hollow wall as an electrified clicking filled the air. Scarlett kicked out, buckling his kneecap. But when she went for his throat, he caught her arm, the self-defence classes with her sister paying off as she used his own weight against him. Although failing to flip the muscular man over, the pressure on Henry's shoulder caused him to cry out in pain, the two of them stumbling in a mess of legs and wires back across the room and through the full-length mirror in the corner.

Scarlett groaned as she felt Henry roll off her and onto the floor. Bent awkwardly around the broken frame, she had hit her head against the wall. She tried to get up but was unable to free her foot, glass falling like rain in time to her every movement. She lay motionless for several seconds... then heard Henry ask in a strained voice: 'You alright there, slugger?'

Scarlett merely coughed in response, freeing even more glass from the frame.

Crawling back over, he held his hand out to her. 'Come on.'

She tentatively reached out and took it. But as he went to pull her towards him, she brought her other hand out from beneath her, attempting to drive the taser's direct-contact electrodes into his body. Grabbing her arm, he twisted her wrist back until she dropped it, sliding the weapon a safe distance away.

He sat back and shook his head, amazed by her refusal to quit. 'Should we try that again?' he asked, watching her grope around on the floor for the largest shard of glass she could find. 'God, you're stubborn,' he told her in exasperation, glancing at the doorway on hearing voices close by. He looked back at her regretfully. 'OK. Have it your way. You take care of yourself, Detective Delaney,' he told her, staggering to his feet and limping out, the door closing behind him as Scarlett finally allowed herself to lose consciousness.

It was early evening by the time she came back around. Unravelling her limbs from the wooden frame, she crawled into the centre of the room and rolled onto her back. Her hair was encrusted with dried blood, a hundred tiny cuts decorated her arms and a lump the size of a golf ball had come up on the back of her head.

'*Shit,*' she whispered, on the verge of tears. 'Why am I so *stupid?*'

She removed her phone from her pocket, seeing the fresh crack in the screen and discovering that she had four missed calls from Frank. Knowing he'd be worried, she went to phone him back... but then hesitated, embarrassed by her handling of the situation – going in alone, allowing an unarmed suspect to get the drop on her like that. There was no way that this latest development could remain between the two of them and she, of all people, couldn't afford another mark against her name.

But accepting there was no way around it, she dialled his number, her eyes falling upon the black duffle bag still sitting against the wall.

'Scarlett?' Frank's voice buzzed from the speaker.

'I'll call you back,' she mumbled, hanging up on him as she dragged herself over to it and ripped open the zip to unpack the contents: a professional lock-picking kit, a pair of black gloves, a bottle of oral morphine, a hunting knife, a crowbar and three cheap mobile phones – clearly burners.

Excitedly, she picked up the first: locked.

The second: also locked.

And then the third: locked... but the most recent text message still displayed on the screen:

Today: 0794647241
We have things to discuss.
The Mendeleev – 8:30pm

The numbers adjusted in the top right-hand corner of the display. Whatever this meeting was, it would take place in just two hours' time, she realised, heart beating faster – partly for having an opportunity to redeem herself before anyone could find out that 'Deranged Delaney' had severely screwed up, partly for having reason to go to one of the city's most renowned and exclusive restaurants, and if she was being completely honest with herself, partly in anticipation of seeing the mysterious stranger again.

Wobbling slightly, Scarlett struggled to her feet, glass showering over the floor as she did so. She looked down at herself: blouse torn and spotted with blood, her dark trousers covered in dust and God knows what else. There was no way she could walk into The Mendeleev dressed as she was: she'd stick out like a sore thumb. He'd spot her coming from a mile off. And should she lose him again after failing to alert the team, she could kiss her career goodbye.

So, if she was going to risk everything she had worked so hard for on a single roll of the dice, she was going to need something to wear...

TWELVE

THE GIRL IN THE DEAD GIRL'S DRESS

Scarlett climbed out of the black cab and into the drizzle falling over Marylebone High Street. As it pulled away, she caught sight of herself in a darkened shop window, despite the rain, staring at her reflection as if it didn't belong to her. Playing with her hair where it fell in loose curls down her neck, she wondered how she'd even ended up there, having spent the previous two hours in a dreamlike daze.

She worried what it said about her that the most beautiful she'd ever looked was when wearing a dead girl's dress, adorned in her jewellery, rooting through her most treasured possessions just as The Jackdaw must have done.

She had silenced the nagging doubts in her mind, justifying her actions through necessity: her resolution not to live up to the black cloud of a reputation she'd inherited, the frivolous purchase-prohibiting depths of her overdraft, the fact that she couldn't get home and back within the tight timeframe, let alone get made up for the night without Mark asking questions from his spot in front of the television.

But that's all they were – an attempt to justify it.

The truth was: she'd wanted to play dress-up in the swanky

penthouse more than anything in the world, that she had googled the emerald Victor & Rolf dress six times since that morning, and would have paid spa-day money just to have that bathroom to herself while the sunset ignited the clouds beyond the skylights. She'd been owed this one night. She'd owed it to Eleanor. But now, standing out in the rain, the magic was beginning to lift.

'What are you doing?' she asked her reflection, the full weight of her reckless behaviour suddenly dawning on her. *Perhaps 'Deranged Delaney' wasn't so far off the mark after all.*

She turned to call the cab back, watching it disappear round the corner just as the heavens opened. More concerned about the dress than herself, she hurried across the street to shelter beneath the upmarket restaurant's canvas canopy, the man seeing a couple into a limousine rushing over to open the door for her, apologising as if he hadn't done it promptly enough... as if she belonged there.

'Oh. No. I'm just...' she started, spotting a taxi a little further down the street, the cold rain sparkling in its headlights. But then she looked back at the inviting doorway, the sound of a piano carrying on the escaping warm air... 'Thank you,' she smiled, stepping inside.

Scarlett's pulse quickened, the room having an instant ambience – the gentle roar of conversation, laughter and music an intoxicating cocktail. Grand chandeliers burned lazily over the distinguished clientele, each unique and casting the room in a faux candlelight. At the far end, a wide staircase curved up to an intimate bar area, where the people waiting to be seated flickered in and out of the clusters of light as if they were sitting amongst the stars.

* * *

At a table in the centre of the room, Henry was momentarily distracted by the vision of emerald and fire gracefully climbing the stairs towards the bar.

'I'm sorry?' he asked, turning back to the Russian sitting across from him, who smelled like a distillery and clearly hadn't changed his clothes since their meeting the previous day.

'I said, you've not touched your food,' he told Henry while using his hands to gnaw the meat off a chicken leg.

'No. It feels like it's missing something.'

The Russian shrugged. 'So... today was a bad day. These things happen.'

Leaning to see round the other man's head, Henry watched the woman in green take a seat at the bar. 'Obviously, my employer will no longer be paying you the other half of the money.'

The Russian nodded enthusiastically, his mouth full. 'Of course. And *obviously*, I will not be returning what has already been paid.'

Henry frowned. 'You know, I'm not so sure that *is* quite as obvious,' he replied, moving his soup aside to conduct their business.

'This is a risky game, my friend. I am now eight men down and have my entire operation plastered all over the news.' He pointed at Henry with the knife he'd apparently only just realised was there. 'That initial payment was for *me* taking that risk for *you* in the first place, allowing people in fancy suits like yourself to keep your hands clean,' he said, looking Henry up and down with a derisive sneer. He sighed. 'Tell your people I can get them more girls. Same terms as before but with a five per cent discount for... unforeseen supply-chain disruptions.'

'Five per cent,' nodded Henry. 'That's very generous of you.'

The other man raised his hands as if to say, 'Well, that's just the kind of guy I am.'

'The thing is,' continued Henry, rubbing his chin for dramatic effect, 'we don't *actually* want any girls... never did, in fact... just one, and we got her back this morning.'

Setting his cutlery down, the Russian sat up straight, watching Henry as he took a sip of his drink and checked his watch.

'Five minutes ago, a team of my associates stormed the Value-Clean Carwash and Automotive Centre in Stratford,' Henry continued in a pleasant tone. 'A front for your more nefarious business endeavours, I believe?' The man didn't respond. 'I'd say it's safe to assume that everybody there is now dead, and they have recovered the money along with anything else you might have been stashing on the premises.'

The Russian visibly tensed up, beads of sweat forming on his flustered face.

'That good, *huh*?' teased Henry. 'I suppose it would be stating the obvious at this point to say that it was *me* who despatched your eight employees this morning. *Me* who concealed a tracker in yesterday's payment to locate your base of operations. *Me* who broke in last night to obtain details of the shipping container you were using to traffic women into the country. And, of course, *me* who poisoned that chicken you've been devouring for the past ten minutes while you were ogling that lovely waitress over there.'

Coughing, the Russian stared down at the plate in front of him in horror before pushing it away. Now sweating profusely, he loosened another button on his already half-open shirt, gold chains tangling in thick chest hair as his shaking hand struggled to lift his glass of water to his lips.

Henry swirled his drink calmly as he watched the man across from him lose control of his hands altogether, his panicked breathing the only sound he could muster. 'That's the paralysis setting in,' Henry explained cheerily. 'It should reach your lungs in approximately three to five minutes, at which point you'll lose the ability to breathe and...' – he picked up his untouched bowl of soup and carefully positioned it in front of the other man – '...*splash*,' he smiled darkly.

The Russian looked at him with desperate eyes, his face now so red he looked as though he might explode.

Leisurely finishing the rest of his drink, Henry got up to button his jacket. 'Now, if you'll excuse me, Mr Pavlov, I think I might head upstairs.'

* * *

Unaccustomed to the sensation of being watched, Scarlett nursed a drink at the ornate bar, already tiring of the attention. Feeling self-conscious, she pretended to scrutinise the cocktail list, but then glanced back over the restaurant to discover that Henry was no longer in his seat. Her eyes darted from the restrooms – to the smaller restaurant bar – to the main doors, but he was nowhere to be found, the only thing quelling her panic the fact that his dinner guest was still seated at the table.

...And then she heard a familiar voice behind her.

'A double Scotch on the rocks.'

'The Macallan, sir?'

'Perfect... The eighteen not the twelve.'

'An excellent choice.'

Forcing herself not to react, Scarlett slowly turned back to the menu in her hands, obscuring her face from him as the rain intensified against the glass roof above, smearing the moon across the sky. She flipped the page, sensing him staring at her.

'How is it *even* possible,' he began, 'that a dress as stunning as that is still only the fifth most striking thing about the person wearing it?'

She fought the smirk attempting to form on her face. 'Only the fifth?' she replied in feigned confidence without taking her eyes off the cocktail menu.

'My mistake: sixth... I just noticed your smile.'

She looked decidedly unimpressed. 'And what do you think of my eye roll?'

Henry laughed, handing the barman his credit card without even waiting to hear the price when he brought his drink over. 'May I?' he asked, gesturing to the stool beside her.

'You may,' she replied, trying not to breathe in the appealing mix of sandalwood and cedar that suddenly filled the air between them. Mark, in comparison, tended to smell of Lynx body spray and burnt toast.

'So, are you waiting for someone?'

'Perhaps,' she answered coyly.

'Husband? Boyfriend?... Date?'

She remained silent.

'...Girlfriend?' he asked, losing hope. '...A fellow nun?'

Despite herself, Scarlett laughed. 'Perhaps,' she smiled. 'You?'

'No. I was here for a... *thing*, but they should be leaving us...' – he straightened up to peer over the tables below – 'yeah... *any* minute now,' he told her, tapping his watch to ensure it was still running before giving her his full attention once more, the hammering rain drowning out the hushed conversations around them, it suddenly feeling as though they were the only two people in the crowded room. 'Are you hurt?'

'Huh?'

He gently touched the inside of her wrist, where dozens of tiny cuts that the make-up had failed to conceal climbed her forearm. Flinching as though he'd just burned her, she pulled her hand away.

'Oh. Right. No... Alkie... My cat,' she explained, thinking on her feet. 'Something... *bad* happened to him once. He's only got three legs,' she added, aware that she was babbling. Somehow she'd forgotten while preparing for her undercover mission that lying had never been her strong suit.

'A three-legged cat named Alkie,' he chuckled. 'Now you've *got* to tell me more.'

'No. I don't.'

'...Or not,' he laughed again, appearing mildly entertained by her mood swings. 'So, what do I call you?'

'How about *failed conquest from the bar this evening*?' she suggested, sliding back into character.

'*Ouch*,' he said, staring into the amber liquid at the bottom of his glass.

'Scarlett,' she told him on realising she'd gone too far.

'Scarlett,' he nodded, watching her in fascination. 'It's pretty.'

'Thank you.'

'Well, Scarlett, I'm Henry Macallan,' he introduced himself, holding a hand out to her.

'Macallan?'

'Macallan,' he confirmed.

'Wasn't that Macallan Scotch he just poured you?'

'So it was.' He shrugged innocently. 'No relation.'

'*Uh huh*. Then I'll be Scarlett Malibu-Coke... It's hyphenated,' she informed him, seizing her opportunity and finally turning to face Henry as she took his hand, recognition dawning over his face as the handcuff clicked tightly around his wrist.

He looked down at their linked hands in interest. 'Just to make *absolutely* sure I'm not misreading the situation...'

'I'm *arresting* you,' she snapped back.

A sigh. 'Well, that's one way to ruin a perfectly pleasant conversation, Detective Delaney,' he smiled, impressed. Again, he appeared to be enjoying himself far more than he ought to have been. 'I didn't... You look incredible. It would seem falling through furniture becomes you,' he joked, reaching for his drink but then frowning in frustration when the handcuffs pulled taut. 'Did you really have to cuff both our drinking hands though?'

'I didn't,' she grinned, taunting him by taking a sip from her glass as he stretched awkwardly for his own.

'Oh, because your left is my...' He trailed off. They'd already been over all of that once already. 'So, what now? You've been drinking. Are we to get the Tube like this?'

Ignoring him, Scarlett tried to wave the barman over between rooting through her bag for her Metropolitan Police ID, cursing under her breath on realising it wasn't there.

'I find it interesting you'd come after me alone,' Henry continued as the young man prepared cocktails for another customer. He watched her closely when she didn't respond. 'Shall we at least get another drink while we're waiting?... My treat.'

'Thanks, but I'm working,' she replied distractedly, trying again to catch the bartender's attention. Giving up, she struggled to take out and unlock her phone one-handed, deciding it was easier to just make the call herself.

'*Yeah*, I actually need to speak to you about that,' Henry started in his loaded way. 'That Russian gentleman I was having dinner with is *not* my friend. In fact, I'd go as far as to say that he *might* be the very worst human being I have ever come into contact with.'

Phone to her ear, Scarlett peered down at the man he was referring to, only half-listening as she formulated what she was going to say to her backup when they arrived.

'What I'm trying to tell you is that I wasn't here for social reasons. I too am working.'

'You were... investigating him?' she asked innocently.

'Is that *still* what you think I do?' laughed Henry. 'No... No. I was here to *kill* him.' Scarlett looked appalled. 'Well, technically,' – he looked a little awkward – 'I already have: poison. To tell you the truth, I have absolutely no idea how he's even still upright.'

'*Jesus Christ!*' she whispered, looking back down at the

dead-man-sitting. 'We've got to do something!' she said, hanging up on her call to dial 999 instead.

Henry sucked his teeth. 'Even if I wanted to, which I really, really don't, he'll be long dead before anyone gets here.' He reached out and gently lowered Scarlett's phone hand to the bar. 'This presents us with a small, yet entirely manageable, problem: when the police start questioning people, which they will, they're going to tell them that *I* was the one having dinner with him. And after they speak to our barman friend here, they're going to know that a non-uniformed police officer... *that's you*... was sitting here drinking and flirting with her suspect... *that's me*... while a man died just twenty feet away. Speaking objectively: doesn't sound good.'

'I was undercover! I was trying to get close to you!'

Henry held up his hands in peace. 'Hey, *I* know that... I won't be passing it on, of course. But I do know it.'

'*Shit*,' complained Scarlett, putting her head in her hands.

'May I offer a solution?'

'Let me guess: let you go?'

He shrugged. 'OK. You don't sound particularly enamoured. We'll put a pin in that for now. But what I *was* going to say is that we should leave... quickly.'

'Leave?'

'Quickly,' he reiterated. 'I think it would be better for *both* our sakes if we weren't in the building when he... you know.'

'Dies.'

'Yes – dies. I have a *very* capable lawyer, who has informed me on more than one occasion that a little bit of distance goes a long, long way. We'll just head down the street. You keep the cuffs on me at all times, and we tell your backup that after confirming my identity, you followed me out to make your arrest. Naturally, in return, I'll misplace all memory of this conversation as well as any details you'd like forgotten from our encounter earlier in the day... *surely* the reason behind you deciding to come after me alone this evening.' Torn, Scarlett looked again at the man below. 'This is sort of time sensitive,' he pushed her.

'I know that! But how am I supposed to trust you?'

'Oh, you can't. And you definitely shouldn't. But in this *particular* case, I assure you that you *can* and you definitely *should*. Come on. Don't forget your coat.'

Looking pained, Scarlett watched the man sitting alone amid the packed restaurant out of the corner of her eye.

'He's drooling,' she whispered. 'Like, *a lot.*'

'Yeah. That's not good... Time to go,' Henry pressed her.

'Oh, God!' gasped Scarlett, getting to her feet, the metal chain between them pulling Henry up from his chair, both of them watching the Russian sway uncontrollably... then miraculously look as though he might be alright for a moment... before landing face down in a bowl of soup.

As unfortunate as this development was, Henry couldn't help but chuckle, forgetting he was still attached to Scarlett when he celebrated with a mini fist pump. The disapproving look she shot him was interrupted when, within the space of a few seconds, everything went to hell.

A woman at a neighbouring table started to scream, her husband heroically rushing over to pull the man from his minestrone-flavoured end. Several other people leapt to their feet, including the man about to receive his flambéed Bombe Alaska, knocking it clean out of the waiter's hands and all over the drowned Russian on the floor, whose penchant for bad vodka and aversion to changing his clothes meant that he went up like a wicker man. As the room descended into blind panic and the fire alarms tripped, the sprinklers were activated – shorting out the chandeliers as they swung and flickered over the indoor storm.

'*Wow.* That escalated quickly,' said Henry, brushing his

soaked hair off his face as he turned to Scarlett. 'I swear, I'm usually far neater than that.'

Dazed, she didn't seem to hear him, too distracted watching people stampede towards the exit to notice his expression change as a new plan formed in his mind.

'Detective Delaney?' She didn't respond. 'Detective!' This time she gazed up at him. 'Don't fight me.'

'What?' But before the confused frown had even reached her face, Henry had pulled her into him, spinning her round so that her back was pressed up against his chest as he wrapped a powerful arm around her neck, her futile attempts to fight him off growing weaker and weaker until, finally, she felt herself black out.

THIRTEEN

THE ASPHYXIATION SITUATION

Scarlett's eyelids fluttered open, the tap of lazy rain all she could hear as she gazed out at the twinkling city below. Raising her hand to her swimming head, she winced, the pillow beneath her damp, her hair still wet.

When she struggled to sit up, the bed springs pinged beneath her shifting weight as she found her left hand caught on something. In confusion, she tugged again, disturbing Henry who was dozing in the chair beside the bed.

Disorientated, but now very much awake, Scarlett leapt to her feet and made for the door, travelling all of two steps before the chain pulled taut. A spectacularly ungraceful somersault later, she landed in a heap on the floor.

'*Oww!*' she complained.

'*Ahh!*' concurred Henry, rubbing his shoulder. He'd removed his wet jacket (as far as possible) as well as his shoes and rolled up the sleeves of his white shirt. In irritation, he peered down at her. 'What on *earth* are you doing?' he asked, receiving a vicious kick to the thigh in response, which he suspected had been intended for another target altogether.

'What am *I* doing?...What am *I* doing?!' she spat back up at him. 'Trying to escape my captor!'

'*You're* the one who handcuffed *me*, remember?!'

'You tried to kill me!'

'No, I didn't.'

'You strangled me!'

'More of a "hold". But, yes. And I apologise for that, but the situation was beginning to get away from us. I thought we could use a little time to... regroup,' he told her pleasantly.

'Give me *one* good reason why I shouldn't just scream for help right now,' demanded Scarlett.

'Be my guest. I very much doubt anyone would hear you anyway,' shrugged Henry, reaching for the TV remote.

She pressed her free hand to her temple and closed her eyes, trying to force her scattered thoughts into some sort of order. 'Where the hell are we?' she asked him. 'And why are we so high up?... I thought I'd died and was on my way up to heaven when I first opened my eyes.'

'Well, you're not far off there,' he told her. 'This *is* the Presidential Suite at the Hilton on Park Lane, twenty-eight stories up.'

'And how did I get here?' she asked through gritted teeth, the fog not lifting any.

'You were carried.'

Scarlett opened her mouth to say something but faltered, the idea of this dangerous stranger carrying her through the rainy streets of the capital tripping her up.

'...By a drunk man I tipped twenty pounds,' Henry added, obliterating that image. He reached for his drink, the glass besieged by a collection of empty miniatures, making Scarlett wonder how long she'd been out for. 'Can I tempt you with something?'

'No,' she replied shortly.

'Helping you off the floor perhaps?'

'...Fine,' she mumbled, ignoring the amused look on his face as he pulled her up onto the edge of the bed. 'Thanks. But don't you *ever* touch me again,' she warned him. 'Understood?'

'Understood,' nodded Henry sincerely.

Scarlett looked down at the beautiful dress, already knowing that it was ruined: neither emerald nor floaty anymore, it now resembled a soggy piece of seaweed she'd become tangled up in. Finding the sight of it too depressing, she instead took in her surroundings, making a mental note of the shiny letter opener lying out on the bureau before watching a wispy cloud pass by the living-room window as the city lights sparkled in all directions, tiny cars zipping about in the darkness like fireflies.

'I looked for the key in your handbag,' said Henry, snapping her out of her daze. 'Hope you don't mind. Didn't find it... *obviously*,' he added, jangling the chain between them. 'Otherwise I would have ordered us some room service.'

'We literally just came from a restaurant,' she said distractedly, reaching across the bed for her bag.

'Yes. I did order a bowl of soup... but there was something floating in it,' he smirked.

'...Was that a dead Russian joke?'

'It was, yeah.'

'Funny,' she said, in a way that suggested she'd found it anything but. 'It was right here!' she shouted in frustration, emptying the contents of the bag all over the duvet. '*Argh!* Can't you just pick it or something?'

'I *could*... but you've got my kit,' he reminded her.

'*Argh!* This is just *perfect*,' she laughed bitterly. 'Trapped half a mile up in the air handcuffed to an assassin.'

'Technically,' Henry interjected, 'I'm a *fixer* not an assassin. There's a difference.'

'*Oh!* I'm *very* sorry if I offended you,' she retorted sarcastically. 'Please, enlighten me on the nuances of your particular criminal activities. How is it, *exactly*, that you "fix" things?'

Henry looked as though he regretted opening his mouth. 'Usually by assassinating them,' he mumbled. 'It's a... subtle difference.'

Scarlett shook her head in exasperation. 'What a mess!' she said, falling backwards onto the bed, almost pulling Henry's arm from its socket in the process. 'What were you *really* doing in that dressing room this afternoon?... The truth this time.'

'I told you: investigating Francesca Labelle's murder. I do tell the truth ninety-nine per cent of the time.'

'You also told me you were a PI.'

'OK. That was a one per center,' he conceded. 'But Edgar Crews did hire me to hunt down a serial killer.'

'Then the two of you can share a cell together,' she said, sitting back up and looking around the room anxiously.

'Everything alright?' Henry asked her.

She looked uncomfortable: 'Yeah. It's just... I really need to use the bathroom.'

'Second door on the left,' he told her.

Raising her shackled hand, she shot him an impatient look.

'Oh,' said Henry before pulling a troubled face. '...*Oh*.'

'Don't look!'

'I'm not looking!'

'You're listening!'

'Well, what do you want me to do?'

'Sing something,' Scarlett told him, arm stretched across the room from where she had insisted he stand in the bathtub and pull the shower curtain between them. 'God, this is so degrading.'

'It's no picnic for me either, you know?'

'Sing!'

Of course he can hold a tune as well, Scarlett thought bitterly as she provided an unwelcome accompaniment to his rendition of Bill Withers' 'Ain't No Sunshine'.

'OK!' she called, standing back up and flushing the chain. 'That wasn't so bad, was it?'

'I'm glad you feel that way,' said Henry, holding the shower curtain back for her like a gentleman. 'In you get then.'

'Huh?'

'My turn.'

Scarlett's smile crumpled.

'...Come on!' he hurried her.

With a hefty sigh, she nodded, climbed into the bath, and pulled the curtain closed.

Scarlett had finally allowed Henry to fix her a drink. Sitting on the bed, she used her free hand to write out a short text message to Mark telling him she loved him and not to wait up, while Henry struggled to pick the lock from his spot on the floor.

'So,' he started, concentrating intensely on the bent hair pin between his fingers as her hand hung limply over his chest, 'I've got a confession to make.'

With exhausted eyes, Scarlett looked down at him.

'...While you were out—'

'*Knocked-out*... by you.'

He huffed and started again. 'While you were *knocked-out*... *by me*, I made a couple of calls. It's only natural to want to know who one's handcuffed to, after all.'

Scarlett shuffled uncomfortably. 'And?'

He didn't answer right away, looking hopefully at the pin in the lock before hearing a snap and placing it with the other three he'd already broken. He held his hand out expectantly. Rolling her eyes, Scarlett released another tangle of hair and handed him a replacement.

'I know who you are.'

'And who am I?' she asked defiantly.

'Well, for starters, I know that *Delaney* was your mother's maiden name, that you were an only child and that you moved over from Ireland when you were six. Your actual name is Scarlett O'Callaghan and your father was Kieran O'Callaghan aka The Four-Leaf Cleaver.'

Scarlett didn't respond as her breathing quickened, her face taut to conceal any emotion.

'...The unfittingly blithe nickname he picked up along the way,' Henry continued, 'on account of him being Irish and avoiding capture for so long on blind luck and very little else. He would stalk, bind and torture his victims – eight women over the course of seven months, all redheads... like his daughter. All except the last one: your mother, who he killed while you were playing in the back garden.'

'Stop,' Scarlett whispered.

'They think she must have found out and—'

'Stop it!' she shouted over him. She wanted to storm off, but having to take him with her seemed to rather defeat the point. Neither of them spoke for several moments. 'Congratulations, you did your homework.'

'It wasn't my intention to upset you,' Henry told her evenly, returning to the lock. 'I just wanted you to know that I think you're pretty remarkable.'

Reaching for her gin and tonic, Scarlett scoffed.

'I mean it: the daughter of a serial killer becoming a homicide detective,' he said, shaking his head in disbelief. 'That's the stuff of trashy novels. I couldn't work out for the life of me why you had come after me alone tonight. It was... reckless. But I think I understand it now. You must have to work *ten times* harder than everybody else to prove yourself. All of them waiting... *hoping* you'll finally snap and confirm what they've been whispering behind your back this entire time: that whatever was wrong with your father, whatever gene, whatever misfire in the brain, will one day reveal itself in you.'

Scarlett felt a lump in her throat, feeling as though her innermost thoughts were being aired out loud and yet, rather than being admonished for them, she was being applauded.

'We're from different worlds,' he told her, 'but it seems to me that, right now, our interests are aligned. I think we can help each other here, pool our resources – legitimate and... less so – in pursuit of a common goal.'

'And what resources *specifically* are you bringing to the table in exchange for those of the *entire* Metropolitan Police Service?' she asked him derisively.

'Well, for one: I know how The Jackdaw pulled off the murder at The Old Playhouse,' he replied smugly, watching her expression change. 'Something that the *entire* Metropolitan Police Service *doesn't*. I'm very good at what I do.'

'Even if you've got a theory, it doesn't mean—'

'I found the body.' He cut her off to save her wasting her breath. 'I *know* how she did it.'

'...She?'

'Just a hunch. And I *know* I can work out how she did the others. We could make one *hell* of a team, you and I. You want to stop The Jackdaw? *This* is how you do it.'

'Stop, or kill?'

Henry considered his reply. 'Would the world be a better place now had your father been locked in a cage for the rest of his days rather than being gunned down in the street like he was? Honestly, if you could go back and change it, would you even want to?'

Scarlett looked away from him.

'...I propose a truce – a temporary partnership. You, Scarlett *O'Callaghan*, will be the detective who single-handedly hunted down The Jackdaw – irrefutable proof that you deserve your place on the force more than anyone.'

'And when we find them?' she asked in a hoarse whisper, amazed to hear the words leaving her mouth.

Henry's self-assured smile flickered for the most fleeting of moments. 'Then we're done,' he shrugged simply. 'All bets are off.'

'I won't let you kill them.'

'And I won't let you take her alive.'

'Best deceit wins then?' she suggested, meeting his eye.

Henry smiled, Scarlett yet again surprising him with her unflinching determination. 'Why don't you get some rest? I'll keep working on this, and we'll head to the theatre first thing.'

Yawning at the mere mention of sleep, Scarlett knocked back the rest of her drink and made herself a little more comfortable on the bed, the rain intensifying as if on cue. 'If you think I'm closing my eyes for *one second* with you around, you've got another thing coming.'

'Suit yourself.'

'So... how did they do it?' she mumbled.

'Tomorrow,' said Henry, but already talking to himself, as within seconds of her head hitting the pillow, Scarlett was snoring gently.

He removed the hair pin from the lock and placed it on the side with the others before reaching into his pocket to find the small silver key. Loosening the metal from around his wrist, he retrieved his jacket from the chain, pausing to watch Scarlett sleep for a few moments. And then, smiling sadly, he draped it over her, leaning in to whisper in her ear, 'Best deceit wins.'

FOURTEEN

GRAVITY'S A BITCH

Scarlett was woken by a knock at the door.

Forgetting where she was entirely, she watched as Henry crossed the room to answer it, tipping someone a crisp note before taking a trolley from them.

'*Ah*. You're up!' he greeted her. 'Breakfast on the balcony?' he suggested, not waiting for an answer as he wheeled the loaded cart out into the sunshine.

Piece by piece, the fragmented night started coming back to her: the dress... the bar... the burning man... the awkward bathroom visit... and finally – the agreement that she'd come to with a cold-blooded killer: partners, for as long as it suited both their needs.

'*Oh, shit,*' she gasped, grabbing her phone and firing off an apologetic text to Mark, noticing her freed wrist and rubbing the tender skin as the open handcuffs waited like a primed trap upon the unit beside her.

'Coffee?' Henry called through the doors.

'I'll just be a minute!' Scarlett shouted back, realising the blanket she'd been sleeping beneath all night wasn't, in fact, a blanket at all. Pulling the suit jacket off her, she sat up and climbed off the bed, stopping by the bathroom to take a swig of mouthwash and wipe away some of the previous evening's make-up.

She stared at herself in the mirror: the green dress looked dreadful from where she'd slept in it while damp – creased to the point where it now resembled crinkled tissue paper. Unable to salvage it, she slipped it off, pulling one of the thick dressing gowns around her before heading out to join Henry on the balcony.

'Morning,' he smiled as she took a seat. He removed the metal lid from a tray of hot food, Scarlett taking one look at it and then helping herself to a croissant instead.

'You picked the lock then?' she said, stating the obvious.

'Yes. Both of them. Eventually... Milk?' he offered, holding it over her coffee cup.

'No, thank you. How long did it take you?'

'A while... Sugar?'

'No.'

He shrugged and placed it back on the table. '...Juice?'

'No! Would you stop trying to force-feed me and just answer the *bloody* question!'

He placed the jug down. 'It took me hours.'

'You should've woken me up.'

'It was the middle of the night and we have somewhere to be this morning. Besides, you clearly needed some sleep... Eat,' he told her, helping himself to some food from the hotplate before realising she was still staring at him. 'Yes?'

'Could you pass the juice please?' she mumbled. '...And the milk... and sugar.'

Ten minutes later, Henry dabbed his mouth with a napkin. 'I want to show you something,' he said with a boyish grin, getting up from the table. Taking a cold slice of toast with him, he walked over to the railing and the thin pane of glass that separated them from the sky. When Scarlett failed to move, he looked back at her impatiently until she finally got up to join him.

'If I drop this, what will happen?' he asked.

It was her turn to give him an impatient look.

'Come on. Humour me,' he prompted her.

'Well, it'll fall thirty-odd floors and...' – she peered over the edge, her eyesight blurring as the vertigo set in – 'probably knock out one of those people climbing out of that tour bus down there,' she said, having to take a steadying breath.

'You're absolutely sure about that?'

'Can I finish my coffee now?' Scarlett replied, bored, as Henry tossed the slice of toast out into the void. 'No! Don't!' she gasped, holding her hand to her mouth like a naughty child as she watched it twisting in the air away from them. 'I can't believe you did that!'

He gave her a funny look. 'You *do* remember the drowned, poisoned, burning Russian from the bar last night, right?'

'Yes... But still.'

Suddenly, a dark shadow flickered across the treetops. Plummeting towards the concrete below, a large bird snatched the bread out of the air before soaring away.

Scarlett laughed out loud. Henry watching the wonder on her face, also unable to help but smile. 'Try it,' he told her, nodding encouragingly as she tentatively dropped the rest of her croissant over the side; it only made a few floors before being ripped from the sky. 'Again?' he asked her.

She nodded enthusiastically, grabbing another slice of toast off the table and returning to the railing.

As she tore it in half, Henry moved beside her. 'I *had* intended to use this as some sort of metaphor to put your mind at ease, something about how – as certain as it might seem that this arrangement of ours is going to end in disaster, it's a long way down and no one knows what might happen along the way.'

'*Oh!* Here he comes!' she said, pointing to where another overfed bird glided between two buildings, dropping it on the first pass but catching it on the second. She watched it with a melancholy expression as it flew away over the park. 'I'm surprised,' she said, looking up at Henry. 'I wouldn't have you pegged for an optimist, Mr Devlin.'

Henry frowned. 'Why? What do *you* see?' he asked in interest.

'I see... that the toast is doomed either way... free-falling towards an inevitable end and there's nothing she can do to stop it.'

'*She?*' he asked in concern.

'All the birds are doing is putting her out of her misery before she gets the chance to hit the ground. But, ultimately, the outcome's still the same: no more toast... Gravity's a bitch.'

They stood in silence for a few moments, Henry thinking on what she'd said, when a warm breeze blew over the empty juice bottle on the table.

'Can I throw something else over?' Scarlett asked him, the rebellious grin returning to her face.

'Be my guest.'

Walking back over to the breakfast table, she agonised over her choice until finally settling on a black pudding, which she pitched into the sky just as another tour bus started to offload below. 'Hey, where are you going?' she asked Henry, who'd grabbed his coffee and was already halfway to the door.

'Oh, I'm hiding in here. The birds don't like black pudding,' he informed her, Scarlett's face dropping as he shoved a pain au chocolat into his mouth and hurried inside.

FIFTEEN

SMOKE AND MIRRORS

Scarlett had borrowed one of Henry's jumpers, which she'd paired with his workout trousers and some ill-fitting trainers from the display beside reception. While not ideal, the ensemble was, at least, more appropriate crime-scene wear, and less likely to prompt questions than a ruined evening dress.

They hailed a black cab outside the hotel, using the ride over to concoct a convoluted story to explain Scarlett's appearance, Henry's presence and the 'funny' incident that had led to a Metropolitan Police detective not having any ID on her; the truth – that she'd left it in a dead woman's apartment while stealing a dress – not sounding that great when said out loud. This had all turned out to be a complete waste of time, however, when the sweaty young man that came to The Old Playhouse's stage door let them in without so much as a grunt in acknowledgement.

Scarlett and Henry shared a look, the gloomy corridors feeling all the more claustrophobic when following downwind of their aromatic guide.

'You know this is an active crime scene, right?' asked Scarlett, slightly muffled by the hand covering her nose and mouth. 'You can't just let *anybody* in here.'

Glancing over at her, Henry mouthed the words *what the hell?* as the man came to an abrupt stop, both of them taking a tactical step back as he turned to address them. 'Alright then. Let's see some ID.'

Scarlett shuffled uncomfortably. '*Actually*, there's a funny story about that. You see, we were staying at a hotel... Well, not both of us... I mean, yes, we were both staying at a hotel but separately. They were separate hotels, which we were both staying in and—'

'Whatever,' their fragrant escort huffed before continuing on his listless trudge along the corridor.

'Nicely done,' Henry whispered sarcastically, Scarlett glaring at him as they reached the dressing-room door.

'Thank you!' she called after the apathetic employee shuffling away without pausing, as if he'd forgotten they were even there.

'Now that's a young man who *really* doesn't give a shit,' said Henry as they regarded the doorway with ripped tape curling around the frame like cheap decorations. 'Ladies first,' he insisted, pushing the door open and following her inside, neither of them commenting on the destroyed mirror in the corner of the room.

'OK. Impress me,' said Scarlett.

'Talk me through the timeframe once more,' said Henry, walking a lap of the room.

'At intermission, Dame Edith Donohue gets off stage and comes here, where she has a brief interaction with her assistant. Seven minutes later, she is heard ranting at someone over the phone... a voicemail to her husband, if memory serves. Towards the end of the intermission, the assistant returns to hear the victim still on the phone and doesn't move from outside the door. There is a minute or so's gap between the end of the phone call and the assistant finally entering the room to find it empty, at which point she rushes into the auditorium just in time to catch the reveal of the decapitated head. No body was recovered. Security bars on both the windows in here.'

'And where's your investigation at?' asked Henry as he continued to pace.

Scarlett sighed. 'We know the decapitation took place in the bathroom,' she said, walking through into the chilly tiled room. 'The shower had been washed out but lit up like a Tokyo strip joint under luminol. The wound around the decapitation was clean – not a saw – more like serrated piano wire, as with The Jackdaw's other victims. About a million prints, none of them useful. Aside from that...' She shrugged. 'It's physically impossible.'

'No. It's not,' Henry corrected her, thinking. 'But it *is* very clever.'

'I'm all ears,' said Scarlett, folding her arms.

'What's the first question we should be asking ourselves here?'

'I thought you said you *knew* how they did it. I'm not interested in playing games or being patronised.'

'I'm not patronising you,' Henry told her evenly. 'I'm trying to *teach* you.'

'Teach me what, exactly?'

'How to stop thinking like a police officer... and start thinking like a criminal. So, what's our first question here?'

Scarlett huffed. 'How could our killer possibly murder someone, behead them, dispose of the body, escape an effectively locked room *and* deposit the head on the stage in under ninety seconds?'

'No,' said Henry.

'No?'

'You're letting yourself get distracted by the smoke and mirrors. That's precisely what she wants. Clearly neither the victim nor her killer were still in this room by the time the assistant was waiting outside that door... whatever she might have heard. So, what's our first question?'

'How did the assistant hear a dead woman's voice?'

Henry nodded.

With an impatient frown, Scarlett cast her eye around the room – over the vase of wilted flowers on the table, the open script book beside it, the fragranced candles on the shelf, the collection of less-damning newspaper clippings and... 'The speaker!' she blurted, walking over to inspect it, noting a metal dock for some now-obsolete smartphone and the grey aux wire trailing out from behind. As she regarded it, the device made three loud chimes before a deep, husky voice resonated from somewhere inside:

'I think we never stop learning, whatever discipline we specialise in. Perhaps our craft invites criticism more than most, but when one is fully invested in a role—'

Scarlett gave Henry an enquiring look.

He held his mobile phone up to show her. 'Bluetooth,' he explained. 'That was just an interview I found on the internet, but you get the idea. With the right soundbites, it wouldn't be difficult to recreate a conversation that never happened... Next question?' he prompted her.

'How did she get the body out?' tried Scarlett.

'It's a packed theatre, remember.'

'Then, where did she... *hide* the body?'

He crouched down, Scarlett doing the same as he pointed to the line of aged sealant filling the gap between the uneven floorboards and the wall. 'Yellowed,' he said, tracing it into the corner and onto the next wall. 'Yellowed.' And then the next. '...Also yellowed.' Getting up, he moved into a small nook where a hanging rail stood opposite a wall-mounted mirror.

'Fresh!' gasped Scarlett, knocking against the hollow wall.

Henry removed a flick knife from his pocket and handed it to her. 'All yours, Detective.'

Carefully, she opened it up, staring down at the bloody blade in alarm.

'Oh. Sorry. Let me get that for you,' he said, wiping it on one of the coats on the rail before returning it to her and taking a step back into the main room.

Sinking the blade into the fresh sealant, Scarlett sliced a dark line all the way around the flimsy wall. Heart pounding, she looked over at Henry, who smiled encouragingly. Turning back to the false wall, she managed to use the knife to break off a corner large enough to peer through...

'I can see something! There's something back there!' she told him excitedly, squeezing her fingers through to break away a little more of the wall until she was able to get a whole hand inside. 'It feels... smooth... hard,' she announced in confusion, reaching in, oblivious to the revolted face Henry was pulling.

She started snapping more away, a cloud of dust spilling from the nook as she used both hands to pull on the wall.

'Detective Delaney,' said Henry. 'I'm not so sure that...' He trailed off, not that she was listening anyway as bit by bit the wedged piece of hardboard started to move. 'Seriously, Detective, would you like me to—'

But then, the whole thing suddenly gave way as something heavy toppled out on top of her. Falling back into the clothing rack, Scarlett kicked out futilely, pinned beneath the weight of what she knew to be a headless cadaver wrapped tightly in thick plastic. 'Henry!' she called, unable to wriggle out from under it. 'Henry!'

The pressure eased and she was able to breathe again as Henry lifted the packaged corpse off her and propped it back into the foot-and-a-half of additional space that the false wall had been concealing. 'Are you alright?' he asked.

'*Uh huh,*' she replied, getting back up and brushing herself off repeatedly, as if still covered in something that neither of them could see. '*Jesus!*' she whispered, breathing heavily as they regarded the otherworldly body – beheaded and ethereal – shimmering like water where the light diffracted through the plastic.

'You're sure?'

'Yeah,' she said, puffing out her cheeks.

'Looks as though this was made here,' Henry commented, looking at the colourfully painted reverse side of the hardboard. 'Part of an old background, perhaps?'

'OK,' replied Scarlett, still a little distracted.

'My best guess,' started Henry, walking back out into the main space, 'our killer was already in here when the actress and her assistant came in at the beginning of the intermission... most likely in the bathroom,' he added, working it out as he spoke. 'The victim makes her phone call. We could do with a transcript of that,' he told Scarlett.

She nodded.

'And our killer...' – he frowned – '...starts playing the audio through the speaker as she comes out from the bathroom and throttles the victim from behind,' he continued, following The Jackdaw's steps into the tiled room. 'She... drags her into the shower, the pre-recorded voice still talking away while she removes the head and wraps up the body, which she puts...' – he marched back over to the macabre cadaver standing to attention in the far corner of the room – 'behind this pre-prepared section of wall before sealing it in place.'

Almost walking straight through Scarlett, he spun on the spot. 'She washes away the blood, takes her customary trophy and conceals the head in something before leaving the room.' He moved out into the corridor and took two steps before stopping. 'Which way to the stage?'

Scarlett pointed the way he was heading.

'She's dressed as one of the crew. She'd have seen their

uniforms while planning the murder. She closes the door behind her, leaving the dead woman's voice echoing down the hallway while she adds the finishing touch,' he said, hurrying through a door and up the wooden steps onto the stage. 'She places the head here, obscured by the folds of the curtain and then simply walks out,' he told her excitedly, following the illuminated fire-exit signs and shoving the door open to emerge out into blinding sunlight.

'All she has to do is walk away, the staged phone call falling silent as the Bluetooth connection is lost. It's brilliant,' he laughed, shaking his head in awe, Scarlett regarding him with much the same expression. 'Congratulations, Detective Delaney. You'd better call in your find,' he smiled. 'I think it best I make myself scarce but should you need me, I'll be staying at The Shangri-La at The Shard tonight.'

Scarlett nodded. '...Hey, Henry,' she said, touching his arm when he went to walk away. '...Thank you.'

* * *

Across the street, a camera with a telephoto lens snapped greedily, capturing every micro-expression on the two faces: the beat longer than necessary that the redhead's hand lingered on his arm, the smile creasing his eyes enduring long after he'd walked away... and the abruptness with which it crumpled on looking directly into the camera – on realising that he'd just been caught red-handed.

SIXTEEN

CRIME SCENE ETIQUETTE

Standing over the darkening bloodstain on Francesca Labelle's bedroom floor, Frank stared down at the black duffle bag he'd just found at the bottom of the wardrobe. His phone went off and he answered without even looking at the screen. 'Frank Ash.'

'Frank, it's me,' Scarlett greeted him as he carried the bag over to the bed and began unpacking the contents. 'Where are you right now?'

'I'm...' With a frown, he placed a vaguely familiar blouse to one side. 'I'm just grabbing a coffee,' he lied.

'There's been a development.'

'Go on,' he said distractedly, checking the three cheap phones in turn, a brief text message still trapped behind the glass on the Nokia's lock screen.

'I need you down at The Old Playhouse.'

'That's not our scene,' he reminded her, dropping the lock-picking kit onto the bed.

'It is now,' she told him. 'I just found Dame Edith Donohue's body.' At the very bottom of the bag, he discovered a thin black wallet, recognising what it was immediately – identical to the one in his own jacket pocket and carried by every officer in the Metropolitan Police Service. 'Frank? You still there?'

'Yeah,' he said, heart sinking when he opened it up, his suspicions confirmed on seeing the photograph in the top right corner of the ID card. 'I'm on my way.'

* * *

The roads encircling The Old Playhouse had all been closed off by the time Frank ducked beneath the cordon, knees clicking again in protest, making him feel old. The excessive police presence at one of The Jackdaw's previous murder scenes had predictably attracted the attention of the press along with a few hundred gormless passers-by with nothing better to do with their lives.

As he made his way over to the stage door, he received an insincere round of applause from Richardson and Murphy as they perched against the bonnet of their car. Clearly they'd stepped outside to smoke and bad-mouth their glory-hunting colleagues who'd made them look incompetent. Sympathising, Frank ignored them all the same and entered the maze of dark hallways, stepping aside when the coroners, unable to squeeze their trolley around the tight corners, had to physically carry the body bag out.

He followed the sound of Scarlett's voice into the dressing room, glancing from the broken mirror in one corner to the damaged piece of hardboard propped up against the wall. Realising he was in the way, he moved out of the crime scene photographer's shot while the forensic team crawled around in their matching protective gear.

'Detective!' one of the masked people called, raising a hand when it wasn't immediately obvious which one of them had spoken. 'Had you seen this?'

Using a pen, Scarlett carefully lifted the broken piece of

costume jewellery to inspect it more closely. 'No, I hadn't,' she told him. 'Would you bag it, please?'

Somebody tapped Frank on the shoulder. 'Could I get by?'

'Sorry,' he said, stepping out of one person's way only to plant himself directly in another's.

'Excuse me.'

'Sorry.'

'Frank!' called Scarlett, finally spotting him. Unable to hide the troubled expression on his face, he simply responded with a nod. 'I did it! I worked out how The Jackdaw killed her!' she told him, her smile becoming a little forced.

'Looks like you've got everything in hand,' he said, looking around. 'We need to talk though. I'll be outside. Come find me when you're done.'

'OK. But I'm probably going to be a while; this is my first time in charge of one of these,' she said, clearly confused by his tone. 'Do you want to head back to base and—'

'Scarlett,' he interrupted, meeting her eye. 'We... need... to... talk.'

*　*　*

'Hey. Seen Frank?'

'Not for a while.'

Walking over to another colleague, who was on his phone a little further along the street, she asked: 'Have you seen Frank?' He pointed her towards the solitary figure sitting halfway up the steps to the theatre's main entrance. 'Thanks,' she said, making her way over, the cordon surrounding them creating a surreally peaceful spot at the very heart of the city.

Looking lost in thought, Frank stared into his takeaway coffee.

'Thought you'd be pleased,' she greeted him.

He looked up and gave her a weak smile. 'It's just... there's a certain *etiquette* to be followed in situations like this. This was Richardson and Murphy's scene.'

'Is *that* what this is about?' Scarlett snapped back at him. 'Those two miserable shits sulking because I made them look bad?' She laughed bitterly. 'Which one of them was it again who refused to work with me because I was, and I quote, "a psychotic time bomb waiting to go off"?' She waited for an answer.

'Murphy,' mumbled Frank.

'Screw them,' she spat. '*I* broke the case today. And if they don't like that, maybe—'

'It's not just them though, is it?' Frank interrupted her. '*I'm* your supervisor.'

Scarlett sighed. 'I phoned you the *moment* I found the body... before I even called it in,' she said, taking a seat on the step beside him.

'What the hell were you even doing here?'

'You know what I was doing: following my skip lead – looking for scratch marks on the ground. I thought I saw a light on in the dressing-room window, so went in to investigate, which is when I discovered the fake wall and...' Realising she'd been drowned out by the thoughts in his head, she trailed off.

The sun finally climbed high enough in the sky to flood their shady side street, the light reflecting off the cobbles combined with the smell of Frank's coffee lending the scene a pleasantly Parisian feel.

'What's wrong, Frank?'

'Why are you dressed like that?' Scarlett opened her mouth to answer with another lie but then hesitated. 'I wasn't getting coffee when you called me earlier,' he revealed. 'I was at the crime scene... *our* crime scene.' He paused, but Scarlett let her cue to come clean pass by. 'The bathroom looked to have been disturbed: water around the plughole of the bath, the make-up rearranged. Someone had been there.'

She looked away guiltily.

'So, I had another look around,' he continued. 'The next thing I know, I've found a bag of your clothes along with three burner phones and your ID at the bottom of Francesca Labelle's wardrobe. And then I get a call from you to say you've just found a body at a crime scene you shouldn't have even been at.' He huffed. 'What are you up to, girl?'

Scarlett lowered her eyes to the ground.

'Look at me,' Frank told her. 'Scarlett, look at me.' She met his eye. 'There is *nothing* in this world you could do that would make me turn my back on you. There is no trouble you could get yourself into that I wouldn't get you out of.' Her eyes began to well up with tears. 'But I can't protect you if you don't tell me what this is.'

She looked torn, her lips parting as if about to let it all out, when a car door slammed nearby, an engine starting up as some of their colleagues were called away to another job.

The moment gone, she stood back up. 'Where's the bag now?'

'In the boot. I'm parked on Agar Street.' Looking wounded, Frank tossed her his car keys.

Scarlett went to walk away... then paused. 'Hey Frank, I *will* tell you everything. I swear. Just... not yet. Please can you just trust me?'

He gave her a sad smile and nodded.

'Would you like me to apologise to Richardson and Murphy?' she offered.

He considered it for a moment but then shook his head and chuckled. '*Nah*. Screw 'em.'

SEVENTEEN

SAMSON AND DELILAH

Henry had always considered Le Français à l'étranger one of London's more pleasant establishments on a sunny day. In contrast to the capital's standard outdoor dining option – four tables crammed between the pavement and an A-road – it was a place where one could while away the hours, read a newspaper undisturbed and simply enjoy its enviable position looking out over the Barracks' field on the fringe of Duke of York Square.

Unfortunately, on this occasion Henry had barely ordered, read only the front page of his paper and was yet to even look up at the tranquil setting, before there was a sharp click as something solid was pressed into his back.

'Colour me surprised,' a man with a thick Eastern-European accent said in his ear. 'Did I just sneak up on the great Henry Devlin?'

'*Ah*, Felix,' said Henry without turning around. 'Very impressive. And excellent use of a British colloquialism to boot; although I'm not entirely sure what colour surprise is these days.'

'Red. Always red in our business.'

'Touché,' he said, gesturing to the empty chair beside him. 'Won't you join me?'

Keeping the concealed gun trained on Henry, the enormous European took a seat. A steroid-guzzling, gym-addicted giant of a man, he was bursting out of his T-shirt, a large camera looking more like a necklace where it dangled over his chest. Intricate tattoos weaved up his arms, painting an eclectic picture-book story of his life thus far: a tale of gangs, redemption, military service, the undoing of that redemption and professional cage-fighting. He was clean shaven with close-cropped hair – force of habit – one less thing for his enemies to grab hold of.

He laughed triumphantly. 'I could have killed you. Right then. *Bang!* No more Mr arrogant Englishman. You are losing your touch, Henry.'

Smiling patiently as the man gloated, Henry moved his newspaper aside when the waitress came back over holding a tray. Passing him a flat white with the letter *H* crafted into the froth, she then placed a large cappuccino with an *F* formed in cocoa powder in front of Felix, who looked at her as if she'd just slapped him.

'Skimmed milk and one shot of sugar-free hazelnut syrup, right?' she double-checked on noticing his expression.

'Yes... That is right,' he conceded, tucking the gun away as the waitress walked off.

'Fancy camera,' commented Henry, taking a sip of his coffee.

'Yes. I use it to photograph kill confirmations, husbands doing sex with hookers and the astounding beauty of the natural world.'

'Nature, huh?' Henry asked the ex-gang member, and cage-fighting war survivor.

'The other day: a blue jay on my neighbour's fencepost.'

'Lovely.'

'I show you.'

'Alright,' said Henry, leaning over obligingly to watch the other man flick through his most recent photos.

'That is pigeon.'

'Yes.'

'That is also pigeon.'

'Yes.'

'That is you... you... you... There are many of these. ...*Ah!* The blue jay,' he said excitedly, turning the camera to show Henry the blurry rear end of what appeared to be a defecating bird.

Henry nodded politely. 'You're very talented.'

'Yes. I have "the eye"', Felix agreed, switching off the camera and placing it on the table. 'She wants to see you.'

'I thought she might.'

'This is not good for you.'

'No. I suspect not.'

'Know that, if I must kill you, it is business only. No hard feelings.'

'No hard feelings,' nodded Henry as he picked up his coffee cup, surprised to feel the air of irreverent confidence that had always carried him through life abandon him for the first time in a very long while.

* * *

Henry and Felix had cut through Victoria and the labyrinthine backstreets that years of unscrupulous dealings had taught them to navigate. When the Latvian stopped to take a picture of a bedraggled crow on a railing, Henry used the delay to check his phone, neither of them noticing the man with a switchblade and long dirty deadlocks approaching.

'Wah gawaan, my friend. You gotta give up yuh coil.'

'Sorry. One second,' Henry told him, reading over his text message one last time before hitting *send*. 'How can I help you?'

he asked the garishly dressed man, Felix still clambering over rubbish bags in the background as he struggled to frame his shot.

'Yuh coil. Yuh stash. Give it up,' said the man, head constantly bobbing as if he could hear music playing somewhere. '...And di phone and all.'

Henry looked utterly bemused.

'What does he want?' called Felix, now no more than a pair of legs amid the mountain of black bags.

'I can't be sure,' said Henry, 'but I *think* he's trying to mug us.'

'You *think*?!' shouted the man, scaring the bird away before rapidly losing confidence as Felix got larger and larger with every step he took towards them.

'Hello,' he greeted the mugger.

'Yo, you be a giant, brother. But still – give up the camera.'

'I actually think that's an *excellent* idea,' smiled Henry, Felix ignoring them both as he scrolled through the library of failed shots he'd just taken.

'Yo!' said the man, becoming irate now. 'Eyes on me! I am *trying* to conduct business here!'

'He's doing that thing with the knife,' said Felix, zooming in on one shot where he'd somehow managed to miss the bird altogether.

'I know,' nodded Henry.

'Why do people always do that?'

'I have no idea.'

Calmly, Felix reached out and bent the man's hand back until he started to gasp and gave up the weapon.

'*Jeeeeesus!*' complained the mugger, rubbing his injured hand.

'Far too easy to take like that,' said Felix, handing him back the knife.

'Yes, but look,' started Henry. 'Now you've given him a

complex about it and he's holding it like the killer in *Psycho*. Take away the height advantage and...' He forced the man's hand downwards and the knife dropped to the ground.

'*Ah!*' frowned the mugger, shaking off the pain.

'I like that,' nodded Felix, picking the knife back up and handing it to their assailant. 'OK. Now you come at me like that.'

'No!' shouted the man in frustration, his Jamaican accent now sounding a little more South London. 'I don't feel you're taking me seriously. This is a mugging!'

'Told you,' said Henry, nudging Felix. 'Want me to do the honours?'

'Why should you have all the fun? I could take him down in half the time.'

'Perhaps. But you always make such a mess,' said Henry, turning to argue the point with his colleague. 'Let me guess: you disarm him because, let's face it, he's holding the knife like that again...'

Their mugger self-consciously repositioned his fingers.

'You drive him into that wall repeatedly until either you impale him on that pipe sticking out there or his head explodes. And then you drop what's left into the nearest rubbish bin... that big blue one over there.'

The man glanced back at it, now looking understandably worried.

'And I suppose you have a better idea?' asked Felix.

'I do actually. By employing a little *finesse*,' said Henry, 'you let him come towards you. He can only swing from one direction holding the knife that way...'

Looking pained, the man changed position yet again.

'...With gloves on,' he continued, suddenly wearing a pair, 'you grasp his knife hand and drive it into his liver.'

'Is that on the right or left side again?'

'Right. Just under the ribcage. With only *his* prints on the weapon, we allow him to "escape". He runs out into the high street looking for help while we carry on on our merry way. He collapses within two to three minutes and has bled out by the time the ambulance arrives. We're in the clear: nowhere near him and, as far as anyone is concerned, we never touched him.'

'Perhaps we should let *him* decide,' suggested Felix.

'I think that's a fine idea,' agreed Henry, both of them turning back to see the man shrinking into the distance as he sprinted away from them. '*Huh.*'

'We overthought it,' said Felix in disappointment.

'Yes... Yes, I think we did.'

* * *

Henry sensed Felix stop walking as he continued through the doorway into Room 18 and the pink fabric walls of the National Gallery's Yves Saint Laurent Room. The arched glass roof above was acting like a greenhouse – drowning the gallery in light as he passed a bookish man with a scarred face, whose intensity and silence he knew to be rooted in something far darker than mere introversion. 'Linus,' he nodded in greeting.

'Henry.'

In the next doorway along, he spotted a tall woman wearing a form-fitting dress: Sofia. With bleached-blonde hair and bright-red heels, she was making little effort to blend in and probably wouldn't know how to anyway. Like all good honey traps, every inch of her was intended to catch the eye, to draw in those men... and women whose naivety and arrogance fools them into believing that some things *can* be too good to be true.

She gave him a playful wave as he proceeded towards the far end of the room and the silver-haired woman sitting with her back to him, whose gaze was fixed upon the painting that filled the back wall. Having been stripped of his weapons, the contents of his pockets and even his shoelaces, she allowed him to approach, Henry reaching the end of the bench before she finally got to her feet – an unspoken instruction to come no closer. Aging gracefully and dressed in coordinated designer clothing, the handsome woman looked well at home amid such surroundings, the fact that she was over a foot shorter than Henry in no way diminishing her undisputed dominance over the room.

Out of the corner of his eye, he saw Sofia take out her weapon, knowing that the others would be doing the same.

'Henry, my dear!' the woman greeted him affectionately despite the five-metre gap between them.

'Rebecca,' he smiled back, looking past her to the painting she'd been admiring: lit by candlelight, a wavy-haired warrior slept in his lover's arms while dubious characters crept about in the shadows.

'You like this piece?' she asked him.

He turned to fully appreciate it. 'Rubens?' he asked.

She nodded, also taking it in one last time. 'Do you know the story behind it?'

'Vaguely,' he replied. 'It's Samson and Delilah. If memory serves, Samson was once a great warrior who fell for the wrong girl. She betrayed his secret to his enemies and used it to put him in a cage.' He had to hand it to her – Rebecca had always had a flair for the dramatic. 'Interestingly, Rubens included a sculpture of Cupid in the background, but instead of wearing the blindfold over his eyes, as is customary, it's wrapped tightly around his mouth.'

A tense silence ensued as they both took a moment to contemplate the significance of the myth behind the painting.

'Have you something you wish to tell me, Henry?'

He could feel the weapons raised expectantly around him and was under no illusion as to what Rebecca was concealing behind her back. 'Nothing springs to mind,' he replied casually.

Revealing one of her hands, Rebecca produced a pile of

photographs: Henry and Scarlett out on the pavement behind the theatre, their genuine smiles captured in vivid colour and framed with the precision of a professional wedding picture. *It was sod's bloody law that the first decent photo Felix had ever managed to take was the thing to seal his fate.*

'Scarlett Delaney,' said Rebecca. 'A detective with the Metropolitan Police... She's pretty. But then, you always did like pretty things.'

'Have *you* something you want to ask *me*, Rebecca?'

'Would I receive a word of truth back in return if I were to?'

'Only one way to find out,' he shrugged.

'OK. I'll bite,' she said. 'Would you *please* explain these photographs to me, Henry?'

'Of course. She caught me working a job... *The* job. There was an altercation, and I escaped. I thought that was the end of it until she turned up again at The Mendeleev...'

'Yes, I'd been meaning to compliment you on your discreet work with the Russian,' she deadpanned.

'I defused the situation, overpowered her and took her back to my hotel.'

'You should have killed her then and there!' snapped the formidable woman in a rare display of emotion. 'In fact, you should have done it the first time.'

'I saw an opportunity,' replied Henry evenly. 'She's impulsive, reckless even, driven by personal issues and out to make a name for herself at any cost. She wants The Jackdaw so badly that everything else is just background noise... making her an ideal candidate to be manipulated.'

'So, your plan was to turn her then?' Rebecca laughed sceptically.

'As a matter of fact, I already have,' said Henry, somehow managing to conjure a fleeting glimmer of his usual confidence. 'And now she owes me. You've given me an almost impossible task to carry out—'

'Are we forgetting that *you* volunteered for it?'

'Just imagine how much easier it would be to pull off with the police on side.'

She watched him for a moment and then looked back down at the pictures in her hand: 'So pretty,' she sighed regretfully before addressing the bespectacled man Henry had passed on his way in. 'Kill her.'

'I think that would be a mistake,' blurted Henry, prompting Rebecca to finally reveal her other hand as she pointed a dainty gun at his forehead.

'There seems to be a lot of those going around at the moment,' she said.

'Maybe so, but this is too good an opportunity to just throw away. I have got a *homicide detective* wrapped around my little finger. I mean, look at her!' he said, gesturing to the top photograph. 'The stupid girl is already besotted with me! We can *use* this... We can use *her*.'

'You are aware that she's living with someone?'

'You've seen me, right?' he replied cockily, a smile breaking across Rebecca's face as she lowered the weapon.

'Expect us to be watching,' she told him.

'I wouldn't expect anything else.'

'Please don't make me kill you, Henry.'

He nodded and went to leave.

'Oh, and Henry,' she called after him. He stopped and turned back to face her. 'You use her up and spit her back out. The moment the job is done, I want you to put a bullet in her head like you should have done in the first place. She's already on borrowed time.'

'Of course,' he shrugged, turning on his heel and walking out.

EIGHTEEN
TWENTY-PENCE-WORTH OF PLATED GOLD

Frank sat down at his desk and switched the computer on, regarding the bustling office with disdain as the ancient machine booted up. The boss looked to be in a jovial mood, wearing a big grin on his face while pacing his goldfish bowl of a room. In fact, everyone appeared to be buzzing over Scarlett and this much-needed break in The Jackdaw case.

'Fickle bastards,' he muttered under his breath, watching the same people coo over her now who only a few weeks earlier had set up the pool still taped to the back of the men's-room door. Over half the department had got involved, placing bets on when 'Deranged Delaney' would finally snap and, for double points, the name of her ill-fated victim – with answers as wide-ranging as herself to the President of the United States. Frank had left it up, as, angry as it made him every time he had to go for a piss, he'd decided it better to be privy to what they were saying behind her back rather than blustering in futility and rendering them *both* blind to the next attack.

He removed a crumpled slip of paper from his pocket, struggling to decipher his own clumsy scrawl:

The Mendeleev 8:30pm

Entering the name onto the system, he was surprised when an incident report came up straight away, and then even more so on realising that it had only been logged the previous evening. With a growing sense of unease, he double-clicked on the document and started to read.

'Hey, Fernandez!' he called, waving someone over. 'What was this Mendeleev job last night?'

'Dmitry Pavlov,' the moustached detective told him, pausing as though Frank should recognise the name. 'Russian mob, human trafficker and all round piece of shit. I guess you heard about that shootout near Dover where they found all those girls in the back of a truck?' Frank nodded. 'Someone was out to mess with his operation, big time. First that, then later at dinner he face-plants his starter and somehow ends up catching on fire!' he laughed. 'No great loss for the world there.'

Frank glanced back at the report on his screen. 'Are you heading up the investigation then?'

'As much as anyone is,' replied Fernandez. 'You know how these mob jobs go. No one's crying over this guy. All the evidence was burned to a crisp anyway. It's not going anywhere.'

'No leads then?' Frank asked him, trying, but failing, to sound casual.

Fernandez frowned but didn't question his colleague's interest, years of history between the two men buying Frank the benefit of the doubt. 'A couple... Literally – a couple: a man and a woman.' He took out his notebook. 'The male was described as "the most handsome man I've ever seen. And I've seen Magic Mike... twice. He kind of looked like if you took Superman and

Mr Darcy and mashed them together and then sprinkled some Edward Cullen on top for good measure," whatever one of those is,' he shrugged. 'He was seen having dinner with Pavlov before he died and then at the bar with "an attractive redhead."'

'A redhead?' asked Frank, feeling sick.

'Yeah: green dress, five-ten,' he continued. 'Apparently she and Super-Darcy were seen leaving together a minute or so before the Russian went up in flames. I've requested the security footage.' Frank was unable to keep the pained expression from his face. 'What's with all the questions, Frank?'

'Sorry. I was planning on taking someone there for dinner at the weekend,' he lied.

'Yeah?' the man smiled encouragingly. 'Fancy. Getting back in the game?'

'Something like that,' replied Frank self-consciously.

'Good for you. It's about time,' the other detective told him. 'But unless she's happy to sit in a giant ashtray, I'd suggest you book somewhere else.'

* * *

Scarlett was sitting with her legs dangling over the edge of the stage, the moodily lit auditorium the perfect place to think as a murdered woman's parting words filled her ears. With the wire of the headphones trailing down her neck, she restarted the recording that Richardson had begrudgingly sent over, turning up the volume on the voicemail message Edith Donohue had left her husband while she died:

'Stephen, it's Edith. I'm trying your mobile because your landline is engaged despite being told that you wanted to speak with me... It's not fair, and I won't tolerate it—'

Taking it back a few seconds, Scarlett closed her eyes to listen more closely – the abrupt change in the woman's tone and timbre undoubtedly the point at which the recording took over:

'...that you wanted to speak with me... It's not—'

She shook her head and played it again:

'...speak with me... It's—'

There was a definite creak, *a faint gasp perhaps?* Again:

'...with me...'

A creak, a sharp intake of breath, *maybe even the sound of feet scrabbling across floorboards before the pre-recorded message drowned it out?*

Removing the headphones, she scrolled through her contact list to find the number for Technical Services. 'Hi, Chris? It's Detective Delaney... Yeah... Yeah. Thank you. It's been an interesting day. Speaking of which, could I send you over an audio file? Great. Think you could bring up all the background and ambient noise for me?... Thanks,' she said, hanging up, rather pleased to hear news of her discovery had already reached other departments beyond Homicide.

She forwarded the file on to him and then hesitated, her thumb hovering over an unsaved number on her call log. Biting her lip in nervous excitement, she made sure she was alone before holding the phone up to her ear.

* * *

There are blue rivers and there are very, very brown rivers.

The Thames comfortably falls into that second category, thought Henry as he tried his utmost not to fall in from the second-storey window he was unsuccessfully attempting to access. When his phone started buzzing in his pocket, he tapped the button on his hands-free earpiece.

'Hello?' he answered, quite calmly considering he was hanging off the side of a building.

'...It's Scarlett.'

'*Ah.* Detective Delaney,' he said, voice growing a little strained now. 'How does it feel to be the toast of the Met?'

'Honestly?... Pretty great.'

'I'm glad to hea— *Oh, shit!*' he gasped, losing his footing and dropping ten feet through the air before catching a ledge one floor below.

'Henry? Are you still there?'

'Yeah,' he replied, feet scrambling against the wall, his shoulder agony again. 'Still here.'

'Where are you?'

He managed to pull himself back up. 'On a warehouse down by the river.'

'What are you doing in—'

'*On,*' he corrected her.

'Know what? Don't tell me. I don't even want to know.' She took a deep breath. 'I... want to do another one.'

'I thought you might say that,' he told her while attempting to jimmy the lock. 'Find anything useful from the scene today?'

'Yes, actually. Forensics found a broken necklace in the wall with the body. Could be The Jackdaw's first misstep... So, can we do another?'

'We can,' said Henry, hand slipping, his tool falling into the water below. '*Shit.*'

'Did I hear a splash?'

'You did.' Losing patience, he just put his fist through one of the panes of glass instead. 'How about tonight?'

'Where shall I meet you?'

'My place?' he suggested, reaching through for the handle and finally clambering inside.

'Seven o'clock?' suggested Scarlett.

'It's a date.'

'No. It isn—' she managed to get out before he hung up on her.

Photo: 273
Francesca Labelle

Audrey Wilmore
Chris Heathcoat

Frank couldn't concentrate on anything.

Looking at the clock, he realised he'd just lost another twenty minutes to staring into space. The monotonous task, which had consumed the past three days of his life, now seemed inconsequential in light of Scarlett's discovery: an actual body lying in the lab, a broken necklace being subjected to every test under the sun and, perhaps even more importantly, confirmation that The Jackdaw, whoever they may be and as clever as they were, wasn't infallible after all.

He hit the *enter* button and didn't even need to refer to his list to complete the next entry, the photograph a carbon copy of the one that had preceded it apart from, excitingly, the young man had now raised his drink in the air. Rapidly losing the will to live, he hit the *enter* button once again.

One of his more computer-savvy colleagues had performed some wizardry and reordered the pictures according to their timestamp thus providing a chronological visual diary of the night Francesca Labelle had died. As helpful as that had been, it had made Frank's job even more unbearable as he waded through dozens of almost identical photos in succession, it feeling like an unending game of vain-spoilt-rich-kid spot-the-difference.

He rubbed his eyes, needing a break, and made his way out to the toilets, finding little solace there however on being confronted with the hateful pool taped to the back of the door. It struck a nerve in his current frame of mind. Tearing it down, Frank stuffed it into the bin, throwing the door open as he stormed back out.

'For Christ's sake, Frank!' complained Murphy, shirt soaked in hot coffee. 'Watch where you're going, will you?'

'What did you say to me?' Frank asked him, his tone

attracting several enquiring looks as he squared up to the other man in the corridor.

Murphy took a conciliatory step back and smiled. 'Don't worry about it. Just be a bit more careful next time,' he said, giving him a friendly slap on the shoulder.

Lashing out without warning, Frank shoved Murphy into the wall, grabbing him by the scruff of the neck and dragging him through the door into the toilets, both men landing a couple of solid punches as they wrestled on the floor until being separated by their colleagues.

'Hey! Hey!' someone bellowed, the crowd parting to allow DCI Griffiths through, who looked from Murphy on the floor to Frank panting heavily while being restrained by two men. 'What the *hell*'s going on here?!'

Murphy wiped his face then looked down at his bloody hand. 'Nothing boss,' he said. 'I slipped, didn't I? And Frank came to help me back up.'

'Is that so?' asked Griffiths, the lie far easier to process than the weeks of paperwork and disciplinary meetings that the truth would undoubtedly entail. 'Frank?'

'Yeah. Helping him up,' he said, shrugging off his colleagues and straightening his tie.

'I want you to take the rest of the day off,' Griffiths told him.

'I'm fine.'

'Take the rest of the day, Frank!' he barked over him. 'In fourteen years, I've never *once* known you to "help anyone up". I don't know what's going on with you but sort it out. I want you back to your old self tomorrow. OK?'

'Yes, sir.'

'OK then. Everybody back to work!'

* * *

Forty minutes later, Frank approached the door of his neglected family home, finally appreciating what his neighbours had been complaining about for years: walls shedding paint over a sea of overgrown grass, the house a living mausoleum to best-laid plans both inside and out.

He'd only taken half-a-step over the threshold before being greeted by Max, his excitable Staffordshire bull terrier, the two of them play-fighting for a few minutes in the hallway. With a groan, Frank got back to his feet and headed into the kitchen. The remnants of a week's worth of microwavable meals festered in the sink as he poured out a mountain of dog biscuits and walked through to the living room, the day's events pulling him over to the mantelpiece.

A yellowed photograph of his wedding day stood among more recent pictures of a red-haired girl as she grew up from one frame to the next... *and bounced between one foster family and the next*, he recalled with regret. And at the far end, collecting dust, stood his medal, presented to him by the commissioner himself: twenty-pence-worth of plated gold in frugal recognition of his 'outstanding bravery'.

Frank picked it up to look at it as he contemplated ridding himself of the unpleasant memory for at least the thousandth time. It wasn't that he felt he hadn't earned it. He *had* been brave that day, had stood his ground where most would have fled. His issue was that bravery came in many different forms and nothing he did that day had been rooted in selflessness or virtue, but was borne out of frustration, vengeance and wrath.

It was an unamusing irony that the one time he'd truly let go, had felt himself lose control, had forsaken his career and acted out of pure emotion, was the one occasion on which he'd ever been recognised for his thirty years of service – a depressing commentary on the moral ambiguity of a police service working with one hand tied behind its back, if ever there was one.

Placing it back in its neat square cut from the dust, he headed out to the shed to see whether the lawnmower still worked.

* * *

Mark was having a good day... a *great* day even.

Not only had he made the earlier bus, but he'd been promoted to *Assistant to the Head of Year* 3. While not an official title, and therefore not subject to any physical rise in pay or points, it did involve a significant rise in both responsibility and meetings. And even though he'd lose four to six inset days to admin a year, it would look very impressive on his CV, which he wouldn't be needing anytime soon, already being at the best school in the area. That being said, there was no denying it put him in good standing for the role of *Head of Year* 3 when the current holder, by far the youngest and healthiest Head of Year Clapham Town Primary School had ever employed, either retired... or died.

'Oh, bugger it!' he blurted on realising he'd been screwed over, startling an old lady as he stepped off the bus.

Checking, as always, no one was sleeping in the void below the steps, he let himself into the house. Scarlett's handbag and shoes were in their usual spot – dumped on the floor beside the staircase as the shower leaked through the ceiling into a bucket by the door.

'Hey!' he called up.

Receiving no reply, he scratched Alkie's head affectionately and made his way downstairs.

Almost twenty minutes later, Scarlett came down the creaky staircase that led to their cosy basement kitchen. Eclipsed by tall walls at either end, only the most determined of natural light ever made it beyond the windows, the room existing in a perpetual state of dinnertime darkness.

She was wearing her favourite pair of jeans – 'the ones that made her bum look good' – and an off-the-shoulder jumper, and had done her hair in the relaxed half-up style that Mark liked.

'You look nice,' he said, an edge of panic to his voice as he racked his brain trying to work out which birthday, anniversary or generic-greeting-card-guilt-day he'd forgotten.

'I'm going out for a bit tonight.'

'Oh,' he said in disappointment, looking down at the onion he'd just diced as if he'd killed it for nothing.

'With the girls from work,' she added quickly. 'We're celebrating... I had a good day.'

'Me too,' he told her. Although his dubious 'promotion' had been a bust, Andrew Ramsbottom had only wet himself twice before the end of the day (the one as he was walking out of the school gates didn't count) and making that earlier bus was still a solid win. 'You go. You go,' he said, wiping his hands on his apron.

'Well, you know the Edith Donohue murder?'

'Yeah,' he replied enthusiastically.

'I found the rest of her body behind a fake wall this morning!'

'Oh!... How great!' he tried, the nauseated look on his face perhaps making it feel a little insincere.

'Right? It was wrapped up in plastic, which is why no one had smelt it decomposing back there.' Mark just stared at her, unable to come up with an appropriate response. 'OK. Now you go,' she told him.

'*Nah*. It's not important. Have you got time to eat something before you go?'

'I'm already late.'

'I've hardly seen you.'

'I know, but I'll make it up to you... if you know what I mean,' she added with a sly smile.

'You mean?...'

She nodded. '*X-Files*, pyjamas and Dominos pizza night.' Mark looked as though all his Christmases had come at once. 'But I've got to go now,' she said, making her way back to the stairs. He followed her up.

'Shall I wait up for you?'

'No,' she told him, grabbing her keys off the side as she stepped into her suede boots.

'Want me to save you some dinner?'

'A little bit, but only if there's some left over,' she told him, heading outside. 'Bye!'

'Love you!' he called as the door slammed in his face.

Her perfume lingered in the empty space she'd left behind – a ghost in the quiet house. Faced with the prospect of yet another night alone, he just stood there for a moment, breathing her in and missing her already.

Suddenly, the front door burst open and Scarlett marched back inside, throwing her arms around him and squeezing tightly.

'Is everything alright?' Mark asked her when she still hadn't let go of him, but she just squeezed him tighter. '...Scarlett?'

'Everything's fine, and I love you too,' she told him, releasing her hold and planting a kiss on his cheek before hurrying back out.

NINETEEN

WHAT HAPPENED ON THE RED CARPET

Tony Wilson could barely keep his eyes open, a hastily cobbled-together radio show taking a rose-tinted look back at the life of the late Dame Edith Donohue doing little to help.

Up ahead, flashing orange lights made a spectacle of the handful of cones set out to barricade the road as a solitary figure worked into the evening. Watching the rear end in the side mirror, he turned the wheel, parking the limousine outside the brand new apartment complex.

As usual, he had googled his celebrity passenger ahead of time, his teenage daughter never failing to get a kick out of her dad driving her idols around the city. Tonight, he would be collecting the pop star Keeya Rose, currently sitting pretty at the top of the charts, and taking her to a glitzy awards ceremony being held at the O2 Arena.

If she seemed nice, he'd ask her to sign his daughter's autograph book, which he already had out on the passenger seat. Depending on how she responded to that, he might even ask for a cheeky picture together.

It was going to be a long night, these things always were – the end of the awards show only the beginning of the festivities for the young, beautiful and famous. Once he'd safely delivered her to whichever bar or club was hosting the best after-party, Tony could look forward to hours sitting outside chain smoking with the rest of the hired help while they awaited the return of their inebriated clients.

It might be a blessing in disguise, Tony realised, *a chance to catch up on some sleep*, even the thought of it teasing out another yawn as he glanced at the digital display set into the dashboard:

19:00

The sight of the numbers glowing in the dark like warm embers proved too much for him, his heavy eyelids sliding closed. But just as he slumped down in his seat, Tony jolted awake. Sitting up, he gave himself a firm slap to the face to ensure he stayed that way.

'What the hell's wrong with me?' he muttered, almost forgetting his hat as he checked the time once more and stepped out onto the pavement:

19:01

The cool air was invigorating as he stared up at the blank sky. Eight years in the capital: he could handle the relentless traffic, the gritty air and the contagious hostility, but not a day went by that he didn't miss seeing the stars. He took in his unfavourable surroundings and then swiftly locked the doors. The smart new complex was clearly spearheading the area's rejuvenation efforts, the rest of it still looking in dire need of some shameless corporate gentrification. Walking up to the gate, he pushed a button labelled *Haven 6*.

'Hello?'

'Good evening, Ms Rose. This is Tony. I'll be your driver tonight,' he announced, reciting his company-dictated greeting.

'I thought we said seven o'clock,' the voice replied, a little unfairly seeing as he was only a minute late. Nevertheless, Tony remained courteous and professional.

'Have you any personal possessions you would like help with?' he asked the metal box.

'No,' the voice buzzed back. 'Wait there. I'll be out in a moment.'

Refusing to be told to sit and stay like a dog, Tony ambled back over to the car, smiling smugly at his small victory as he buffed a smudge from the paintwork and regarded the road-works at the end of the street. For one nerve-wracking moment, he thought he might have to perform a thirty-three-point turn in the narrow street but then noticed a diversion sign pointing off to the right.

He was just about to check the route on a map when the gate rattled shut behind an outlandishly dressed woman, who didn't even look at him once as he held the rear door open for her. After ensuring that her dress was safely inside, Tony hurried round to the front of the car and climbed in, watching his passenger in the rear-view mirror as he gave his second scripted interaction of the night. 'I hope you're comfortable back there. There's a fridge just beside your feet. Please help yourself to champagne and water.' The starlet didn't need much encouragement, already reaching for the bottle. 'Is the temperature to your liking?'

'It's fine.'

'You can use the tablet in the door to choose between the radio and the music library. I think we might even have one of yours on there,' he told her with a smile, ad-libbing.

'Can we just go please?' the woman asked, apparently bored of him.

'Of course,' replied Tony, tucking the autograph book back into his bag. 'I'll give you some privacy.'

'Great.'

He raised the tinted screen between them: 'What... a... bitch,' he whispered, setting the satnav and logging the time on his job sheet:

19:03

Pulling out onto the quiet street, he rolled them towards the hypnotic lights blocking their path, taking a wide swing as he followed the diversion into a small side road – only to be confronted with a set of temporary traffic signals.

With a hefty sigh, he pulled the handbrake on, tapping his fingers against the steering wheel as he looked up and down the deserted street, his eyes straining the longer he stared into the stubborn red light burning in the darkness.

A car horn sounded from behind.

'Shit!' gasped Tony, the driver's cabin now cast in an other-worldly green as he released the handbrake and pulled away. Seriously wondering whether he was coming down with something, he checked the clock:

19:03

He must have only closed his eyes for a matter of seconds.

Feeling more awake, he pulled onto the main road and built up some speed as he drove them towards the brightest cluster of stars on the horizon.

. . .

Twenty-five minutes later, they joined the back of the queue of limousines waiting to deposit their passengers – an unglamorous peek behind the curtain of engineered fame – a few dozen chosen celebrities trapped in a cloud of exhaust fumes, waiting to be led out and judged like cattle at a farmers' market, all in service of their 'grand entrance' on the red carpet.

Finally, it was their turn, Tony's heart pounding nervously as he followed the directions of various waving people. Parking up, he quickly put his hat back on and climbed out, feeling the crush of cameras watching expectantly as he made his way to the rear of the vehicle, grasped the handle and pulled the door open.

There was a surreal beat, a moment of pure silence in which no cameras flashed, in which no one called the arriving A-lister's name, in which the collective eye of the penned-in press dropped to the ground as something rolled against his foot. Tony glanced downwards, unable to even process what he was seeing before the world erupted into a disorientating mess of light and sound, the limousine's empty interior thrown into stark illumination as the severed head rocked to a gentle stop at his feet.

Staring down at the calling-card scratches torn across the pretty face, Tony just stood there, frozen, inadvertently posing for his picture with Keeya Rose after all.

TWENTY

BLACKOUT

Following Henry's last-minute instructions, Scarlett walked through the doors of the GŎNG bar and spotted him waiting for her. Having put a lot of effort into her *looking nice without making an effort* outfit, she now felt embarrassingly under-dressed as she entered The Shard's romantically lit fifty-second-floor establishment.

'Drink?' he offered, already well into what looked to be his second glass of Scotch of the evening.

'I thought we were walking the crime scene,' she replied impatiently, pulling her jumper up to cover her bra strap.

Henry seemed in a melancholy mood, surprising her when, rather than coming back with a playful remark, he simply nodded and waved the bartender over.

'Water,' she told the smartly dressed woman sporting both a bow tie and braces, taking enjoyment from the look of disapproval as it crossed Henry's face. 'Tap,' she added, just to really twist the knife.

They got up and moved to a quiet booth beside the window. The twinkling cityscape was at its most alluring – the sky still bright somewhere far off in the distance while the twilight teased the monochrome formations to bloom electric colours. Not that either of them noticed as their dying candle sang its swansong, the warm circle of light enveloping them shrinking by the second.

'You look beautiful,' Henry complimented her, Scarlett tucking a loose curl behind her ear bashfully.

'And you look like a walking cliché,' she informed him, his suit jacket draped over the back of the seat, the top two buttons of his white shirt hanging open, sleeves rolled up beneath a matching waistcoat. He stopped swirling his glass and smiled. 'Did you look over the things I sent through?' she asked him.

'I did. Did you get hold of what I asked?'

'I did,' she replied, moving her glass aside to make room for the sheaf of paperwork she produced from her bag. 'But it took some convincing. They couldn't see why I needed it when we already had the driver's statement, his handwritten job sheet *and* the satnav. And to be perfectly honest, neither could I,' she told him, smouldering over the flame.

'Just a hunch,' shrugged Henry, sounding more like his normal self as he leaned back in his seat and finished the rest of his drink. 'After all, timing is everything.'

The second he placed his empty glass down, the bartender appeared as if from nowhere, placing a fresh Scotch in front of him and an elaborate-looking gin and tonic in Scarlett's general vicinity. She would have protested had she not been distracted by the assortment of sticks, leaves and berries floating about on the surface; it looked like a glass of river water.

'We know how she works now,' said Henry. 'So, let's apply what we learned the first time around to this murder. What question does she want us asking?'

Scarlett considered her reply. 'How did she get into a moving limousine, strangle, behead and remove the body of its passenger, leaving no more than a few drops of blood, and escape without the driver noticing?'

Henry remained quiet as he watched her think.

'But that's impossible,' she said, frowning. 'And there's no way the head was removed in the back of that spotless limo. So, the real question is: how did the killer make the car stop *long* enough to retrieve the body, perform the decapitation and then *replace* the head, on what was made to *appear* as an unbroken journey, without the driver noticing?'

Henry reached across the table to move the wedge of satnav information to one side. 'If it was in the vehicle, we can't trust it,' he explained. 'You take the driver's job sheet. I'll take the GPS data from the tracker,' he told her, helping himself to the printout she'd managed to acquire for them. 'Let's compare, shall we?'

'What are we looking for?' she asked, casting her eye over the scrawled piece of paper in front of her.

'Lost time,' said Henry. 'Arrival at collection point?' he asked.

'19:00.'

'18:54,' he countered, as if they were playing a game of cards.

Scarlett shrugged. 'Human error perhaps? A slow clock?'

'Perhaps,' he replied, moving on. 'Departure at collection point?'

'19:03,' read Scarlett.

'18:57,' Henry fired back. 'A difference of six minutes again.' Scarlett counted it up in her head. 'Arrival at drop-off?'

'19:28.'

'19:28,' he confirmed, raising his eyebrows.

'We've caught up,' said Scarlett, in her excitement braving a sip of her G&T.

'So it would seem,' Henry nodded. 'Which means somewhere between leaving the collection point and arriving at the drop-off, our driver lost an entire six minutes.'

He flicked through the pages of GPS data before turning

back to the start with a frown. 'Here,' he said, tapping his finger
on the set of identical coordinates repeated time and time again,
even spilling over onto a second page. 'Right at the very beginning of their journey he drives for about twenty seconds and
then remains in the exact same location for well over five
minutes. Remind me what his statement says?'

Scarlett slid the seven-page document out from the pile and
started to skim read. 'He says the street was closed due to roadworks so he followed the diversion onto a side road and' – she
turned the page – 'stopped at a set of temporary traffic lights for
a matter of seconds...There was an impatient vehicle behind
him, which used its horn when he didn't move off quickly
enough.'

'That's got to be it,' said Henry confidently, eyes following
the gentleman in the corner as he finished his drink and went
up to the bar to settle his tab.

Looking confused, Scarlett placed the statement down. 'But
he said it himself: they only stopped for a few seconds.'

'And as *I* said before,' replied Henry distractedly, 'if it was
in the vehicle, we can't trust it.'

Scarlett now looked even more perplexed. 'People don't just
lose six minutes of their lives and know nothing about it.'

The stranger donned his coat and hat then left.

'...Do they?'

'I'm so sorry; you're going to have to excuse me,' said Henry,
getting up from the table and walking away, Scarlett watching
him disappear through the exit.

Somewhat perturbed, she sighed and took a long sip of her
drink, with only his discarded suit jacket for company...

...Her gaze returned to it...

Setting down her glass, she glanced back at the door and
then reached across the table to pull the jacket over to her side,
her hand already in the first pocket: a Shangri-La keycard. Next,
she removed an unnaturally tidy wallet containing approxi-

mately three hundred pounds in cash and two driving licences in different names with credit cards to match. And then, with a puzzled expression, she produced a small solid disc from one of the inside pockets, the line of tiny vents encircling the smooth metal only baffling her more.

With another quick look back over her shoulder, Scarlett shook the contraption next to her ear, as if trying to guess a Christmas present, before attempting to gently prise it apart. When that failed to work, she tried twisting it instead, the two halves springing open, giving her a start as a soft beeping sound faded away to nothing... and the room around her drained of all colour until everything went black.

* * *

Scarlett felt a cool breeze on her face as she opened her eyes.

She was outside... on an unfamiliar street... with no recollection of how she came to be there. Gripped by panic on feeling the foreign concrete beneath her palms and something solid at her back, she started to hyperventilate.

'Hey! Hey!' said Henry, crouching down to take her hand as she regarded her surroundings like a blind person seeing the world for the very first time. 'You're OK. You're OK... You're safe.'

As she slowly brought her breathing under control, Scarlett turned to him and panted: 'But we were just... and I was sitting at...' She looked down at her watch, the sight of it only disorientating her further, the hands positioned exactly as they'd been when she'd last checked. 'No... No. That can't be right,' she muttered, feeling light-headed as she stared at Henry. 'You're bleeding!'

He looked down at his white shirt. 'Oh, it's not mine.' Eyes wide, Scarlett frantically started patting herself down. 'Detective Delaney... Scarlett!' he said firmly, grasping both of her hands. 'It's not yours either.' He lifted her chin. 'I wouldn't let anything happen to you. You'll be fine in a few minutes. And look on the bright side, at least you weren't—'

'I don't feel so good,' she announced, giving him all of half-a-second's notice before retching into the gutter.

'...sick,' he mumbled, handing her his pocket square.

'Thanks... Wait... No,' she said, fighting to organise her thoughts. She felt drunk. 'What did you do to me?'

'*I* didn't do anything,' he replied defensively, moving his shoe. 'I came back to find all of my things spread across the table and you passed out beside them!'

'So, you thought you'd move me?!' she snapped, making her headache infinitely worse. Placing an uncoordinated finger to her lips, she shushed herself.

'Well,' started Henry guiltily, 'we needed to leave. I made rather a mess in the restroom.'

'The bleedy man?' Scarlett asked, gesturing to his stained shirt.

He smiled. 'Yes. The bleedy man.'

She groaned. 'How did I get here?'

'We got a taxi to the end of the road and then you were carried.'

'...*By?*' she asked suspiciously.

'By me this time,' he assured her. 'Look: your jumper's ruined to prove it.'

Scarlett huffed and attempted to get to her feet, having to hold onto Henry for the first few seconds just to stay upright. 'What the hell was in that thing?... Some sort of drug?'

'Not exactly. Absorption rates and several other factors make drugs far too unpredictable for a job like this. If you want to steal six minutes of someone's life without them realising, it takes precision timing,' he said, handing her the small metal disc. 'It takes something like this.'

'Why do you even have it?' she asked accusingly.

'Because we were coming here,' Henry answered simply. 'They're quite popular in my line of business. It's an incapacitation agent split into several chambers and operated remotely, allowing one to alter the dose as required.'

Happy to put some distance between herself and the faint frisbee, Scarlett handed it back.

'So... where are we?' she asked as he dropped it back into his pocket.

'The crime scene, and it's actually twenty-past eight. I changed your watch on the way over to demonstrate how time is merely a matter of perspective. That was the collection point,' he said, gesturing to the only building on the street that didn't look like a squat house. 'The roadblock,' he told her, pointing to the end of the road. 'And the diversion,' he continued as they walked round the corner. 'This must be where they stopped for those missing minutes.'

The street consisted of little more than the wall of a derelict factory on one side and a security fence surrounding a warehouse on the other.

Scarlett looked back at the corner. 'If the traffic lights were staged, the roadworks probably were as well.'

'Certainly worth looking into,' said Henry as he regarded the uninviting street.

'There's just one problem with your whole theory though,' she told him, still unsteady, still holding her head. 'I feel *bloody* awful and definitely noticed being knocked out.'

'Which is where the precision timing comes in. Plus, you were out a lot longer than he would have been... and I moved you across the city,' reasoned Henry. 'Did you see what the driver said in his statement? He was "unusually tired" that evening and "couldn't stop yawning".'

'Seems coincidental.'

'Not when we know The Jackdaw must have already gained access to the limousine beforehand to alter the clocks and plant one of these or something similar,' he said, retrieving the disc from his pocket. 'Maybe two: one in the front and one in the rear,' he added, thinking it through. 'Remember how I said you could regulate the dose administered? A tiny amount released into the air will just make one feel drowsy.'

'Drowsy enough to not even question it when they close their eyes for a few moments at a set of traffic lights!' said Scarlett, catching up.

'She activates the incapacitation agent,' said Henry, walking through the murder as if he were watching it happen. 'She drags the unconscious victim out of the back of the limo and presumably into another vehicle in order to dispose of the body. There, she strangles her, leaves her trademark scratches and performs the decapitation before returning with the head. She then removes whatever incapacitation device she used, sets the clocks back to the correct time and walks away... Six minutes gone in the blink of an eye,' he finished with a snap of his fingers.

'What about waking the driver precisely six minutes later?' she asked him.

'Didn't the statement mention something about there being a vehicle behind honking its horn?'

'That was the killer!' gasped Scarlett, all of the pieces falling into place. 'And the body must have been in the back!'

'Presumably a van of some sort, if one plans to do a spot of decapitating of an evening... and doubles as a roadworks vehicle.'

'So, find the van and we find her,' she said excitedly while optimistically looking up at the forgotten buildings for cameras.

Henry took out his phone and turned on the torch function, scanning the pavement as he made his way back over to her. 'Probably worth coming back in the daylight. If this *is* the spot, van or not, there *will* be blood.'

'I'll get forensics down here in the morning,' she said, gazing out over the desolate street as though it were paved with gold. 'Thank you.'

'You're very welcome,' replied Henry. 'Although, as much as I enjoy playing *cops and serial beheaders* with you, and I do, I'm not doing this out of the kindness of my heart.' Scarlett felt her stomach twist, having been dreading this moment ever since first striking their illicit deal. 'There's something I'm going to need you to do for me...'

TWENTY-ONE

BACK HAS LICE

'*Christ*,' muttered Frank on seeing the circus that Scarlett had created this time.

Lit by flashing lights, an evidence tent adopted the role of a big top around which clowns in matching facemasks and over-alls bustled about – one walking the perimeter looking set to jump up on his measuring wheel cum unicycle at any moment.

He parked as close as he could get and climbed out, making it only a few steps before hearing his name called. Walking back to the plume of smoke escaping a beaten-up estate car, he leaned down to where DCI Griffiths was smoking in the front seat.

'Morning, boss.'

'Morning. How are you feeling today?' the other man asked before breaking into a fit of rattling coughs.

'Yeah. Better. Thanks.'

'Glad to hear it,' Griffiths told him, 'because I've just made you and Delaney lead on The Jackdaw murders going forward.'

'Lead?' asked Frank dubiously, knowing the title made little difference bar the size of the target on one's back when the inevitable shit started hitting the ever-spinning fan. 'She's only a constable.'

'Good thing you're not then,' said Griffiths as he dropped his cigarette butt out of the window and started up the engine. 'No need to thank me.'

Coughing on fumes as the wreck of a car pulled away to wage war on the environment once more, Frank sighed heavily. 'Wasn't going to.'

Heading into the frenzy, he spotted Scarlett right away as she held court over senior officers of various disciplines. Smiling in his direction, she wrapped up her briefing and made her way over. 'Hey.'

'Hey.'

'Reckon these human lie detectors realise I am *way* out of my depth here and just *trying* to sound like I know what I'm talking about?'

'Looked like you were holding your own from where I was standing,' he replied, taking in the hectic scene. 'I didn't even know we had this many officers,' he deadpanned.

'We found blood,' she explained, pointing to where the white tent had been erected.

'How about that,' Frank nodded. 'Looks like you've done it again.'

Evidently picking up on his tone, Scarlett hesitated before continuing. 'We think they must've used a van to set up the roadworks and traffic lights, and then to perform the actual murder in, so we've got people canvassing the neighbours, getting hold of camera footage and even analysing a set of tyre tracks but, to be honest, I think that guy was just looking for something to do. I was thinking—'

'The Mendeleev,' he interrupted her.

Scarlett's face betrayed her long before the unconvincing attempt at confusion. 'I'm sorry?'

'The Mendeleev,' Frank repeated. 'The night a member of the Russian mob was assassinated and set alight.'

Scarlett frowned. 'What about it?'

'A witness said he saw the Russian's dining companion at the bar with a redhead.' He looked at her impatiently. 'Are you going to make me watch the CCTV?'

She folded her arms defensively. 'Fine!' she whispered. 'I was there.'

'Who's the man you were with?'

'Nobody. Just an acquaintance.'

'And does Mark know about this... *acquaintance?*'

'There's no reason why he should.'

'So, he's *not* the most handsome man short of a cinema screen?'

'*Errm...*' she started, as though the thought had never occurred to her. 'I *suppose...* if you like that sort of thing.'

'Handsomeness?'

'Yes. I thought we talked about this already,' she snapped. 'I asked you to trust me on this and you said you would.'

'That was before I knew a Russian had turned into a literal Molotov cocktail before your eyes.'

One of the forensic team moseyed over to them. 'Excuse me, Detective Delaney?'

'Not now!' they barked in unison.

'Look, we're making progress here,' Scarlett told Frank. 'I'm the *lead* on a high-profile serial-killer investigation! This is what I've always wanted. Maybe you should just trust that whatever I'm doing is working.'

'Some things aren't worth the cost.'

She scoffed at that. 'Easy for you to say. You don't have everyone you work with treating you like a pariah. You've already had your career-making case. Did you follow every rule and procedure to the letter back when you were hunting my father?'

Frank didn't respond.

'And if someone had told you to pull back – inaction through obedience – would you have done it?'

Again, he remained quiet.

'I'm hunting a monster, Frank, and your newfound conscience is the very *last* thing I need right now. And if you can't support me, the *least* you can do is stay out of my way,' she finished, leaving him with tears prickling his eyes as he watched her storm off.

* * *

Shortly after arriving back at New Scotland Yard, Scarlett exited the evidence room and headed straight into the toilets across the hall. Ensuring she was alone, she hurried into the end cubicle, locking the door before opening up the file she'd just signed out on Henry's behalf: Paul Williams, twenty-eight. Freelance investigative reporter found dead in his basement flat – overdose.

Skipping past the macabre photographs, she moved on to a previous encounter between Mr Williams and the police, which had been linked to the investigation and was dated only a couple of weeks earlier. She turned the page and started to read through the officer's report.

Mr Williams self-presented at Charing Cross Police Station... appeared extremely agitated... displaying clear signs of paranoia and sleep deprivation... During the interview, Mr Williams was seen to take prescription medication of an undocumented type.

She paused to listen when she heard a door slam nearby.

Mr Williams claimed to be fearing for his life, believing that he would be 'taken out' by an organisation of criminals operating out of the city after inadvertently uncovering their existence while working another story. He went on to say: 'This thing is far bigger than you can imagine. I'm talking large-scale corruption here.' He could not say how many were involved but stated that they utilised several big businesses and charities to operate in plain sight... went on to describe one of the 'operatives': Male, mid-20s, Eastern European. Tall, very muscular, cropped hair, tattoos.

The door swung open as loud voices entered the room mid-conversation.

Quickly packing up the file, Scarlett stuffed it into her bag and walked out.

Her desk had amassed a disproportionate amount of paperwork in the three hours since her elevation to 'co-lead' detective on The Jackdaw murders. Without sitting down, she flicked through her post tray and then attempted to decipher the scrawled note attached to the most intimidating stack of papers.

Back has lice.
This is it –
– Arse

She shook her head and gave up, spotting Frank at his desk on the other side of the room. He cut a depressing silhouette, staring down at the floor while shovelling a supermarket own-brand pasta pot into his face. Feeling guilty, she went over.

'"Slim a Noodle,"' she greeted him, reading the unappealing packaging which, to be fair, was always going to be fighting a losing battle. '"For One." I'm glad they made that clear because I was *this* close to grabbing a fork and joining you.'

He gave her a weak smile.

'About earlier,' she started, but Frank waved it off. 'So, are we good?' she asked.

'Always,' he told her.

'How are the party photos coming?'

'So far today I've catalogued fifty-three.'

'Not bad.'

'Although fifty-four new ones came in, giving me a tally of minus one. But the day's still youn— *Oh, Jesus!*' he exclaimed on realising the time. 'Any more news from the crime scene?'

'Forensics are still doing their thing. Definitely two different people's blood but that's as much as we know at present,' she told him. 'What about the broken necklace from the theatre?'

'Same as before: they've lifted a partial print, not Dame Edith's, but no matches yet.'

Scarlett groaned. 'Why is this stuff all so slow?'

'Many have tried and *all* have failed to expedite the glacial pace of the forensics department,' he told her wisely.

They shared a smile, but it still felt weird between them – superficial and forced.

'I'm heading out for a bit,' said Scarlett.

'Anywhere more interesting than here?'

'Thought I might take the necklace round some jewellers if forensics have what they need. See if they can tell me anything more about it.'

'Want some company?'

'No,' she replied a little too quickly. '...Thank you. I wouldn't want to keep you from your photos. Anyway, I'll only be a couple of hours. We'll catch up again then,' she said, picking up her bag and hurrying out before he could argue.

* * *

Having known Scarlett since she was a little girl, Frank could always tell when she was lying. Abandoning the remainder of his Slim a Noodle – For One (with a considerably stronger stomach than himself), he gave her a thirty-second head start to reach the lifts before grabbing his keys and following her out.

* * *

Frank unenthusiastically took a seat on a bench that the pigeons had been using for target practice. From across the water, he watched Scarlett find a table at a café overlooking the lake in St James's Park, wishing he'd stopped at the ice-cream van by the entrance when several uneventful minutes passed. Eventually, she was joined by a well-dressed man, the two of them appearing friendly, close even, as they ordered.

He glanced back in the van's direction – only flashes of yellow visible through the trees – like trying to spot a leopard in the wild. Stomach rumbling, he turned back to the café just as Scarlett opened up her bag and produced what he instantly recognised to be a crumpled case file. The man flicked through it, nodded and then set it to one side as their drinks came out.

Fifteen minutes later, Frank had just finished naming every duck on the lake when he saw them getting up from the table. Also getting to his feet, he set off on a leisurely amble towards the café, watching as the two of them said their goodbyes and split off in opposite directions, Scarlett heading deeper into the park as her mystery man started to approach.

Stopping to look out over the water, Frank sensed the man pass behind him and counted to ten. Apparently growing tired of the vista, he then followed him out towards the grand façade of Admiralty Arch, which stood like an unmovable last line of defence before the vulnerable palace... and the ice-cream van parked in its shadow.

Disguised behind a Mr Whippy moustache, Frank crossed the road into Trafalgar Square, the history buff in him inevitably taking over; the base of Nelson's Column, as usual, was buried beneath a dogpile of tourists as he stalked the suited man past one of the four bronze statues failing to guard it.

Legend had it that should Big Ben ever strike thirteen, the giant Landseer Lions would come to life and, presumably, eat the disrespectful little bastards, backpacks and all. And over in the south-east corner of the square, missed by most, stood the lamppost with a door in it, rumoured to be the world's smallest police station. Binning his cone, Frank headed up the steps towards the National Gallery.

When the man waltzed past the entrance queue with no more than a nod in the staff's direction, he was tempted to use his badge... but decided against it, collecting his ticket and passing through the security check with the rest of the public. Worried he'd lost him, Frank hurried over to the map in the entrance hall, spotting the man already at the far end of the East Corridor. He picked up his pace, affording priceless master-pieces as little attention as one would street-art caricatures, reaching the corner just in time to watch the man enter a roped-off hallway.

Frank approached cautiously, stepping past the *No Entry* sign before following the hum of voices along an unlit corridor that opened into an ornate gallery bathed in natural light. A muscular man was standing guard in the doorway with his back to Frank as he dashed into one of the darkened alcoves: perhaps twenty feet from the entrance, he was able to see much of the room and had a good view of the suited man but not the person with whom he was speaking. In the doorway opposite stood an attractive woman, while another man in glasses flickered in and out of sight against the back wall. The combination of the distance and echo melded their words into an incomprehensible drone, but it was unsafe to move any closer with one of them so near.

Carefully taking out his phone, Frank opened up the camera app, stepping out as far as he dared from the wall. Zooming in over the muscular man's shoulder, he positioned Scarlett's suited acquaintance dead centre, framing the other two either side as he waited for the perfect shot...

Click.

The artificial camera noise reverberated down the corridor as Frank dived back behind the wall, swearing under his breath as he doused the light of his phone screen against his chest.

The man standing guard had heard it.

They had all heard it.

The gallery fell silent, five sets of eyes focussed on the dark hallway, the blade of the serrated knife singing a metallic chime as it was unsheathed.

'Shit,' whispered Frank, his clumsy fingers unsuccessfully scrolling through the innumerable screens of settings and menus as he tried to dull the backlight or switch off the sound effects but achieving neither. 'Come on... Come on.'

For such an imposing figure, the enormous man moved with surprising stealth as he crept further into the darkness, the corridor a confusing melange of nooks and displays set into the walls.

Giving up on his phone, Frank stood with his back pressed into the wall. As he attempted to quiet his breathing, he was acutely aware that the hum of conversation had been replaced with a foreboding silence. In the gloom, he could just about make out the painting on the wall beside him: a vase containing a bunch of dying flowers, just one still clinging to life – one spark of colour defiant in the face of inevitability, the scene reminiscent of a ticking clock...

* * *

Felix peered behind a free-standing display, the space unoccupied but the angle providing him with a view of the next recess along: deeper – large enough to conceal a person. Looking back to the others in the main room, he waved for assistance but none of them responded.

He tried again.

Realising they couldn't see him, he turned back to the dark corridor and started edging towards the void, knife raised, primed to strike. He paused... and then stepped around the corner, discovering only a painting of wilted flowers. Above him, the pipes and vents of the ventilation system clicked and whirred intermittently. Shaking his head, he sheathed his weapon, frowned at the ugly picture and then returned to the gallery.

TWENTY-TWO

THE BROWN JEWELS

Scarlett had trekked over to Hatton Garden, London's jewellery quarter seeming a logical place to start looking for information on the broken necklace recovered from The Old Playhouse. She stepped off the bus and pulled out her phone, dropping the garish piece of costume jewellery to the ground for the third time in two hours. Crouching down, she wiped away what she could of whatever sludge it had landed in this time and then stared at it with disdain – large cuts of glass intended to impress betraying their utter lack of value, the pendant reminding her of a poker player attempting to buy their way out of a bluff.

Dropping it back into her pocket, she checked the map, following her phone down the street as if it were a dowsing rod until an engraved plaque announced her arrival at Fellow & Sons Jeweller.

The spritely proprietor must have been in his early eighties and had been in the back for over fifteen minutes while Scarlett checked her emails. A member of staff, presumably one of the advertised sons, was dealing with the only other customer in the little shop, allowing her to take a few moments out to message Mark.

Hey x

> Hey you
>
> Good day?

Yes

Found blood ☺

> Ciol
>
> *Cool
>
> Found poo
>
> Under my desk

At home?!

> At school.
>
> Went in to prepare for parents' evening

Gross

> Definitely Andrew
>
> Little shit
>
> Well, it was a big shit actually.
>
> I mean...

Gotta go x

> Oh. OK. Bye
>
> Love you x

'Sorry to have kept you so long,' apologised the owner, having reappeared behind the counter. He seemed different somehow – a serious tone flattening out the musicality of his voice. 'I just wanted to be sure what it was before talking to you.'

'So, you found something that might help us?'

The old man forced a smile. 'Perhaps it would be best we speak in private,' he suggested, gesturing in the direction of the other customer, who was making no effort to hide the fact that he was listening to their every word. 'Please,' he said, gesturing to a door and leading her through to the tiny workshop at the rear.

Ever the professional, the man had laid the piece of tat out over a velvet cushion as one would the Crown Jewels and even donned a pair of cotton gloves before sitting down to handle it again. When he frowned, the fault lines in his forehead were emphasised by the enormous magnifying glass between them, Scarlett waiting patiently as he gave it one final assessment before delivering his verdict.

'It's a shame it's broken,' he said, staring down at it under the bright light – a surgeon with a patient on his operating table. 'I don't suppose you still have the missing piece?'

'Afraid not,' she replied. 'If it ever *was* at the crime scene, it either dropped between the floorboards or got swept up and binned somewhere along the way.'

The man, who clearly took his job a little too seriously, looked physically pained. 'That *is* a pity.'

'So... what can you tell me about it?' she prompted him.

'I'm sorry,' he said, snapping out of his daze. 'It's just this is a first for me.' Scarlett looked confused. 'As a damaged piece, it is made up of five exceptional twenty-two-carat examples surrounded by clusters of circular-cut diamonds, emeralds and rubies of the highest—'

'Diamonds?' she interrupted him. 'As in – real ones?'

'Oh yes,' replied the man animatedly.

'Even the big ones?'

'Well... yes,' he told her, surprised that she didn't know. 'All set into a platinum housing. It's Middle Eastern in both style and unabashed excess – a statement of one's standing for all to see.'

Sitting up, Scarlett regarded the hideous pendant, unable to resist asking the inevitable next question. 'And how much is something like this worth?'

The man reached for a scrap of paper, having apparently wondered the same thing, a page of scrawled calculations annotating a rough sketch. 'A conservative estimate... in its current condition, of course,' – he took a sharp intake of breath – 'four to four-and-a-half perhaps.'

'Oh,' she said, mildly impressed. It was an insanely expensive piece of jewellery, no doubt, but the way the old man had been building it up, she'd almost expected more. She took out her pen to make a note. 'Current condition: four to four-and-a-half thousand.'

'Million.'

'I'm sorry?'

'Million,' the jeweller corrected her. 'Four to four-and-a-half *million* pounds.'

'*Jesus shitting Christ!*' blurted Scarlett. 'I'm so sorry. That was unprofessional of me, but... *Jesus shitting Christ!*' she reblurted, gazing down at the fist of diamonds she'd had to fish out of a puddle of bin juice back in the park.

'Best guess: five to six if it were complete,' the man continued, passing it back to her as if it were made of... exactly what it *was* made of. 'You asked me to help you find the owner of this piece but something tells me you won't have to. They'll find you. Somebody out there is *definitely* going to be looking for this.'

* * *

The moment Frank got back to the office, he made a beeline for Olsen, the skinny jeans, retro-T-shirt-wearing man-child he went to with all his IT issues. Infinitely patient with him, the socially awkward youngster was an acquired taste but for some reason had taken pity on the old man gradually being rendered obsolete by the modern world.

'Olsen!' Frank greeted him enthusiastically.

'Frank,' he smiled back. He stopped what he was working on and spun on his chair to face him. 'What you got for me today?'

'Am I *that* obvious?'

'You're holding your phone.'

'Oh. Right,' mumbled Frank, hating always feeling like such a burden. 'It's a photo I took. I need to separate the faces and get them onto the system.'

'Shouldn't be a problem,' Olsen told him. 'Good resolution?'

'Well, I snapped my picture and managed to get out of there without anyone seeing me so, yeah, not bad.'

Trying to hide his smile, Olsen held out his hand. 'Password still one, two, three, four?'

'And I've not forgotten it yet,' Frank told him proudly.

Unlocking it, the young man brought up the most recent photograph, zooming in on each of the visible faces in turn. 'OK. OK. This'll work,' he said, swiping his fingers across the screen and handing the phone back to Frank.

'That's it?' he asked in surprise.

'That's it,' shrugged Olsen. 'I've emailed it to myself. I'll split it up and put it on the system for you. What case number do you want it linked to?'

'Same as before?' replied Frank with a hopeful smile.

'...OK,' Olsen chuckled, the crate of his favourite beer going down nicely the last time he'd bent the rules on Frank's behalf. 'I'll give you a shout if anything comes up.'

* * *

'Frank!' Scarlett called to him, poking her head round the door to the office. 'I've got something I need your help with,' she said, extending an olive branch.

Taking it, he got straight to his feet and followed her out towards the lifts. 'Where are we going?' he asked.

'Robbery,' she replied, pressing the button.

'Because?'

She handed him the broken necklace. 'Careful with that,' she warned him. 'It's worth over four million pounds.'

He dropped it immediately, back clicking twice as he bent over to scoop it up. 'Four million?!' he stage-whispered, only about half the people in the corridor overhearing as he stared at it open-mouthed, any animosity between the two of them at least temporarily forgotten about.

'We're going to speak to Robbery because *they're* the ones who'll be able to tell us who reported it missing.'

It took less than two minutes to locate the stolen-property report for so distinctive and expensive a piece of jewellery.

'So, we believe the owner's alive?' asked Scarlett in surprise.

'And kicking us in the balls,' replied the robbery detective as he squinted at his computer screen. 'According to this, she phoned yesterday to give one of my colleagues an earful for not recovering it yet. Hey, McGregor!' he called, waving someone over. 'You dealing with that massive diamond necklace?'

'Yeah, why?'

Frank held up the broken pendant, the man's eyes lighting up appropriately. He hadn't loosened his grip since being entrusted with it by the lifts: it felt surreal to hold everything he'd ever coveted – every unticked bucket-list entry – in his hands, if only for a little while. His mind kept wandering –

daydreaming about the life he could have given Eleanor before he lost her, her 'one day' dreams of visiting Japan or going on safari always just a couple of payslips out of reach until it was too late. And all the while, this eyesore was dangling uselessly around some rich woman's neck.

'We're working The Jackdaw murders,' explained Scarlett. 'The necklace was found at one of the crime scenes. What can you tell us about the owner?'

'Ameera Abdalla,' read the man at the computer.

'Saudi-born heiress to a sheik and richer than God,' his colleague took over. 'For the past couple of years, she's been renting out the entire top two floors of The Mountbatten Hotel. And, yes, she is every bit as entitled, dismissive and unpleasant as you'd expect her to be.'

'What are you thinking?' Frank asked Scarlett. 'If she's alive, could she be The Jackdaw?'

'It's possible, but I doubt it. While she's certainly got the means, I can't imagine someone who walks around in things like this getting their hands dirty.'

'A victim then?'

'A *future* victim,' she agreed. 'The *next* victim perhaps? We know The Jackdaw must get close to their kills in order to plan such meticulous murders.'

'True. But as far as we know, she's always taken her trophy *after* their deaths,' Frank pointed out.

'But none of those trinkets were ever worth millions of pounds before, were they?'

'Fair point.'

'Maybe they couldn't resist,' reasoned Scarlett, turning back to the two robbery detectives, who'd been listening to their exchange in fascination. 'Do you have some contact details for us?'

TWENTY-THREE

THE INDIGNANT DIGNITARY

'Ridiculous,' grumbled Frank, looking at his watch again as they waited in The Mountbatten Hotel's lavish lobby. 'Forty minutes we've been sitting here. She only has to drag her rich arse downstairs.'

'*Uh huh,*' replied Scarlett, personally welcoming the breather to catch up on the latest influx of emails. It reminded her of trying to stay on top of the leaky shower at home; every time she went to check her inbox feeling the same stab of apprehension as when she walked through the front door to discover whether the unrelenting drip had finally overwhelmed the bucket by the stairs. 'Forensics say one of the blood samples taken off the street matches our pop star,' she read aloud. 'Still waiting on the other one.'

Frank nodded in acknowledgement before checking the time again. 'I say we let The Jackdaw have her.'

As if on cue, the lift doors parted and a handful of imposing men dressed in identical suits fanned out across the reception area. One made his way straight outside, his rear end facing the window beside Frank's head as he watched the rooftops.

'What the hell's all this?' Frank asked Scarlett as a second lift opened onto the lobby, the people within lingering inside the metal box until receiving the all-clear from their colleagues.

Flanked by her bodyguards, an immaculate dark-skinned woman strode confidently across the reception area. Her monochrome make-up and hair contrasting with a pristine white dress made her look like the star of an old black-and-white movie superimposed into a colourful setting. Her men broke off in turn as if choreographed, surrounding the seating area as she sat down opposite the two dumbfounded detectives. Crossing her legs, she tapped her long fingernails impatiently.

'*Errm*... Ms Abdalla,' started Scarlett unsurely. 'I'm Detective Delaney and this is—'

'I was told by the other one,' the woman interrupted her, 'that you were responsible for finding my necklace... well, most of it anyway. So, you have my gratitude... or most of it, anyway. *That* is the *only* reason I agreed to this meeting. You have three minutes.'

'OK,' said Scarlett, leaning forward to address the terrifying woman, the nearest bodyguard watching her closely. 'We're here because of *where* we found your necklace. We have reason to believe—'

'And where *did* you find it?'

'Beneath a dead body.'

She pulled an appalled face. 'I hope you cleaned it. Although I suppose that would explain why I have two homicide, rather than robbery, detectives recovering my possessions.'

'...Leading us to believe,' Scarlett continued as though she hadn't been rudely interrupted *again*, 'that there may be a very credible threat against your life.'

This revelation only seemed to amuse her. 'Detective, do you have *any* idea how many people out there wish me harm? Want to kidnap me? Use me against my father? Take his only daughter from him in retribution for some ancient business deal that went sour? Why do you think I keep *them* around?' she asked, gesturing to her entourage spaced out around them.

'I take it you've heard of The Jackdaw?' said Scarlett, changing tack, the woman's utter self-assurance slipping for the first time.

'Of course,' she replied, shifting uncomfortably in her seat. 'Is that... Why is that relev—'

'Your necklace,' Scarlett continued over her, taking control of the conversation, 'was found beneath the decapitated corpse of one of The Jackdaw's victims.'

Taking a nervous glance around at the bustling lobby, Ameera Abdalla forced a smile onto her flawless face. 'It doesn't matter who it is. The top two floors of this hotel are a fortress. No one can get to me.'

'They can, and they will,' Scarlett assured her. Frank, sitting silently at her side, raised an eyebrow at the blunt approach. 'The Metropolitan Police would like to provide you with twenty-four-hour protection.'

'Out of the question.'

'I'm not asking,' Scarlett told her firmly. The taciturn woman looked taken aback, being told *no* apparently an entirely new experience for her. 'This isn't just about you. There is a *serial killer* out there, who has already murdered three people. And this necklace... and you, is the first time we've ever been a step ahead. The Jackdaw *is* going to come for you. There is a *very* strong possibility that they *are* going to remove your head, and should they escape, how many other people are going to die because you naively thought you were untouchable?'

She knew she'd gone too far even before Frank stamped on her foot, the indignant dignitary getting to her feet. 'This conversation is over,' she said, nodding to one of her men.

'Ms Abdalla,' blurted Scarlett, standing as three identical Range Rovers pulled up outside, blacked-out windows matching the paintwork and wheels. 'I am the *lead* detective on this case for a reason. I, alone, have unravelled not *one* but *two* of The Jackdaw's previous murders. I understand them. I know how they think. And I'm telling you that *I* can protect you.'

The formidable woman huffed and regarded her for a long moment... then she turned to address Frank, silky hair cascading over her shoulder like a waterfall. 'Is that true?'

'Every word,' he nodded.

'And, if she's been doing all that, what's your role here?'

He regarded Scarlett. 'Moral support, cheerleader... and conscience,' he replied, the answer more for his partner's benefit than hers.

She looked back to Scarlett. 'I like you. No bullshit. So, let me extend you the same courtesy: no police. I have my own militia up there, most of them armed, and each and every one of whom I would trust with my life.' Scarlett opened her mouth to protest, but she continued over her. 'I will, however, on your advice, confine myself to the hotel for the next week. I will cease *all* contact with those both inside and outside of this building once we have gathered enough provisions to comfortably see us through. Finally, I will permit you to come up and take a final walkthrough before we go into lockdown. You'll have the opportunity to highlight anything we might have missed and to brief my men as required. Is that acceptable to you?'

Scarlett looked to Frank, who shrugged back in response. 'It is.'

'Very well. I have some errands to run and then we'll need a couple of hours to prepare, so I'll expect you back here at eight o'clock,' she told Scarlett finally before turning on her heel, a shadow of dark suits falling into line behind her as she marched outside and climbed into one of the waiting vehicles.

* * *

Purchasing a rust-red Ford Mondeo back in the mid-nineties had either been a stroke of genius – disguising the tired vehicle's corroded blemishes as she aged gracefully – or its owner had been driving about for over a quarter of a century in a car that had looked like crap from day one. Frank chose to believe the former.

Parked a little way down the street from the hotel, he'd just unlocked all of the doors at once with the cutting-edge 'central locking' feature when his phone went off. 'Frank Ash,' he answered, Scarlett perching against the bonnet as she waited for him.

'Frank, it's Barry.'

'...'

'...Barry Olsen.'

'Oh! What's up?' he asked, conscious of his partner listening in.

'Those photos I put on the system for you, I've had a hit back from one of them already.'

'That was quick,' said Frank carefully. 'Which?'

'Male – glasses, blond hair, scars on his face.'

'I know the one.'

'I'll fill you in when I see you, but...' – Olsen paused, the crinkle of paper filling the silence as he presumably looked over the report – 'he's a pretty bad character. Like... *bad*, bad.' He huffed. 'Look, Frank, it's none of my business, but if whatever you're working on doesn't have a case number, it really, *really* should.'

'Noted,' said Frank, giving Scarlett a *just one second* gesture.

'I'm only bringing it up because I'm concerned about you.'

'And I appreciate that,' Frank told him. 'Tell you what, let's talk about it when I get in. I'm heading there now anyway.'

'See you soon.'

'OK. Thanks,' he said, putting his phone away and turning

to Scarlett. 'Sorry about that. I need to get back. Problem with another case,' he explained vaguely. 'You coming?'

'I think I'll make my own way,' she told him. 'Might pick up something to eat.'

'I'll see you back there then,' he said, climbing in and firing up the spluttering engine. He waved to Scarlett then pulled away, watching in his rear-view mirror as she immediately took out her phone and held it up to her ear.

* * *

Enjoying the sensation of sand between his toes, Henry was standing on an almost deserted beach watching the sunlight float on the surface of the water like an oil spill, when his phone started to vibrate. Setting down the bright pink bucket he'd just found, he answered it.

'Detective Delaney!' he greeted her enthusiastically, closing his eyes and taking a deep breath of fresh air.

'There's been a development.'

'That's encouraging.'

'We've found who the broken necklace belongs to,' Scarlett told him, the sounds of London – engines and anger – almost drowning her out. 'Ameera Abdalla. She's very much alive and, therefore, presumably the next target. I've just met with her and she's... *difficult*, to say the least.'

Two seagulls started squawking at each other as they fought over a box of chips.

'What's that?' she asked him.

'Seagulls.'

'Where are you?'

'The Norfolk coast,' he told her, looking around at the rugged bay he'd discovered by chance. 'Day off,' he explained. 'I was just thinking about how if you bury a person in the sand, to extract information from them for example, you don't actually need to cover them any deeper than their shoulders in order to asphyxiate them.'

'*That's* what you were thinking about?'

'It's all to do with the rise and fall of the chest when we breathe. As soon as the sand is above their ribcage, every time they exhale, the finer grains slip down to fill the void left behind until, bit by bit, there's no room left for the lungs to inflate and one suffocates with both their airways completely clear. Isn't that amazing?'

'Maybe you should try reading a book or something next time?' suggested Scarlett. 'Anyway... Ameera Abdalla,' she said, getting back to the point, 'has her own personal army of body-guards who never leave her side, and isn't remotely interested in our protection. It was all I could do just to convince her to let me assess her place tonight before they lock it down.'

'So, where is she now?' Henry asked in confusion.

'Out.'

'Out?'

'Carrying on with her day as usual, I guess. As I mentioned – she's difficult.'

'What time do you want me and where?'

'That's going to be problematic.'

'Maybe so, but what time do you want me and where?' he asked again.

'She doesn't even want *me* there!'

'Make it work. If that necklace belongs to this woman then The Jackdaw *will* come for her, and I need to be there when she does. We had a deal, Detective Delaney.'

'I know that!' She huffed. '...Eight o'clock. The Mount-batten Hotel. I'll meet you in the lobby at ten-to.'

'I'll see you there.' He went to hang up.

'Hey, Henry!'

'I'm still here.'

'I know you've got a job to do and nothing I say will change your mind. And I know you don't owe me anything, but... let me arrest them first... The Jackdaw. Just let me put the handcuffs on and walk them out before you do anything.'

There was a long pause.

'I'll think about it,' he said, ending the call and frowning down at the screen. Checking his watch, he quickly dialled another number from memory.

'Yes?' a female voice answered.

'That thing we spoke about,' Henry greeted her cryptically. 'I was hoping I could borrow Sofia for it this afternoon.'

'I'll have her contact you.'

The line went dead.

Taking another greedy breath of sea air, Henry looked down at the man at his feet: eyes vacant as a gentle breeze caught his wispy hair, only his head, neck and shoulders still protruding from the sand. It might have just been optimism on Henry's part, but the lolling mouth looked as though it had been on the verge of spilling whatever secrets he'd been sent to acquire. He'd put it down as a 'near miss'.

'*Shit*,' he tutted, placing the colourful bucket over the unsightly head before collecting his shoes and walking away.

TWENTY-FOUR
SHOP TILL YOU DROP

Kamil Dagher had been on Ms Abdalla's protection detail ever since the unsettled situation in Riyadh had necessitated her abrupt relocation to London. In that time, there had been three serious breaches of their security: two that she knew of, and one that she didn't – involving a journalist posing as a member of the hotel staff.

All had been handled.

Today, however, he was anxious.

Not only would it be his first real test as her newly appointed head of security, but his client appeared to be in an especially counterproductive mood – stubbornly carrying out her usual routine as though it were any other day. His most trusted men were laden with shopping bags, the highly trained team reduced to porters trudging between hairdressing appointments and pedicures via every shoe shop en route.

Spread out around the make-up counter, the team watched a steady stream of people pass through Selfridges' labyrinthine ground floor, Kamil's men constantly having to divert customers away from the stand where Ms Abdalla was being poked at with various brushes and pencils, her head of security finally running out of patience.

'How much longer is this going to take?' he barked.

'We're almost done,' the woman armed with a speckling brush smiled back.

'I don't like this,' he said, foot tapping anxiously as he watched one of his men argue with a woman determined to reach another stand.

'Oh, relax, Kamil,' Ms Abdalla told him from her horizontal position on the leather chair. 'Why don't you go and get yourself a coffee or something?'

'We shouldn't be here. It's too open.'

'Perfect!' announced the make-up artist, stepping back to allow her canvas to sit up and look at herself in the mirror.

'Can we go now?' Kamil asked while the other woman went to bag up the products they'd been discussing for over half an hour.

'Yes. We can go,' his employer told him, getting up. '...to the champagne bar,' she added, Kamil muttering under his breath as he collected up her purchases and followed her towards the web of escalators spun across the great void at the heart of the store.

* * *

The ringing tone drowned out the road noise as Henry sped along the duel carriageway back to London.

'Good afternoon. The Mountbatten,' someone answered in a faux-genteel manner.

'I was wondering whether you could help me,' started Henry. 'I was hoping to book a room with a view for this evening. Do you have anything available on your upper floors?'

'Let me just check for you. *Ah!* You're in luck. We have one room left on our forty-ninth floor, the highest level we offer out to the public.'

'That'll do nicely.'

'It's an executive suite, which is charged at—'

'That's fine.'

'And what name should I put it under?'

'Henry Devlin.'

'That's all done for you, Mr Devlin. We look forward to welcoming you later.'

* * *

'Thanks. I owe you,' said Scarlett, hanging up the phone.

Stuffing the bullet-proof vest into a bag before anyone saw her, she closed up the locker belonging to her heavily pregnant friend who, quite sensibly, was intending to avoid gunfights for the foreseeable future.

Zipping up the fraying rucksack, she flung it over her shoulder and hurried out of the changing rooms.

* * *

Frank had been wearing a frown ever since Olsen had handed him the report on his photograph suspect Linus Bergman, his young colleague's unease now completely understandable on seeing the extent of the elusive Swedish national's chequered past. Pacifying him with a lie, Frank had told Olsen that he was still in the very early stages of building a case against the group in the picture but *had* promised not to take any further snap-shots of *any* of them without a small army present.

When Scarlett entered the office carrying a grubby ruck-sack, he quickly folded up the printout and tucked it into a drawer.

'Half-six,' she announced, looking at the clock. 'Thought I

might head over to the hotel soon, see what the management can offer in the way of additional security.'

'Five quid says bugger all.'

'No deal,' she replied, suspecting he was right.

'New bag?' Frank asked, tongue in cheek.

'Just a change of clothes,' she lied, sounding unusually convincing, although she'd had an awful lot of practice in a very short space of time. 'Me and Mark might still get an evening yet. You clocking off soon?'

Frank looked confused. 'Aren't I coming with you?'

'Don't be silly,' she told him. 'There's no point *both* of us wasting our night on a five-minute stroll through a hotel. What day is it?'

He had to think about it. 'Saturday.'

'Then you've got your book club. You haven't been in weeks. Go to that.' Frank looked torn. 'I'll be fine,' she assured him. 'Nothing's going to happen in the few minutes I'm in there with her.'

'You're sure?'

'Of course!' She smiled at him and went to walk away.

'Scarlett!' Frank called after her, unsure himself what he wanted to say as she turned back, the list of atrocities attributed to the Swede still playing on his mind. But he also knew their relationship couldn't take another big argument so soon. In the end, he settled on: 'Be careful.'

* * *

Scarlett was shown through to the loading bay, The Mountbatten's duty manager accommodating her unorthodox request on the most limited of information.

'So, we could bring a police car in here?' she asked him.

'It shouldn't be a problem unless there's already a delivery being unloaded.'

'And where are we exactly?' The manager responded with a blank expression. 'In relation to the rest of the hotel, I mean. Front? Back? Side?'

'Back,' he informed her. 'There's a service road that runs the length of the building.'

'Is it private?'

'Accessed via a barrier-controlled gate. There's an intercom at the entrance.'

Scarlett nodded. 'I'm going to need you to brief your staff. Tell them to send any police vehicles round the back to here.'

'Of course.'

'Could I leave this in here somewhere?' she asked him, sliding the tatty rucksack off her shoulder.

'Be my guest,' the man replied, watching her push it out of sight atop a metal cabinet.

'Thank you. You've been very helpful.'

The moment they resurfaced from the concrete warren beneath the hotel, Scarlett's phone pinged:

Room 497

She scowled down at the message, thanked the obliging man once again and made her way across the lobby to the lifts. Ears popping as she ascended the building, she focussed on the seam between the shiny doors, feeling the metal box slow as it approached its destination. Relieved to step back out onto solid ground, she rapped against the door to the nearest room.

Henry greeted her with a warm smile before stepping aside to allow her into the plush suite, the only luggage he'd brought with him his suit jacket laid out across the foot of the bed and the long rifle propped beside the windows.

'It's booked for the next week. I figured if this is where she's going to be, it's where *we* need to be, whenever we can. It's no good us being across town when the call comes in,' he reasoned. 'We've got twenty minutes. Can I offer you a drink?'

'You can offer,' replied Scarlett as she walked over to the windows, a smile curling at the corners of her mouth on looking out over the busy high street to the *front* of the building. 'But I'll decline.'

Opening up the mini fridge, Henry removed a small bottle of champagne and popped the cork, pouring out two glasses anyway.

'I was thinking about what you said,' he told her, placing one of the glasses down on the table next to her. 'And you're right – there's no reason that both of us can't come out of this with what we want. The only question is whether *you're* going to have a last-minute moral crisis when it comes to actually pulling the trigger.'

She looked unconcerned. 'But *I'm* not the one pulling the trigger – you are.'

'I was speaking figuratively,' said Henry, watching her as she watched the rambunctious city below.

'I knew what I was getting into,' she said defiantly, picking up the glass and meeting his eye. 'No moral crisis here,' she assured him as the rifle stood between them like a line in the sand – the ethical boundary that he was asking her to cross forever.

After a few moments Henry nodded. 'Make your arrest,' he told her. 'Let the world see you not just hunt down but actually *catch* the uncatchable killer.' Scarlett felt her pulse quicken. 'Walk her outside and then take two steps back. I'll take care of the rest.' He raised his drink: 'To a fruitful partnership.'

Picturing the bullet-proof vest she'd stashed in the loading bay to the rear of the building, she smiled. Scarlett had compromised herself time and time again in aid of this case, so it was reassuring to know that, at its close, she hadn't lost herself entirely.

'To a fruitful partnership,' she echoed, toasting glasses with him.

Best deceit wins.

TWENTY-FIVE

ABDALLA FALLS

Henry gazed up at Ameera Abdalla's head of security in awe, the monster of a man looking like a bigger, badder, beardier Felix.

'Who is this?' demanded Kamil Dagher, addressing Scarlett as his two colleagues moved behind them.

'Henry Devlin,' she told him, closely watching the man invading her personal space. 'He's been consulting on the case.'

'Police?'

'No.'

Standing an entire head taller than Henry, Kamil peered down at him. 'And what *exactly* is your area of expertise, Mr Devlin?'

'Practical Security Management alongside Algorithm-based Risk-adverse Infrastructure,' Henry replied without hesitation, Scarlett looking impressed, the larger man considerably less so.

'Sounds made up.'

'That'll be because it is. *I* made it up... five years ago, when I first started freelancing. It was a toss-up between that and I'll Save Your Life... For a Substantial Fee.'

The man grunted in either mild amusement or outright

fury; it was hard to tell. He looked to his colleagues. 'Search them... thoroughly.'

Raising their hands above their heads, both Scarlett and Henry were subjected to a comprehensive groping.

'I feel compelled to buy you a drink after this,' Henry told the humourless oaf patting him down. '...Oh, that's *all* me,' he assured the man, who appeared unduly suspicious of his under-carriage.

Apparently satisfied, Kamil's subordinates nodded and stepped back, the head of security finally inviting Scarlett and Henry into the lift as he removed a key card from around his neck. Inserting it into an inconspicuous slot, the doors sealed as the motor whirred to life.

'Once the card has been read, the lift won't stop at any other floor,' he informed them.

Scarlett smiled back weakly as she tried to hide her discom-fort at her third dizzying lift journey in twenty minutes. She couldn't help but feel they were putting an awful lot of blind faith in the flimsy floor holding them above the abyss by packing her and Henry in with three of the largest men she'd ever seen.

'So, you're here to tell us how to do our job?' Kamil asked her challengingly.

'Not exactly,' replied Scarlett between controlled breaths.

'Ms Abdalla was alive when you spoke to her earlier, yes?'

'*Uh huh*,' she managed, feeling her ears pop again.

'Then we know our job.'

Several excruciating seconds later, the lift slowed to a stop and Scarlett followed the others out into a long corridor iden-tical in layout to the floor below, except clearly the exclusive guest had been permitted to decorate as she saw fit. Kamil led the way, guiding the group towards an open door at the far end.

'Staff accommodation,' he informed them. 'Cameras,' he said, pointing to the two black domes either end of the hallway. '...Guard dog,' he deadpanned when a fluffy Pomeranian with a bow in its hair came running out of the open doorway and jumped up at him, the terrifying man picking it up and carrying it like a baby as they made their way up a set of stairs to the top floor of the hotel.

The sun was refusing to go down without a fight, casting a stunning array of purples and blues onto the sky above the city as they emerged back out into the cool evening. But the vista wasn't what had taken Scarlett's breath away – it was the dreamlike roof terrace featuring its own woodland garden, where an old-fashioned swing set hung from the branches of an established willow tree. She was struck by the surreal idea of the garden sitting in that precise same spot back when the hotel first broke ground, the building thrusting it up floor by floor into the sky.

A collection of water features trickled down the surrounding walls, converging at one end of an incredible infinity pool, its glass borders only adding to the illusion that it was spilling over the side. Candles flickered in paper lanterns all around them, their light complemented by the cosy glow seeping from the handful of structures that bordered the garden.

'Ms Abdalla's quarters,' announced Kamil, putting the dog down to point to the grandest of the rooftop buildings. 'Guest quarters,' he continued, gesturing to the next one along. 'My quarters,' he said, and then 'Security. Security. Security,' identifying the remaining rooms. 'Seven cameras provide a three-hundred-and-sixty-degree view of the entire rooftop, which itself is surrounded by bullet-proof glass.'

'And where is Ms Abdalla now?' Scarlett asked him while desperately trying to come up with a valid excuse to try out the swing set.

'Meditation,' the head of security informed her. 'And then a swim, a drink and video-call with her mother back in Riyadh, and then bed. The same every night. So, please,' he said, gesturing to his impenetrable fortress, 'do what you came to do.'

Even Henry looked impressed by the unapologetic extravagance as she headed over to join him by the edge of the building, where he was watching the infinity pool pour over the side of the glass and into a trough below.

'How do you want to play this?' she asked him. 'I take upstairs, you take down?' He nodded in agreement. 'Anything in particular I should be looking for?'

'You'll know if you see it,' he assured her. 'Routine is a bad thing. And she shouldn't be on her own for long periods of time. Did you notice the lift doors had locks on them? They need to seal those the moment we're gone. Obvious stuff really.'

Scarlett lowered her voice. 'Honestly, right now, I feel like we *are* wasting their time. It seems impossible that anyone could get to her up here.'

'I agree, but let's keep looking,' he said, heading back over to the stairwell with the intimidating head of security in tow.

* * *

'Can we check these rooms?' Henry asked as they reached the lower floor of Ameera Abdalla's empire.

With a huff, Kamil used his key card to open the nearest door, revealing a suite identical to Henry's below. 'All the windows have already been secured.'

Henry nodded, walking a lap of the room. 'Have you thought about a breach from beneath?' Judging from the other man's expression, he hadn't. 'Might want to think about it. Best to pull up all the carpet on this level, especially under the wardrobes and beds – places where no one's going to notice a gaping hole in the floor.'

Kamil looked around in concern.

'Right,' Henry smiled cheerfully. 'Next?'

* * *

Scarlett was still checking the guest quarters when Ameera Abdalla emerged from the doorway opposite dressed in a white robe. Opening her mouth to greet the reluctant hostess, Scarlett's fascination with the lives of the rich and famous stopped her. Instead, she just stood there, watching through the window as the beautiful woman strode towards the distant sunset. With a champagne flute in one hand and a fluffy towel in the other, it looked like an exotic perfume advert playing out in real life.

The man keeping an eye on Scarlett cleared his throat, snapping her out of her reverie.

She turned to him. 'Everything looks fine in here,' she announced before heading out and walking across the terrace to the woman tucking the last of her dark hair into a swimming cap.

'Detective Delaney,' nodded Ameera Abdalla. 'Any issues?' she asked in feigned interest as she dropped her robe to reveal the simple black swimsuit beneath.

'So far only things I'm sure your men would have identified anyway.'

'Pleased to hear it,' replied the flawless woman.

Conversation apparently over, she pulled her goggles down over her eyes, Scarlett clocking the heart-shaped diamond bracelet most wouldn't dare remove from its box, let alone go swimming in. Diving into the pool, Ameera Abdalla commenced her nightly lengths as Scarlett looked out over the neighbouring rooftops, all of a sudden unable to shake the feeling that they were being watched.

* * *

Henry's word of caution had struck a chord with Kamil, the two men splitting up to more effectively check the less visible areas of floor.

'Anything?' asked the enormous man when they reconvened out in the corridor. Henry shook his head. 'Keep looking,' he said as they split up again to search the next two rooms along.

* * *

Solar-powered illuminations triggered in turn as the light began to wane, stars in the floor sparking to life beneath Scarlett's feet as the willow tree burst out in great clusters of warm lightbulbs. The swimming pool too was now an ever-changing blend of pinks and blues, as if someone were mixing paint.

'I'd like to check Ms Abdalla's quarters next,' Scarlett told the man watching her from a few feet away.

With a curt nod, he updated the team over the radio and then led the way.

* * *

Henry heard Kamil in the hallway. Finding nothing of note, he closed up the wardrobe doors and headed out to speak with him, a look of concern instantly forming on his face. 'Was that door open before?' he asked the distracted head of security, gesturing to the emergency exit standing slightly ajar.

Kamil's eyes grew wide as he unholstered his weapon. 'Stay here!' he barked, Henry nodding obligingly as he watched the goliath cautiously step through the door to the stairwell beyond.

* * *

Scarlett entered the first of Ameera Abdalla's lavish rooms while the billionairess enjoyed her rooftop pool in the background. But far from being overcome with jealousy, she unexpectedly found herself craving fish and chips, her comfy sofa and a night wasted watching rubbish on TV with Mark.

She'd been informed that her host had lived atop the towering hotel for over two years, yet the rooms looked unlived in: no pictures on the walls, no slouchy clothes left out for lounging around in, no friends or family to share her isolation with – only an army of people well compensated to keep her alive.

As Scarlett stared out at Ameera Abdalla performing her regimented laps of the glass pool, she actually felt sorry for her – a woman with everything in the world... and yet nothing at all.

* * *

Henry loitered beside the fire door, watching through the opening for any sign of life. 'Kamil?' he called. '...Kamil?' After glancing back down the empty corridor, he stepped into the silent stairwell. 'Kamil?'

A substantial crimson puddle had spread across the top step, now dripping over the lip as if in pursuit of the other sporadic bloodstains that decorated the route down. Peering over the railings, Henry immediately spotted the enormous man's crumpled body one flight below, framed in his own blood, foamy bubbles forming around his mouth as he struggled to breathe. Rushing down the stairs, Henry got onto his knees beside the dying man, pressing a hand against the puncture wound to his neck, it futile to even attempt to stem the blood flow.

Wiping his hands on his shirt, Henry prised the radio from the other man's grasp and held the *transmit* button. 'Kamil is down! Lower-floor stairwell. She's in the building. The Jackdaw is in the building!' He attached the radio to his own belt, relieved the head of security of his key card and picked up the gun beneath his limp hand. 'I'm sorry,' Henry told him, turning his back on the man with only moments left to live and sprinting back up the stairs.

* * *

'Stay where you are!' a member of the security team barked at his employer, effortlessly falling into Kamil's all-too-recently vacated role, as the rest of Ameera Abdalla's men swarmed around the outer edge of the pool.

Feeling helpless, Scarlett could only stand there watching the shadows with the rest of them.

Suddenly the sound of running footfalls echoed up the stairwell, the security detail and their assorted weapons turning to face it. One of them fired instinctively, shattering the glass behind Henry's head as he emerged onto the rooftop covered in Kamil's blood.

'Don't shoot! Don't shoot!' yelled Scarlett as Henry froze, his hands raised.

'Gun, radio and key card,' he explained, setting them down on the ground. 'Didn't want to leave them for her.'

Slowly backing away, he went over to join Scarlett.

'Cavalry's on its way,' she told him anxiously, the tension in the air palpable.

'You, you, and you: downstairs!' ordered the man in charge, those chosen hurrying away to be swallowed up by the dark stairwell. 'Find them!'

The paper lanterns swayed in the breeze as everything fell silent once more, the terrified woman they were so desperately trying to protect trapped in her watery cell as they all listened in to the crackled radio transmissions:

'Room One clear... Moving on to Room Three.'

'Room Two clear.'

'Room Four clear!'

'The bodyguard?' asked Scarlett in a whisper, Henry shaking his head regretfully. 'We need to lock down the whole hotel,' she said, reawakening her phone screen when she noticed the look on Henry's face as he took a step towards the pool, the click of weapons arming filling the night sky.

'Stay back!' ordered one of the men.

'Her face!' Henry shouted back at him. 'Look at her face!'

As the bemused man turned to look down at his panicking employer, Scarlett caught a glimpse of her through his legs – five fresh scratches that she knew hadn't been there before bleeding across her perfect face.

'Get her out of the pool!' Henry yelled, already running towards them. 'Get her out—'

The explosion scattered the ring of armed men like bowling pins, shards of glass thrown into the air like razor-sharp snowflakes as the water surged like a tsunami, knocking those still standing off their feet. And then Scarlett could only watch in horror as the wave hit the side and began to retreat, draining back out, Ameera Abdalla screaming as she was washed towards the open edge of the building.

* * *

Jumping in after her, Henry had no way of anchoring himself as the shallow water pulled his legs out from under him, dragging him closer to the precipice, yet somehow he managed to grab hold of her wrist as they both went over the side of the building. Clinging onto what little reminded of the glass wall, he cried out in pain, Ameera Abdalla dangling over the city like a ragdoll.

'Henry!' he heard Scarlett scream as the glass started to crack, the panicking woman flailing about in his other hand as water continued to wash over them, his grip on her loosening bit by bit... until finally, he let her go.

* * *

For those fortunate enough to witness it, London had never looked quite so spectacular – a surreal sci-fi dreamscape as a raging waterfall erupted from the top of one of its highest peaks, sparkling with light as it plummeted past fifty floors of illuminated windows, the roar of it crashing against the concrete below carrying for miles, shaking the ground like a thunderclap from the underworld.

And then, as suddenly as it had been created, it was gone, a few puddles and a trail of destruction the only evidence that it had ever existed at all.

TWENTY-SIX

QUOTATION MARKS

'...and may I ask what your relation is to Detective Delaney?'

'Just an old friend,' replied Henry, still picking splinters of glass out of his palms while the Metropolitan Police lightshow illuminated the damp tarmac beneath his feet.

'"Friend,"' the officer said aloud, somehow managing to vocalise the quotation marks as he made a note.

'We were meeting for dinner anyway,' Henry continued. 'So when this work thing came up, I suggested, because of my background, I might be of some use.'

'And what background is that again?'

'Practical Security Management alongside Algorithm-based Risk-adverse Infrastructure.'

'Sounds made-up.'

'So I've been told.'

'Have any ID on you?'

'Of course,' said Henry, taking out his wallet and handing the officer a soggy business card along with an authentically uncared-for driving licence.

'I'll be back in a minute.'

Henry wasn't overly concerned as he watched the man

move away to verify his identity. Their team of computer prodigies were among the best in the business. Responsible for preparing forged documentation, bogus companies, legitimate audit trails, websites and even meticulously scripted call-takers – they were yet to make a single misstep.

* * *

Waves of blue coursed across the empty street like electricity as Frank watched Henry's almost-convincing act in interest. Had he not known better, he too would have believed that death was an entirely new concept to the heroic stranger. However, as the officer stepped away and took out his radio, Frank saw it – the façade slip when he thought no one was watching – a playful smile in Scarlett's direction as she gave him an anxious wave from the other side of the street.

'For Christ's sake,' muttered Frank. But his distaste was short-lived, giving way to concern on realising he hadn't been the only one to have seen it.

Having just arrived on scene, DS Fernandez's gaze panned between the handsome man with a blanket draped over his shoulders to the redheaded detective giving her own statement just ten metres away, the cogs visibly turning as he recalled the witness description from The Mendeleev restaurant... and there was absolutely nothing Frank could do about it.

* * *

'Thank you for that, Mr Devlin,' said the officer as he returned Henry's ID, the notable change in his tone suggesting all had checked out. 'It sounds like you were very brave up there.'

'I only wish I could have done more,' replied Henry with a regretful look over at the white sheet framed in headlight beams, the press waiting like a pack of hungry dogs in the shadows beyond.

The officer nodded understandingly. 'Well, you're free to go and get dry now,' he said as he dismissed Henry, who got up and started making his way towards Scarlett when a stocky, leather-skinned man intercepted him.

'You're Scarlett's friend, right?' the man asked conversationally despite having very purposefully planted himself in Henry's path.

'That's right.' He extended a hand. 'Henry Devlin.'

'Detective Sergeant Ash... Frank,' he added, looking Henry up and down as they shook hands. 'You look cold.'

'I am rather.'

'I won't hold you up for long then,' said Frank. 'I just had one final question for you. Would you mind?' he asked, handing Henry his warm Thermos in order to retrieve the notebook from his inside pocket. 'OK. What was it again?...What was it?' he pondered out loud while Henry shivered in the breeze. 'Ah, yes!... Does the name Dmitry Pavlov mean anything to you?'

There was a beat in which the two men locked eyes, the unconnected question effectively an outright accusation.

After a moment, Henry shook his head. 'Doesn't ring a bell.'

'What about a fire alarm?' the man asked with a smirk.

'I'm sorry. I can't help you.'

'Oh well,' sighed Frank, putting his notebook away and gesturing for his Thermos back. 'Thank you anyway.'

Looking down at the metal container in his hands, Henry hesitated.

'Thank you...' Frank prompted again as Scarlett made her way over.

'My apologies,' Henry told him, thinking on his feet as he unfolded his damp pocket square. 'I seem to have got blood all over your container. Let me just...'

'No. No it's fine,' Frank insisted as he proceeded to wipe the metal Thermos clean before handing it back through the creased material.

'Was there anything else?' asked Henry, far too experienced to be tricked into giving up his prints so easily.

'No,' replied Frank bitterly just as Scarlett reached them.

'Everything OK over here?' she asked, evidently picking up on the tense atmosphere.

'Of course,' answered Henry. 'Shall we?' he said before turning back to Frank. 'Very nice to meet you, Detective Ash.'

'Yeah,' replied Frank. 'Catch you later.'

* * *

As the flashing lights of the crime scene shrank into the rear-view mirror, Scarlett turned up the heater for Henry's bene-fit, taking a right at the junction and heading in the direction of The Shard. Neither of them spoke for a few minutes, this first period of quiet giving them both time to relive the evening's events. Desperately wanting to believe her own bravado, Scarlett realised that she couldn't stop her hands from shaking.

When the temperature bordered on uncomfortable, Henry leaned across and switched the heat off.

'So, what do you know about that old boy who stopped me on the way out: Detective Sergeant... Frank Ash?'

'That he's off limits,' Scarlett fired back, almost ploughing into the rear of a double-decker bus when she turned to look at him. 'Like the outer, outer, outermost limits of off limits. Understand?'

'Understood,' shrugged Henry, as though he'd only been making polite conversation.

'No silk scarf,' muttered Scarlett, thinking out loud.

'I'm sorry?'

'The other victims were strangled with a silk scarf. We

presumed it was symbolic in some way, important to the killer, but now...'

There was another pregnant pause.

'I saw her, if you're interested.'

'Saw who?'

'The Jackdaw.'

Spinning the wheel, Scarlett careered them over two lanes of traffic and bounced them up onto the kerb to give him her full attention, car horns sounding from all directions.

'What do you mean you "saw her"?'

'It was only for a split-second... while I was dangling over the side of that building... But it was her. I'm sure of it.'

'And?'

'She was just standing there watching us from the window. Asian. Korean perhaps? Late twenties, at a guess. Quite tall with striking green eyes. Oh, and her hair was shaved at the sides, long and black on top.'

'Henry!' exclaimed Scarlett excitedly. 'This is huge! You actually *saw* her! Can I pass this on?'

'I already have.'

Waiting for a gap in the traffic, Scarlett put the car in gear and pulled back out onto the road.

'That was very brave, what you did back there,' she told him, 'jumping in after her like that.'

'To be fair, I wasn't expecting to get washed over the edge of a skyscraper like that or I wouldn't have done it.'

'Still, I thought it was very brave. Who knew the cold-blooded Henry Devlin cared so much?' She gave him a fond smile.

'He really doesn't,' Henry assured her. 'I saw our *one* advantage over The Jackdaw getting flushed down the proverbial toilet, and knew the second she hit the ground we'd be back to square one.'

Scarlett's smile crumpled. 'Had to ruin it, didn't you?'

* * *

The evening hush had fallen over the office by the time Frank came hurrying back in. Passing his own desk, he marched towards another beside the window, where Fernandez and his extended family looked out from assorted photo frames. Setting his Thermos down, he began rooting through the files littered around them.

'What a *pig*,' he complained on discovering a flattened jam doughnut, a half-empty crisp packet and what appeared to have at one time been a daddy-long-legs, filed among the bulging folders – but knowing it would only play to his advantage.

He moved on to the drawers, finding what he was searching for in the second one down: the file on Dmitry Pavlov's murder at The Mendeleev. He pulled it open and started flicking through the papers until coming across a CD-R, a marker pen scribble adorning the front:

Security Footage
Cameras 1-6
19:00 – 21:00

Glancing up to ensure no one was watching, he removed the CD from its case and tucked it into his pocket before packing up the file and stuffing it back into the drawer. And then, with a sigh of relief, he headed for the door... the shiny Thermos still warm where he'd left it standing amongst the crumbs, the photographs and the files bleeding paperwork over the desk.

TWENTY-SEVEN

THE THINGS THAT HOLD PEOPLE TOGETHER

Scarlett hadn't been able to bring herself to look at Ameera Abdalla's broken body wherever it had landed the previous evening and felt no more prepared for it now, as the medical examiner went to pull the freezer drawer from the wall. Disconcertingly, only the top third of the metal tray was covered in a stained white cloth, which he whipped away without warning. Feeling bile rise at the back of her throat, Scarlett regarded what little remained of the woman to regard.

'Oh. Brace yourself, by the way,' he mumbled as an afterthought, Scarlett wondering why people kept doing that to her as she shot him a look. 'It would appear she landed legs first,' he explained needlessly, seeing as nothing below the ribcage was left of the once striking woman. And even then, only sporadic lumps of tissue clung desperately to the shattered bones. The head, however, had somehow remained relatively intact. The back of the skull had caved in, but the front was almost recognisable, the five scratches that had appeared from nowhere forming crooked lines across the pallid face.

'This is all that's left, I'm afraid,' said the medical examiner in a bored tone. Now into the twilight years of his career, not even *this* could faze him anymore. 'The volume of water flowing over the street would have washed whatever mush there *had* been straight into the nearest drain. We could ask some poor sod to go down there and start fishing but, honestly, I can't see what we're going to learn after that level of contamination.'

'And why...' She faltered on ill-advisedly looking back down into the drawer. '...Why—'

'Why is only the head left?' he guessed, Scarlett nodding. 'The swimming cap and goggles. They supported it around the top and sides,' he explained. 'Otherwise it would have blown open like a watermelon and gone down the drain with the rest of her.'

'OK,' she said with finality, the man mercifully covering the nauseating corpse back up. 'I spoke to her,' she started as the wall swallowed the metal drawer whole, 'about five minutes before it happened. There weren't any scratches on her face.'

'I was going to ask you about that, actually,' he said, picking up a sandwich and taking a bite without even looking at a bar of soap first. 'Sodium,' he told her with his mouth full. 'It reacted with the chlorinated water. And they're not scratches on this occasion; they're burns.'

'A chemical?' frowned Scarlett. 'So, like a liquid?'

'A powder in this case.'

'And how does one end up with sodium powder all over their face in nice neat lines like that?'

'They don't, Detective Delaney. They really, really don't.'

* * *

From across the office, Frank watched Fernandez turn his desk upside down in search of the misplaced CD. Having almost got into a fight with a wise-cracking colleague who'd made a comment about the state of his workspace, he was still on his feet, going through every piece of unsorted paperwork in the vicinity.

Slouching a little lower in his chair, Frank had just moved his computer monitor a few inches to the right to give him some cover, when Scarlett walked in – timing as impeccable as ever.

'Who are you hiding from?' she blurted, Frank jumping up and taking her arm as he swiftly guided her back out.

'*Oww!* Frank! Where are we going?'

Pressing the lift *call* button repeatedly, he glanced back anxiously through the doorway. 'Anywhere but here.'

Scarlett and Frank crossed the road to the river, it still taking some getting used to that Big Ben's Elizabeth Tower was no longer splinted like a broken limb, the framework of scaffolding scaling the most famous extremity of the Palace of Westminster feeling as permanent a fixture as the clockface itself. When he finally stopped walking, propping himself against the railing to look out over the water, Scarlett followed suit.

'What's all this about, Frank?'

He reached into his pocket and produced the loose CD. 'Know what this is?' he asked, handing it to her. Scarlett flipped it over to read the handwritten label. 'Security footage from The Mendeleev. I took it out of Fernandez's file.'

She looked exasperated with him. 'Why?! I didn't ask you to do that!'

'What choice did you leave me?' he snapped, turning to face her. 'He saw you.'

'Who saw what?'

'Fernandez. He saw you and Henry last night and put two and two together.'

Scarlett rubbed her face. 'Shit.'

'Yeah, shit,' he agreed, his tone softening. 'Look, I have no idea if this is the only copy or if it's on someone's computer already, but I had to do something, didn't I?'

'This isn't your problem, Frank. I've got enough going on. I don't need to be worrying about you risking your job over this as well.'

'I think that ship sailed a *long* time ago,' he smirked, an embarrassed smile breaking across Scarlett's face as they both recalled the 'dead body' that had driven off in her patrol car in her first week on the job. Even Frank didn't know how they'd managed to get away with that one. 'And anyway, you're wrong. Your problems *are* my problems. *You* are, and always will be, my problem.'

'Why have you always acted like you owed me something?' she asked.

Frank looked away guiltily, instantly conscious of the large scar decorating his left cheek, the new skin never properly wearing in, destined to feel forever alien to the rest of his face. He didn't speak for a few moments, but then took a deep breath. 'We were going to adopt you... Eleanor and I. We had the meetings. We filled out the forms. We were going to do it.'

Scarlett was speechless. She'd had no idea.

'But we were going to have this amazing life together,' Frank continued. 'A bright future at the Met was all but guaranteed, and Eleanor – she wanted to travel so badly. I can still remember the night we sat down and talked ourselves out of it, sure you'd end up somewhere better anyway. Only that didn't quite pan out, did it? The promotions never came, Eleanor found out she wasn't going to get better, and you got passed around from one shithole to another with nothing to your name but the clothes on your back. It's no wonder this dashing stranger managed to get under your skin.' He laughed bitterly before turning to her. 'I can honestly say, it's the biggest regret of my life... and there's some stiff competition there. I'm sorry.'

Palm wet from wiping away a tear, Scarlett patted his hand and smiled. 'You were always there, never more than a phone call away when I needed you. You've done enough for me. Put the CD back... please.'

'We don't have time for this,' he said, snatching the disc out of her other hand.

'Frank, don't!' she gasped as he snapped it in two, dropping the pieces into the water below.

'We're in this together now, girl. But you need to tell me everything, and I mean *everything* that's been going on *right now* or neither of us are going to get through it.'

Wearing the exact same expression she had when receiving a telling-off as a teenager, Scarlett's defiant scowl disintegrated when she burst into tears, as, at long last, she let it all out.

* * *

Frank had spent most of the afternoon in a distracted daze, the extent of Scarlett's deceit far worse than anything he'd been expecting. He'd managed to click the mouse occasionally to prevent the screen from timing out and had even cast an eye over a couple of emails. But before long, his mind would inevitably return to Scarlett and the encroaching storm she was about to bring down over them.

In a strange way, a part of him had always suspected his career would end in such fashion: protecting her. Perhaps he'd even hoped for it – a final chance to prove himself... to redeem himself. It would certainly be a poetic end. After all, assuming the role of guardian angel to the daughter of his greatest adversary had been the only thing to give his life any glimmer of meaning after losing Eleanor. But as he watched Scarlett carrying on with her day without a care in the world, he started to question whether he'd ever really known her at all.

His melancholy musings were abruptly interrupted when a

familiar metal container was placed down in front of him. In confusion, he looked up to see Fernandez's smiling face.

'Afternoon,' he said in greeting. 'I believe this is yours.'

'*Hmmm*,' replied Frank noncommittally, his mind working overtime.

'I found it at the crime scene,' the other man explained. 'You must've put it down somewhere.'

'Oh,' said Frank, relaxing a little. 'Thanks.'

Maintaining his friendly demeanour, Fernandez perched on the edge of the desk. 'Thing is, when I say "crime scene", I don't mean beautiful woman falling out of the sky. No. I mean the theft of evidence relating to an active investigation from a case file in my drawer.'

Frank's elephant-hide skin had always complemented his poker face. 'Are you winding me up?' he asked with a laugh.

'All those questions about The Mendeleev the other day,' Fernandez continued over him, 'the redhead and Super-Darcy, the security footage I mentioned to you, gone, and your shitty instant coffee left right where it went missing. I know you're covering for her.'

'For who?' Frank chuckled. 'Are you sure you're feeling alright?'

'We're old friends, Frank. But if a crime's been committed, I *will* report you.'

'I'd expect nothing less,' he said, matching the other detective's calm tone. 'Serious accusations though. I wouldn't want to go to the chief with something like this without a literal mountain of proof.'

'Oh, I'm working on it,' Fernandez assured him, getting back to his feet. 'Don't you worry about that.'

'Still friends for now though?' asked Frank, making him laugh.

'Still friends after, for my part. You take care of yourself, yeah?'

Despite the smile fixed upon his face, Frank couldn't stop his leg from shaking beneath the desk as he watched the other man walk away, his poetic end apparently coming for him even sooner than anticipated.

TWENTY-EIGHT

THE MORNING OF 7TH AUGUST 1996

MET IN CHAOS AS FOUR-LEAF CLEAVER KILLS AGAIN

The attention-grabbing headline was failing to grab Frank's attention as he stared into space after another eighteen-hour shift, the cacophony of the bustling office no more than a background hum, the blood of another innocent young woman still drying on the cuffs of his shirt.

Exhaustion was no good for anybody.

It didn't matter how tough you thought you were – lack of sleep could devastate the brave and the cowardly, the strong and the weak, without prejudice.

His memory of the night was hazy, disjointed – hours reduced to a handful of three-second snippets – the mind's override protocol when faced with adverse trauma. *She had been different to the others – younger – nineteen at most. Red-haired, of course, but this time curly and long.* He wondered whether there was anything in that – *not that it mattered.* She'd suffered the exact same fate as the rest of them.

'Frank?... Frank!'

The noise flooded back into his ears as he blinked dazedly, returning to the little room where his boss looked to be awaiting a response.

'Sorry?'

The older man shook his head. 'Look at yourself, Frank. When was the last time you slept?' he asked, receiving only a shrug in response. 'This isn't your fault. This is on me. Maybe you weren't ready,' he told the young detective, sounding more like a concerned parent than his chief inspector. 'You have to have some sort of detachment. You can't... You can't do *this*. Nobody can. That's seven victims now, and you take each and *every* one as if it was a family member. It's not healthy. Look, I know you've got a lot on at home with Eleanor taking ill and all. Perhaps I need to be cruel to be kind here.'

Frank betrayed no reaction whatsoever.

'Are you hearing what I'm saying to you, Frank? I'm giving the case to someone else.'

'Yes, sir.'

'You've done some fantastic work. Sometimes these things just don't play out as we'd like them to.'

'Yes, sir.'

'Go home. Clean up. And get some rest, will you?'

Frank nodded and got to his feet.

Heading back out into the bull-pen, he was too numb to feel anything – too tired to sleep, but was at least lucid enough to acknowledge his failure and the professional embarrassment to come as he wandered back over to his desk.

'Hey, buddy. I'm sorry. Are you alright?' asked Matthews, his baby-faced friend and partner on the investigation.

News tended to travel fast in the homicide department.

'Let me get you a coffee before you drive home,' he offered, dashing off in the direction of the kitchenette.

'Detective Ash?' asked an officer Frank had never actually been introduced to, the detective constable transferring over only a few weeks prior. 'There was a call for you while you were in with the chief,' she told him, Frank just concentrating on keeping his eyes open. 'A Marie O'Callaghan. Said she needed to speak with you urgently, but then the line went dead before I could get a number.'

'OK. Thanks,' said Frank, finally sitting down just as Matthews returned with two age-stained mugs.

'What is it?' he asked, taking a seat.

'O'Callaghan,' muttered Frank. 'Why's that name familiar?'

'Probably because we've interviewed every *bloody* mick immigrant in Greater London,' his friend suggested before flicking through the documents on his desk. 'Not here. In yours perhaps?'

Frank knocked back half his coffee, the scald doing more to wake him up than the caffeine, and started sorting through his own stack of paperwork... finding a freshly typed report in the name of Kieran O'Callaghan, whose next of kin was listed as his wife Marie. On seeing the two names together, he vaguely recalled the unproductive interview, sitting in the gloominess of their brown wallpapered lounge – *who puts up brown wallpaper?*

With Matthews watching in interest, Frank picked up the phone and dialled the number they had on file, an engaged tone beeping irritatingly in his ear. He replaced the receiver.

'What is it?' asked Matthews.

'Probably nothing. Just returning a call,' he replied; although something in the pit of his stomach told him that wasn't quite true. 'I'll drop by on the way home,' Frank told him, Matthews looking uncomfortable. 'It's on my way anyway,' he said, finishing off his drink and getting to his feet before his friend could protest. 'My last act before they have me working suicides and bar brawls gone bad with the rookies,' he joked, grabbing his jacket and heading out. 'I'll call if anything comes of it.'

* * *

Frank didn't recognise the house he'd parked up outside of, although that was to be expected. They'd interviewed countless people over the past few weeks – casting a preposterously wide net in desperation over a city of seven million in search of any and all Irish-born males between the ages of twenty-five and forty. The house itself was outstandingly unremarkable – one of a hundred two-up, two-down Victorian terraces on that street alone.

Checking the address once more, Frank climbed out and went to shut the car door, noticing the silver VW camper van parked a little way down the road and recalling a detail from a fading witness statement already banished to that abyss of unconnected information at the very back of his mind. As a precaution, he retrieved his service weapon from the glovebox where, against procedure, it tended to live whenever he was on duty. He'd never wanted the awful thing in the first place, but it had been a condition of him taking lead on the investigation.

He supposed he could hand it back now.

Attaching the holster to his waistband, he jotted down the registration number and approached the front door.

He knocked loudly... and then again.

Seeing neither life inside nor a lock on the gate, he took it as an invitation to explore further, losing the sun to the dirty poly-carbonate roof that ran the length of the property and looked likely to collapse on top of him at any moment. When he reached the side door, a handwritten note flapped about in the breeze where the tape had ripped free, Frank having to smooth it down against the glass to read it.

Play outside, honey.
I'll come get you soon. Xxx
Don't come in.

With a frown, he continued to the end of the covered walkway to look out over the rear garden, the knot in his stomach pulling tight on seeing a little girl playing in a paddling pool. No older than six or seven, the sunlight was catching in her long red curls, just as it had on the woman whose blood he still wore as the sun had risen over North London that morning.

The van. The disconcerting note. The red-haired girl.

Unholstering his weapon, Frank retraced his steps back down the walkway, checking the magazine before trying the handle, the patterned glass door swinging open into an empty kitchen.

'Mrs O'Callaghan!' he called, the silence deafening as he made his way through to the small living room, still unable to place the woman's face but remembering the hideous wallpaper well enough.

The curtains were half drawn, allowing an oppressive gloom to settle. Against the far wall a boxy television had been left on, the volume turned right down... *gagged*, while a wisp of smoke escaped a lit cigarette balanced on the edge of an ashtray, as if a ghost were relaxing in the empty armchair in the corner.

'Mrs O'Callaghan!' Frank called again, peering through the window to ensure the little girl was still playing outside before heading up the staircase, the wood groaning beneath his weight with every step.

Silence.

There was a bathroom to his left, a child's bedroom straight ahead of him, and to his right... Frank squinted to focus his tired eyes: a woman's leg hung over the side of a double bed.

'Mrs O'Callaghan?' he tried again, voice cracking and gun raised as he pushed the door open to enter the master bedroom.

Perhaps it was the exhaustion taking its toll, perhaps the sight of his second bloodbath in a day, perhaps even the over-whelming vindication he felt on knowing that he'd finally found him – but Frank lowered his weapon, now remembering the woman staring glassy-eyed at him from across the room. At least twenty separate puncture wounds decorated the front of her body alone; however, a weapon was conspicuously absent as she lay on a bed of polaroid photographs liberated from an upturned box.

Taking a tentative step towards her, Frank placed the gun down to pick up one of the glossy pictures, feeling as though he were holding one of his own memories: the first victim, Jessica Palmer, bound to the bed in her university dorm room, her left wrist hanging limp and broken, having lost the struggle against her restraints – just as Frank had found her. Discarding it onto the duvet with the others, wishing he could rid himself of his own thoughts as easily, he noticed movement in his peripheral vision, watching the mirror on the wall as a coat sleeve swayed in the open wardrobe behind him.

Forcing himself not to react, not to alert the other person in the room with him, Frank very, very slowly reached for his weapon...

The rail of jackets, shirts and dresses suddenly burst free of their confines, their flailing limbs flapping uselessly around Frank, disorientating his already sluggish mind as a bloody blade came at him from nowhere. Catching the tattooed arm, he fell back onto the bed – beneath him the fresh corpse of Marie O'Callaghan surrounded by the haunting images of the souls her husband had taken, while, from above, the man himself drove the knife down towards him.

He was every bit as strong as Frank, if not stronger, and had gravity on his side, the blade inching ever closer to Frank's face as he desperately reached out for his weapon, fingers brushing the metal yet unable to grasp it as the tip of the knife slid through the skin of his cheek.

And then, as he began to tire and his hand started to tremble, he watched a smile form on his attacker's face, both men aware that it was over as O'Callaghan shifted his weight to finish it, the bed springs pinging loudly as Frank felt the handle of the gun slide into his hand. Pushing it into the other man's flank, he pulled back on the trigger.

The crushing weight dissipated as Frank gasped for air, O'Callaghan falling into the bedroom doorframe before retreating down the stairs.

For a heartbeat, Frank considered just lying there – not going after him. *Who would have blamed him under the circumstances?* He'd been moments away from death and had suffered a serious facial wound. But before he'd even made a conscious decision, he was back on his feet pursuing his suspect down the blood-smeared staircase to find him already at the side door.

Frank fired another shot, cracking a yellowed wall tile, poorly aimed but close enough to make O'Callaghan panic, the Irishman shooting a pained look into the rear garden before taking off in the other direction, Frank only moments behind him.

'Call the police!' he bellowed as he passed a stunned neighbour and chased O'Callaghan down the street, gaining with every step as the other man lost more and more blood to the concrete. 'Kieran, stop!' he yelled, tearing across the road in front of an approaching car as his suspect disappeared behind a row of parked vehicles.

Frank raised his weapon and waited, but O'Callaghan never materialised from the other side. Stooping down to look beneath the stationary cars, he cautiously stepped up onto the pavement, following the sound of clinking metal to where the man that had the nation gripped with fear, the now eight-time serial killer, was pathetically attempting to scramble over a fence.

'It's over, Kieran,' he told him, the Irishman's shoulders slumping in acceptance as he gave up his futile escape and stepped back down, raising his hands in the air as he turned to face Frank.

He shook his head. 'Why did she have to go look in that box?' he asked in a strong Cork accent, as if it were all his wife's doing.

Frank pictured Marie O'Callaghan making that desperate call, a call that had ultimately cost her her life.

'You know, I think she knew... deep down,' continued O'Callaghan thoughtfully.

Each of the crime scenes flashed through Frank's mind in quick succession – that initial moment of first laying eyes on evil in its purest form.

'I wouldn't've hurt her if she hadn't fought back,' he went on, wincing as he lowered one arm to the wound in his side.

For some reason Frank pictured Eleanor – not the Eleanor as he knew her now but at her inevitable end – Frank having to stand over her and hold her hand at the moment when the cancer finally won their rigged battle – the godless injustice of her being taken from him while this monster endured filling him with rage. And then he realised why he had so wanted to keep the call to himself that morning, that this was precisely where he'd hoped it would lead: him alone with his monster, alone but for all his wrath...

'I can't help but notice you haven't asked me to drop the knife yet,' said O'Callaghan knowingly.

'No,' replied Frank in a hoarse whisper.

'Or told me I'm under arrest.'

'No.'

His suspect shifted uncomfortably and then asked with a lump in his throat: 'What will become of her... my little girl?'

'I don't give a shit,' Frank told him.

For the first time showing a glimmer of emotion – regret even – O'Callaghan met Frank's eye. 'Yes, you do. Would you do one thing for me though? Could you just tell her that her daddy—'

Frank pulled the trigger – a dark hole appearing in the

centre of the other man's chest, O'Callaghan dropping to his knees and giving him a bloody smile before slumping to the ground.

Closing his eyes, Frank breathed a sigh of relief at knowing he was finally gone... Staggering dazedly back towards the house... Flashing blue lights approaching... Pausing for a moment to cover his unsightly wound in the reflection of the glass door... And then kneeling down to introduce himself to the little red-haired girl playing alone in the paddling pool.

TWENTY-NINE

THE WOMBLES OF WIMBLEDON (EAST)

London was bursting at the seams: stifling, suffocating, the warm weather triggering towering office blocks to empty their guts out onto already crushed streets. The pubs were all full, every faeces-free inch of grass littered with suited sunbathers – the British public claiming any sunny day above twenty-five degrees Celsius as a national holiday by right.

Caught in the flow of foot traffic trudging down Tottenham Court Road, Henry's thoughts turned to Scarlett and her relentless determination. He wondered whether she would have actually gone through with it had they captured their suspect, whether she could have marched The Jackdaw out to her death knowing that Henry was lying in wait.

He supposed neither of them would ever get to find out.

Faces passed by, dozens at once, already forgotten by the time they were out of sight as the communal pace slowed to a shuffle. Glancing across the street to see whether the other side was faring any better, Henry spotted a familiar hulking figure standing an entire head above the crowds, Felix having no problems in matching Henry's pace.

'Curious,' muttered Henry, pretending to find something in

the window of Ole & Steen of particular interest as he passed, noticing Linus's distinctive platinum-blond hair in the reflection approximately ten paces behind. 'Concerning,' he corrected himself, keeping his eyes forward as the crowd parted around the strikingly beautiful woman walking against the current towards him. '...*Cock*.'

Sofia gestured to a quaint bistro set back from the road, Henry now seeing Rebecca already waiting on the lone table set out on their little outdoor terrace. Stepping out of the flow of people, he raised his arms, feeling Sofia's hands all over him before relieving him of both his weapons and his briefcase, Linus and Felix assuming their positions as he approached the table.

'Rebecca,' he smiled. 'What a lovely surprise.'

'Henry, dear. Please do take a seat,' she said, pouring tea out for them both. 'Word on the grapevine is The Jackdaw has struck again.'

'She has.'

Rebecca nodded but then moved on without further comment. 'And how is the beautiful Detective Delaney?'

'Still of use,' he replied, attempting to keep his voice even.

She stopped stirring her tea. 'Define "use".'

'My briefcase...' said Henry, his boss gesturing for Sofia to bring it over. 'There's a nine-millimetre in the pocket,' he told her as she opened it up, removed the weapon and took a step back.

Retrieving a brown cardboard folder from inside, Henry slid it across the table to Rebecca, who picked it up and started flicking through. 'What am I looking at?' she asked.

'I know you've been concerned about how much that journalist might have pieced together and how seriously the police might be taking his claims. This is me taking the "might" out of it for you,' he said, reaching for his cup.

She nodded and placed the file down, looking across at him

fondly. 'Oh, Henry, how I'm going to miss you. Not many of us get to outlive this game.'

'Some of us don't want to,' he replied, in reference to the three separate occasions on which Rebecca had got out only to get drawn back in again.

She smiled bashfully. 'Some of us have been doing this so long we can't imagine what wanting to would even feel like.' She paused. 'The issue I have is that you're my best.'

'I am,' he agreed. 'But the issue you're having is that I'm your *favourite*.' She chuckled at that. '...But I'm tired.'

'Aren't we all, dear?' she said, looking out over the chaotic street as if she didn't even recognise the London she'd once so loved.

'Regardless, I trust our arrangement still stands?' asked Henry.

Rebecca took a long sip of her drink before she answered. 'I'm quite sure the purpose of making an agreement that should be impossible to honour is that it *should* have been impossible to honour,' she mused. 'But yes, Henry. For if we do not have our word, what *do* we have?'

He nodded and finished his tea. 'Was there anything else?'

'As a matter of fact, there was. I wanted to pay you the courtesy of telling you in person that I have asked Linus to take care of our pretty little detective... when the time comes.'

Henry knew he had let his reaction show as he looked over at the Swedish ex-doctor who enjoyed his work a little too much. 'You don't trust me to do it?' he asked her.

Tactfully side-stepping the question, Rebecca smiled. 'My mind is made up. But not to worry, darling. I've told him to be on his very best behaviour. Now, if I'm not mistaken, you still have one-fifth of an impossible task to finish.'

* * *

'You've got a little something on your...' Scarlett pointed, the man smearing oil across his back as he retrieved what turned out to be a used tissue stuffed into the end of a toilet roll core entangled in cotton wool, which had affixed itself to the Velcro of his jacket.

'Ta,' he said, placing it on the desk and shooting her a grime-encrusted smile.

She had hurried straight over to the Wimbledon East Landfill and Recycling Site after receiving a call from 'Dumpy Dave', the site manager there who, against all odds, had located her burnt-orange toaster. She was staring out through the window of the 'office', a prefab box she suspected she could put her foot through without too much effort, watching as a cohort of men in matching hi-vis uniforms climbed across, pointlessly reorganised and rummaged through other people's rubbish like a pack of council-employed Wombles.

'Yep,' announced Dave, rechecking the serial number against the one Scarlett had given him. 'This is it.' Picking it up with his bare hands despite already being told repeatedly not to, he placed it into a plastic bag for her.

'I don't suppose there's any way of knowing who might have brought this in?' she asked, suspecting it was a silly question.

'No. Me neither,' concurred Dave, without even realising it was one.

'Have you found anything... unusual around here over the past few weeks?' she tried.

'Fat Ted found a three-headed Beanie Baby. That thing went *straight* up on eBay.'

'I was thinking more... human remains... body parts.'

'Body parts?' asked Dave, thinking hard, Scarlett sure his memory couldn't be *that* bad. 'Last body part I know of was the big toe I found in that washing machine.'

'And that was recent?' asked Scarlett, not holding out an awful lot of hope.

Dave puffed out his cheeks. 'A good six months back now. Good story though: I've seen a lot of medical shows, me. So the moment I saw it, I said to myself: "Dave, this is your moment. If you act quick enough and get this thing on ice, you could phone round all the local hospitals, find out which had a patient matching that injury, get in the car, belt across town and run into that theatre just in time to get the thing reattached."'

He appeared to have finished talking, but not the story.

'And...' Scarlett prompted him. 'Did you?'

'*Nah*, it got really busy and Steve was off with the... sick, so I just binned it,' he revealed, a not-too-sly glance into the over-flowing waste-paper bin beside him enough to encourage Scarlett back to her feet.

'OK then,' she said, collecting her Tesco bag of evidence. 'Someone will be round later for that security footage, if you could get it ready for them?'

'Right-o.'

'Mind if I have a quick look around before I go?'

'*Mi casa es su casa*,' he announced, gesturing to his empire with a filthy hand as he got the door for her.

* * *

Frank had managed to sit on his reading glasses... twice, and now his face was aching from squinting at the computer screen for hours on end. He was perusing an article about the bitter court battle that had been taking place between pop star Keeya Rose and her ex-manager, a man named Rudy Sinclair. Mr Sinclair claimed to be owed hundreds of thousands of pounds for services rendered after his client had fired him on the eve of her first number-one single, a debt, he alleges, she blew on 'sorting that crooked cocaine hoover on her face'.

He scrolled a little further down the page to a photograph of the cosmetically enhanced star performing on stage in a risqué burlesque outfit, wearing a dazzling smile back in the days when she'd had a head on which to wear one. And dangling around her neck, the chunky gold pendant that she was famously never without – belonging to her brother, killed in a gang-related incident – and never recovered following her murder.

He added another note to his spider diagram of bewilderment.

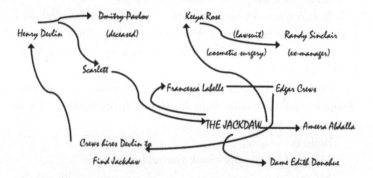

'What you working on?' asked Scarlett, appearing from nowhere and almost giving Frank a heart attack.

He swivelled the notebook to show her. 'Looking for links between our major players.'

'So... what have you got?'

He scoffed. 'What *haven't* I got?'

'No, really,' she said. 'What have you got?'

'Well... they all appear... on my diagram.' Slumping in his chair, he pushed the book to one side. 'Where have you been?'

'With forensics. I dropped off the toaster Francesca Labelle's neighbour threw in the skip outside their building, in the hope they might find something that tells us who ordered it... or collected it or...' She shrugged. 'It's a long shot. What have you got the team working on?'

'Mostly talking to tall, twenty-to-thirty-year-old Asian

women with green eyes, as per your Henry's description. Funny, I haven't heard a word of complaint all morning.'

'Yeah, funny that,' agreed Scarlett. 'What about you?'

'Photos, as if you need to ask, along with trying to track down the explosive used to blow the swimming pool apart. Got a list of chemical companies I'm working through.'

'Well, don't let me keep you,' she said, turning to walk away.

'Hey, Scarlett!' blurted Frank, but then he hesitated before continuing with the thought that had been playing on his mind ever since their heart-to-heart the previous day. 'Henry Devlin killed Dmitry Pavlov, piece of utter shit as he was. And, let's be honest, probably a fair few other people as well.'

She folded her arms defensively.

'I guess what I'm trying to say is – when this is all over, no matter how useful he's been to us, no matter how heroically he tries to save our victims... no matter how you may feel about it...'

She looked uncomfortable.

'I *will* put a pair of cuffs on him as I would any other murderer. I'm not going to look the other way. I'm not wired like that. Just thought you should know.'

'Anything else?' she asked impatiently.

Frank shook his head. 'No.'

Giving him a curt nod, Scarlett walked away, Frank only managing to unlock his screen before being interrupted again, this time by Olsen, the geeky young man's skinny jeans surely cutting off the blood supply to something he needed down there. His visitor went to kneel down... but then thought better of it.

'How's it going, Frank?' he greeted him before lowering his voice. 'Two things: one: that photo you took – I was so busy looking at the faces, I didn't register what was in the foreground. You got a pretty good shot of the back of the big guy's neck.' He handed Frank an enlarged picture of what looked to be a tattoo of a fish. 'It's a black dolphin,' he explained. 'Means he served time in the Russian prison of the same name. But then look at this,' he went on, giving him another picture. 'These are gang brands, area of operation, just across the border: Latvia, Estonia, Belarus. Educated guess: that's where he's from.'

Frank looked impressed. 'And the second thing?'

'Just a heads-up: Fernandez has been sniffing around. He's realised we're good friends.'

That was impressive as Frank hadn't.

'He wanted to know if *I* knew if you were working on anything other than what *he* knew you were supposed to be working on, but didn't want me to let you know.'

Frank looked lost. '...What?'

'He's been sniffing around,' replied Olsen in summation.

'Oh. OK. Thanks,' said Frank, gazing across the office to where Fernandez was engrossed in a telephone conversation. 'I don't expect you to lie for me.'

'It's a bit late for that, I'm afraid,' said Olsen, giving him a gawky smile. 'Between him and Linus Bergman – "The Ghoul of Gothenburg" – you've got trouble coming at you from both sides, so just... watch your back, yeah?' He thought about it for a moment. 'And, by that logic, your front.'

* * *

At a little after 3 p.m. Scarlett's work phone rang.

'Delaney,' she answered. '...You're sure?' she asked excitedly, reaching for a notepad while the person on the other line updated her. 'Yeah... Yes. Thank you.'

Placing the receiver down, she got to her feet but then just stood there for a moment, unsure where to even begin, the brief phone call changing everything. She forced a decision, tearing the scribbled details from her pad and catching the arm of a passing subordinate.

'I need a home address and photograph in the next two

minutes,' she said, the startled young woman just gawping back. 'One minute fifty now,' Scarlett prompted her, providing a gentle shove in the right direction as she made her way over to Frank.

He looked bored.

'Something's come up,' she told him. 'Can I borrow you?'

He'd clearly picked up on her tone, as he got up without argument and followed her back to her workstation, Scarlett watching the flustered officer tear across the room to the printer before giving the temperamental contraption a good kick when she had to fill it up with paper.

'Everything OK?' asked Frank, but Scarlett didn't even hear him as she tried to organise her thoughts.

The perspiring officer came running over with the fruits of her minute-and-a-half's labour, Scarlett dismissing her with a nod, taking a deep breath and turning to Frank.

'Here we go,' she said, taking his hand for balance as she clambered up onto her desk. 'Could I have everyone's attention, please?!' she shouted over the din. 'Excuse me! Can I have everyone's attention?!'

A ripple of hushes spread outwards to the far corners of the room.

She held up a black-and-white photograph, still warm from the innards of the printer. 'Sun Jung Lin,' she announced, showing the picture around. 'This is her, people. *This* is our Jackdaw.'

Excited murmurs broke out all around her.

'She matches the witness description from The Mount-batten Hotel, and it was her blood on the street where we believe Keeya Rose was killed.' She turned to the subordinate, who'd only just sat back down. 'Get Armed Response to her home address immediately.'

The woman nodded and picked up the phone.

'We need you all to stop what you're working on and focus

your efforts on this suspect – the works: family, financials, frequented places, known associates... everything. Detective Ash and I will be on our phones if you need us. Thank you,' she finished, climbing down.

'You're getting good at that,' said Frank as Scarlett grabbed her bag and keys.

'Tell them to wait for us,' she instructed the officer on the phone. 'We're on our way.'

'We?' asked Frank sceptically.

'This is it, Frank. You've got to be there,' she told him, already marching towards the lifts.

'*Nah*. Kicking down doors and jumping on people is a youngster's game,' he said, proving his point by how out of breath he sounded just trying to keep up with her. 'You'll be in good hands. I'll hold the fort here, find you a plan B in case she's not home.' The lift doors opened. 'Besides,' he started as she stepped inside, 'this is all you... always has been.'

She smiled and pushed the button.

'Hey,' he added, catching the doors when they went to close on them. 'You deserve this. You go catch your monster.'

THIRTY

EVERYBODY CONGA!

'Stay at the back. Always at the back. When I say "move" move. When I say "stop" stop. Got it?' asked the Specialist Firearms Command team leader as Scarlett pulled the bullet-proof vest tight around her.

'Got it,' she nodded, peering round the wall at their uninviting destination: to the rear of a parade of downmarket shops, a handful of metal staircases zigzagged up to weathered front doors.

'*Christ*, it's hot,' the man complained before holding a finger to his ear as he looked up at the rooftops opposite. 'Romeo One, visual?'

'That would be a negative,' a distorted voice responded through the radio Scarlett was attaching to her vest.

'Well, we can't just stand about on the street waving our guns at people all day,' he told his team, all looking equally uncomfortable beneath identical black uniforms as he pulled his stifling helmet back on. 'Beta team – on you.'

'Does that make me the boss then?' joked a female officer as she checked her weapon.

'I'm stuck at the back babysitting, aren't I?' he replied, just in case Scarlett hadn't picked up on the *five* previous comments he'd made about how unwelcome she was – not that she gave a toss. He was merely a tool – a means to an end. He hadn't risked his career, jail time and quite possibly his soul in pursuit of this suspect as she had. 'Hand here, so I know where you are,' he told her, placing her hand on his shoulder as the other team scurried across the parking area. 'OK. Alpha team – move.'

Just trying to match the pace of the boots two steps ahead, Scarlett followed the rest of her team to the bottom of the staircase, crouching down in time with the officers as they aimed their weapons up at the doorway above. And then, looking like a conga line at a funeral, Beta team made their way up the metal stairs, fanning out at the top to make room for the ram.

'Hope you're ready,' whispered the team leader, Scarlett's heart beating out of her chest as the officer above counted down on her fingers, the flimsy door bursting open on the first swing. 'Go! Go! Go!' he yelled, Scarlett springing to her feet, focussing only on the boots in front again as they hurried upwards and then in through the broken door.

'Clear!' various voices shouted, the inside of the depressing flat about as unpleasant as she'd been expecting: curtains too thin to even keep out the light hanging off their rails, bins overflowing with days-old rubbish and the remnants of several meals sitting out on the kitchen worktop.

Irrational as it was, she felt a little disappointed in her slovenly monster who, now in possession of a name and unappealing property in Fulham, was starting to feel markedly more human.

'Boss!' someone called.

Scarlett's escort turned to face her. 'You, stay here,' he ordered, leaving her alone in the grotty kitchen as he disappeared round the corner.

Straining to listen in to what they were saying, Scarlett

edged further along the corridor... and then further still as the voices somehow grew more distant. She'd almost made it to the end, when the team leader called back to her:

'Detective Delaney! You'd better see this!'

Straightening up, she waited a couple of seconds and then stepped around the corner, her mouth falling open as her brain attempted to understand the confusion of images before her: the yellowed wall at the far end of the hallway wasn't in fact a wall at all but a thick security door, which was standing wide open to the luxurious room beyond – torn linoleum abutting a dark mahogany floor, peeling wallpaper bathed in the glow of subtly lit exposed brickwork.

Stunned, Scarlett passed through the false wall, feeling like she was passing through a doorway to another dimension as she stepped into the lavish and sprawling space disguised behind a façade of destitution, her opinion of her monster clawing back some ground.

'In here,' said the team leader, beckoning her into the main space: show-home ready bar the bank of computer screens climbing the far wall. 'Is she a hacker or something?' he asked logically, Scarlett's gaze falling to the custom-built towers beneath the desk, fans clicking on and off somewhere inside like mechanical lungs, neon lights glowing in the gloom like the eyes of a predator.

'Not that I was aware of,' she answered honestly, walking over to the desk and pulling on a pair of disposable gloves to sort through the pages of sketches and scribbles piled beside the keyboard.

About halfway through she came across a creased ticket for Edith Donohue's show at The Old Playhouse... and then a business card for the limousine company employed to chauffer Keeya Rose to her awards ceremony. And beneath it all, a small tube of powder labelled *Sodium*.

'This *is* her though, isn't it?' the team leader checked.

'Certainly looks that way,' said Scarlett, moving a sheet of calculations aside to reveal a page from the previous week's newspaper – a story she was already vaguely aware of: news that the controversial activist known only as E.W. intended to finally reveal her identity and give herself up to the police in aid of her cause at an exclusive event taking place in just three days' time.

'Boss!' someone yelled as they came hurrying in carrying what looked to be a children's jewellery box. 'Found this in the other room,' they announced, setting down the collection of trinkets: a blood-smeared brooch beside an oversized golden pendant, a pair of sparkling earrings alongside what Scarlett recognised to be Ameera Abdalla's diamond-encrusted bracelet – each meticulously labelled with the victim's name and placed within a sealed plastic bag, a categorical treasure trove of evidence.

'But that's impossible,' muttered Scarlett, looking again at the heart-shaped bracelet she had last seen washing over the edge of a building while still attached to its owner's wrist. The brooch too was a surprise; they'd been confident that Edith Donohue's wedding band had been taken as the trophy.

'Looks like we just found your Jackdaw's nest,' the team leader announced triumphantly.

'Empty nest,' Scarlett mumbled, still frowning down at the macabre keepsakes.

'Regardless, hope it's enough,' he said over her shoulder, 'because she knows we're here.' He gestured up to the cameras positioned all around the room. 'She won't be coming back now.'

Folding up the newspaper article and sliding it into an evidence bag, Scarlett smiled. 'She doesn't have to... We'll come to her.'

* * *

The evening sunshine poured through the office windows, a slap in the face to those who should have already finished their shifts. Frank didn't care though. He was engrossed in his work, which had veered off on another unexpected tangent, and the revelation that, to this day, the death penalty remained a widely practised form of punishment in Saudi Arabia – public beheadings in the town square the kingdom's favoured method.

Somewhere down this particular rabbit hole, Frank had been surprised to learn of the fate of successful businessman Salmon Fadel, who had been sentenced to death based on the witness testimony of none other than Abbas Abdalla – Ameera Abdalla's father. Following the execution on this particularly bloody day in Riyadh, Fadel's body had been claimed by the crowd, never to be seen again, leaving the family with what they resolutely claimed to be a 'great injustice' as well as an empty grave to mourn over – an eventuality of particular significance to those of Muslim faith.

So, to lighten the mood, he was now reading through the police interview with Dame Edith Donohue's widower, who'd been holding an impromptu dinner party at the family home on the eve of his wife's murder, which, along with the return of his great-great-grandmother's wedding ring, remained bitter sticking points at the centre of the couple's divorce settlement.

Frank was working his way down the list of guests, googling the names in turn, each more affluent and powerful than the last. His thought process: with no clear links between the victims, perhaps there was a connection between the people surrounding them; although, bar their privilege and standing, all he'd really managed to find was a way to waste another half hour of his life.

To postpone having to go back to labelling photographs, he reached for his post tray, removing a weighty printout from the tech team. Having to squint down at the needlessly minuscule writing, it took him a few moments to realise what he was looking at: a complete transcript of text and messenger app correspondence from Francesca Labelle's mobile. He flicked through the pages, more for the waft of cool air than anything else, and went to place it to one side... when he noticed something. Double-checking he wasn't seeing things, he picked up his phone and dialled the number for technical services.

'Hi, it's Frank Ash here from Homicide. Can you put me through to whoever was in charge of the data for the Francesca Labelle murder?'

He was placed on hold for a few seconds before a chirpy-sounding woman picked up. 'Hi, Suzi speaking.'

'I'm just looking at this printout from Francesca Labelle's phone and don't think I completely understand it.'

'We recovered all the messages from the past month as requested. They're displayed in reverse order,' she tried.

'What I mean is the very top entry on here – I've never seen it before.'

There was the click of a computer keyboard in the background. 'What time was the message?'

'12:53 a.m.,' he answered. 'Around the time she was last seen.'

'Ah, yes,' she said. 'So, do you see where it says *recovered* alongside the text? That means we restored it.'

'Restored it?'

'As in, she'd deleted it,' the woman explained. 'Which is why you wouldn't have seen it before.'

'I see. OK. Thanks,' said Frank, hanging up and staring down at the cryptic one-word message that Francesca Labelle had received within minutes of excusing herself for the night and never resurfacing from her room:

+447642367896

00:53 *Rooftop* (recovered)

He hadn't even replaced the receiver before trying the number from which the text had originated, three chimes and a disconnection message greeting him just as Scarlett walked through the door.

'Hey,' she said, looking flustered. 'I got back as quickly as I could. Is everyone still here?'

'Almost.' Frank put the phone down. 'I think Newbury might've broken out – the little shit. Want me to rally the troops?'

'If you could. I'll be in in just a minute.'

* * *

It had, of course, taken Frank over a quarter of an hour to round up everybody working The Jackdaw murders and, even then, he seemed a little light. Scarlett had welcomed the delay however; it gave her the chance to visit the bathroom and cool down before addressing her colleagues, the meeting room falling silent as DCI Griffiths joined them. Closing the door behind him, he assumed his place at the back.

'Right,' started Scarlett with a weary sigh. 'First off – my apologies to those of you who have finished for the day. I wouldn't keep you if it wasn't absolutely necessary. So, as you know, earlier today I joined—'

'Oh, *bollocks*,' someone blurted from the doorway, him and the takeaway coffee in his hand having crashed the meeting. 'I've been sitting out there for over two *bloody* hours, and the five *bloody* minutes I *bloody* well step out...'

'Just sit down, Newbury!' barked Griffiths from somewhere in the room.

Giving a sarcastic salute, the mouthy young officer climbed over three people to reach an empty seat in the middle row.

Once finally settled, he gave Scarlett a *you may continue* gesture.

'OK. As I was saying...'

Over the next ten minutes, Scarlett relayed the details of her operation with SCO19 earlier in the day: the hidden room beyond the false wall, the bank of high-spec computers.

'I take it we can safely say this is her then?' Griffiths asked when she'd finished.

Scarlett nodded. 'The witness description... Her blood at one of the crime scenes, and now evidence related to the previous murders found at her home. Yes, sir. This is her.'

'Then we'll go public with it tonight,' he said decisively. 'We'll have the whole country looking for this Sun Jung Lin by morning. How sure are we this activist is her next target?'

'We'll have a better idea once we've had a proper search through the piles of paperwork I recovered,' she said. 'But for now, it's all we have.'

'OK. Wilkins?...Wilkins, are you in here?' Griffiths called over the sea of heads, an older officer raising his hand.

'Yes, sir.'

'You're the expert. Want to fill us in?' his chief suggested before addressing Scarlett. 'Wilkins was already heading up an investigation into this E.W. character,' he explained, the room turning to face the quiet officer in the corner.

'*Errrm*... Of course,' he started unsurely, getting to his feet. 'Well, this got passed over to Serious Crimes back in February after the incident in the Docklands.'

'Docklands?' Frank prompted him.

'The fire at that distribution centre... with the homeless man inside,' he explained, nods of recognition breaking across the room. 'There's no way she could've known, of course, but manslaughter is manslaughter and somewhat overshadowed the message she was trying to put out there.'

'So, who is she?' asked Frank.

'That's the trouble – nobody knows. All her social media comes through third-party influencers...' Frank nodded along but clearly had no idea what he was talking about. 'What few photographs we have of her in the act tell us nothing: female, ethnicity unknown, five foot five to five foot eight, wears a green balaclava, nondescript jeans and T-shirt,' the officer told them. 'We thought we'd caught a break when the event was announced, but even the money for that was paid from some offshore account we can't trace.'

'Any leads at all?' tried Scarlett.

'Hundreds,' he replied. 'We could use some help though.'

'You'll get it,' she assured him. 'What does E.W. mean? Her initials perhaps?'

'Eco Warrioress – enemy number one to major corporations and unsustainable industries everywhere. Up until the accident with the homeless man, I think it would be fair to say she probably did far more good than harm in the world. She's an inspiration to a lot of people.'

'Sounds like Wilkins has been compromised,' someone teased, the older officer going bright red.

'Errr... Yeah. Hello,' called the tardy officer while waving his cardboard cup in the air. 'I've got a question.'

'What is it, Newbury?' huffed Frank.

'So, if no one knows who this Eco Warrioress is, why would The Jackdaw want her dead?' The room fell silent; it was actually a very good point. Frank opened his mouth to say something... but then frowned. 'I mean, what could *possibly* be her motive?' asked Newbury.

'Precisely the same as the previous murders,' Scarlett countered, taking back control. 'An impossible target in an impossible situation with an audience to witness the genius of it all.

Fits the bill perfectly, if you ask me. And who could be more impossible to get to than a person whose identity is unknown?'

There were murmurs of agreement as several separate conversations broke out around the room, but Newbury wasn't done yet, slopping coffee over the person next to him as he got to his feet.

'Yeah, hello again!' he shouted over the din, the room gradually returning to a hush. 'Just a thought, but if The Jackdaw doesn't even know who this E.W. person is, there doesn't seem much point in us wasting our time and resources trying to find out.'

'What are you on about, you nob?' the person he had just scalded scolded. 'We could warn her ahead of time, tell her not to attend, even cancel the whole thing altogether.'

Newbury chuckled. 'That's sweet – that you'd think for *one second* Detective Delaney or the commissioner would just give up their bait when The Jackdaw is *this* close.' Scarlett looked away guiltily. 'My point is the threat isn't coming from this activist person that no one can identify. The Jackdaw isn't following her about or intending to exploit some aspect of her life. The threat is coming from the event itself: the building, the companies involved in organising it... and the other guests. I'm saying whatever she has planned will already have to be in place before she even knows who her target is. That's what we need to focus on.'

The room looked back to Scarlett expectantly, who was actually starting to quite like the cocky young officer. 'Newbury, is it?' He nodded warily. 'Talk to me after. I might have a job for you.'

Looking pleased with himself, he sat back down.

'We go public with The Jackdaw's image, but our activist's gala goes ahead as planned,' Scarlett told the room. 'We'll comb every last inch of the venue and flood the event with so many police on the night we'll have her in custody before she even steps through the door.' She turned to Frank. 'Anything to add, Detective?' He didn't seem to hear her however, still lost in thought after what Newbury had said. 'Frank?'

Snapping out of it, he shook his head. 'No. Nothing.'

Scarlett's stomach grumbled loudly in conclusion. 'Then, meeting adjourned.'

* * *

The sky was on fire, the sun setting as though for the last time, casting an otherworldly hue over the city as Frank stood alone in Francesca Labelle's penthouse. He reached for a light switch but then thought better of it, finding a rare moment of serenity in watching the long shadows reach across the wooden floors before tangling themselves into patches of gloom. He wasn't entirely sure why he'd made the journey across town, only that the nagging pull in the pit of his stomach wouldn't let up until he'd satisfied it.

After thirty-odd years on the job, one learns to trust their intuition.

He took out his phone and typed a single word: *Rooftop*, the white glow from the screen on his face as he followed Francesca Labelle's journey through to the bedroom, closing the door behind him just as she would have done. Stepping over the dried blood, he approached the window, which looked as secure and undamaged as when he'd first arrived at the scene. The television aerial atop the building next door glowed red in the sunlight; he'd never even noticed it before. A handful of the windows were illuminated and he could see the people inside pottering about as they wound down for the evening.

With a heavy sigh, he turned back to face the room, wondering if after three decades he should be able to tell the difference between intuition and hunger. Heading back out, he was just in the middle of debating whether to cook his lasagne or cottage pie for dinner, when he noticed a fresh pile of post stacked up on the bureau. Clearly the concierge had asked one of his colleagues to bring it up. Supposing he could survive a little longer without starving, he started flicking through, finding the usual assortment of bills and bank statements until coming across something that caught his eye: a single-page note from an upmarket windows company.

Hewlett Glazing Solutions

Dear resident,

As you may be aware, there have been some issues with water ingress in Flat 4, which we have been out to on several occasions. We have been informed that Flat 1 is now experiencing similar issues.
We would therefore recommend that the seals to every window and door in the building be replaced in one consolidated effort. Unfortunately, the warranty period has now lapsed; however, as all of the properties in the block are almost identical in layout, we can offer this service at a discounted rate of £1,995.00 per flat.
Should you wish to take us up on this...

Frowning, Frank headed back to the bedroom doorway, his gut definitely trying to tell him something. In the failing light, he looked from the stain on the floor to the unmade double bed to the large window, only the very tip of the rooftop aerial now glowing like a red-hot poker.

'Son of a bitch,' he exclaimed, it finally coming to him as he shoved the note into his pocket and hurried back to the lift.

* * *

Henry had a relatively good head for heights but still, in the main, tended to avoid falling from them; however, the cramped conditions up in the sultry rafters were making that considerably more difficult.

As he drilled into the beam he was sitting on, there was a disconcerting crack. Henry waited a few moments... Having not plummeted to his death, he wiped the sweat out of his eyes and then very slowly continued, almost jumping out of his skin when his phone started buzzing against the wood. He didn't dare stop, taking his life in his hands with every rotation of the drill bit, the phone vibrating closer and closer to the edge.

He still had time; he had the reflexes of a cat.

The moment the metal pierced the underside of the wood he grasped for the phone, as it dawned on him that even cats get old and slow and a bit shit at everything as he watched it fall through the air and hit the floor thirty feet below.

Quickly switching off his light, he pulled his feet up to lie flat atop the beam as a door opened close by. Unable to do anything other than remain still, Henry watched a torchlight sweep across the cavernous space, the leg of his black trousers illuminated as the security guard moved directly beneath him. Stopping mere inches from the phone, his beam searched the back wall until, finally satisfied, he headed back out, the doors rattling closed behind him.

Puffing out his cheeks, Henry looked down at the little black rectangle below. No doubt smashed to pieces, he knew he would still have to retrieve it one way or another. 'Shit.'

* * *

Scarlett hung up when the phone went to voicemail.

Henry would just have to get an update in the morning.

She was standing on the corner of her road, loitering in the glow of her favourite shop and remembering simpler times. Not two weeks earlier, she and Mark had spent a relaxing afternoon ambling up and down the high street: lunch, shopping, coffee. It had been blissful, as perfect as a day can be, and yet, she wasn't sure she missed it at all. She made her way past cosy houses, the street basking in the dinnertime quiet, and then tutted at the amount of litter that had accumulated beside their basement window as she climbed up to the front door. She'd get it later... or, more accurately, Mark would.

'You're late!' he greeted her the moment she crossed the threshold.

He looked nice – hair coiffured into his 'party' style, which looked deceptively like his everyday style but with an ozone-buggering amount of hairspray. He was even wearing the blazer she'd got him for his birthday, a *sale* tag dangling from the bottom not reflecting particularly well on either of them. She only hoped she'd managed to keep the look of confusion off her face.

'What's with the look of confusion on your face?' he asked.

Shit.

'You forgot, didn't you?'

'No,' she said defensively. 'I didn't forget. It's Sunday—'

'It's Monday.'

'Right, it's Monday, and we said we'd go out tonight. I just got held up at work. Give me twenty minutes and I'll be ready,' she promised, kicking off her boots and hurrying up the stairs.

* * *

'Taxi's five minutes away!' called Mark. 'Did you see they'd changed estate agent over the road?' he asked, engrossed in his phone as he climbed the stairs. 'As if *that's* the problem and not the three-and-a-half grand a month they're asking for it... So, are you feeling like gin or wine tonig—' But he stopped short on finding Scarlett still fully dressed, mouth open and snoring gently where she'd collapsed onto the bed.

With a huff, he looked at his phone, scrolling down to the contact occupying the number three spot on his list of favourites.

'Hello. Domino's Pizza!'

THIRTY-ONE

LEVEL FOOTING

It was 6:52 a.m. when Detective Sergeant Alejandro Fernandez stepped out of the lift at New Scotland Yard, the stink of his spicy breakfast burrito sure to linger in the little metal box for hours to come. He stopped abruptly, a worried look on his face, unsure whether he was suffering a heart attack, a burst lung or merely severe indigestion – a sharp thump to the chest seeming to sort whichever of the three it had been.

He tended to get into work early. Between a wife, a live-in mother-in-law, four kids and two dogs, the perpetual state of chaos they existed in only ever subsided for a few hours each night... if he was lucky. He walked through to the office and stopped again, this time not for a medical emergency but to regard the man sprawled across a desk beside the door: Frank, fast asleep. He looked as though he'd been there all night.

Checking who was about, Fernandez made his way over. The computer screen was blank, no doubt powered down from inactivity, so he moved on to the mess that surrounded the sleeping man: to Frank's left – a fire evacuation floorplan for an apartment building in Knightsbridge. He was both lying on and dribbling over a notebook, where he'd made a series of mildly disturbing notes:

- *Passed-out Bathtub Tutu Man looks a lot like the Vino Vomiter + neither can handle their drink - brothers perhaps?*
- *Where did the tutu come from?! Did he bring it with him?*
- *Stink Breath Kenny isn't even named Kenny! He's called Jeff.*

His balding head was in the way of the next few...

- *Blonde Becky becomes Brunette Becky at 10.50 p.m. but I thought the blonde really brought out her eyes.*
- *I think No Shoes' boyfriend is cheating on her... with someone in shoes.*

'Oh, Frank,' whispered Fernandez in genuine concern as he leaned over his colleague's shoulder to read a tatty scrap of paper:

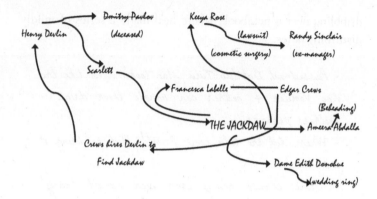

Eyes falling straight to Scarlett's name, he followed the arrow back to Henry Devlin... and then on to the murder of Dmitry Pavlov, a smile breaking across his face as he slid his phone out of his pocket and tapped on the camera app. 'Got you.'

Scarlett closed her eyes, the raucous office disappearing bit by bit as she turned the volume up on her headphones. Days earlier, her colleagues in technical services had sent over the sound file she'd requested, but she'd only now found the time to listen to it. Using some computer magic, they'd effectively inverted the voicemail message Dame Edith Donohue had left her husband, the deceased's husky voice now no more than a muffled crackle in the background of a concerto of footsteps, creaks and thuds.

Scarlett found herself tensing up at the point where the woman's voice gave way to the pre-recorded soundbites, as if hoping it might play out differently this time: that she would turn around, run, at least cry out for help. But, of course, she didn't, an almost inaudible gasp remaining her parting words to a world whose attention she had lost long ago.

Even for a homicide detective, it was a difficult listen. Strangely perhaps even more so than video footage would have been, Scarlett's imagination filling in the gaps between unidentifiable sounds, feeling as though she were in the room with them, as if it were one of her own memories. *Boots?* she scribbled down on hearing the heavy footfalls cross the room... the familiar creak of the floorboard below the light. That wasn't really much of a revelation; she hadn't expected The Jackdaw to behead someone while wearing high heels. She listened closer: the scrape of the hardboard wall being fitted into position. *Strong?* She jotted down next – not because of something she'd heard on the recording but because of something she *hadn't*.

She wondered why the tiny-framed Sun Jung Lin would choose to carry her victim's body across the room rather than drag it. *Perhaps to avoid leaving evidence? Perhaps because she was conscious of the eavesdropping phone? Perhaps she'd been hitting it hard at Legs, Bums and Tums class and was just that fit?* But Frank would think less of her if she didn't at least question it. She underlined the thought and then listened closely as The Jackdaw left the room, closing the door behind her, only the muffled voice remaining now, a binary rant of crackles and pops in the quiet...

'Detective Delaney?'

Scarlett almost fell off her chair. She removed the headphones in irritation and looked up at Newbury, having appointed the mouthy young detective her unofficial second-in-command after he'd impressed at the previous day's meeting. In truth, it was little more than a glorified secretarial job, but that wasn't to say it wasn't helpful. He'd spent the morning deflecting all manner of trivia away on her behalf, in between coordinating the continued stake-out at Sun Jung Lin's Fulham residence – a media-relations-dictated waste of resources for the benefit of the half-dozen television crews parked up in the road outside, who seemed oblivious to the fact that they were somewhat giving the game away. But she appreciated him taking the burden off her all the same.

Their suspect's image had been plastered across the front pages of every newspaper Scarlett had seen, the manhunt officially 'on' with just seventy-two hours to go before Friday night's big 'unmasking' event. Access had been arranged with the organisers and a comprehensive list of companies and personnel involved was already eclipsing the sun beside her monitor. Frustratingly, there was no guest list to work off. In the activist's typical PR-savvy fashion, those invited wouldn't find out until just two hours beforehand, whipping the media into a frenzy while making Scarlett's job infinitely more stressful.

She was worried about Frank. He looked a state, but she hadn't found a free moment to say more than two words to him since arriving at the office. She had, however, ensured she made a little time for Mark that morning, wanting to make up for the previous night. Putting on the dress she'd intended to wear out to dinner and popping open a bottle of Buck's Fizz, she'd surprised him with a candle-lit breakfast before work – his disproportionate gratitude only making her feel worse.

It was a plaster over a chainsaw wound but was the best she could manage for now.

The nightshift had been busy too, an anonymous tip-off leading to a raid on a property in Camden Town, three arrests on drugs charges, one officer with a broken nose, but little else. The boffins, meanwhile, had spent their night utterly stumped by the hacker's military-grade encryption programs – the secrets contained within the recovered hard drives might as well have been on the moon for how close they were to ever gaining access.

'...*Huh?*' asked Scarlett, her mind elsewhere.

'I said I just got off the phone with forensics,' Newbury told her. He seemed energised, excited even. *Clearly she wasn't working him hard enough.* 'They've found Francesca Labelle's DNA on that toaster you brought back from the dump.'

She blinked back at him, her thoughts taking a few moments to catch up. She leapt to her feet. 'But *that* means she must've been in the skip at some point!'

'Right,' he said.

'This is huge!'

'Right,' he agreed.

She formulated a plan on the spot. 'Tell whoever's going through the security video from the dump that it's now a priority,' she said, grabbing her phone and keys off the desk. 'Give them whatever help they need,' she continued, already backing away from him. 'We *need* to know who collected that skip.'

Newbury nodded.

'Frank!' she called across the room, her exhausted mentor looking up from his work. 'Boss's office! We've got something!'

* * *

The engine roared as the Armed Response vehicle accelerated past the traffic on Westminster Bridge, the wail of their convoy calling across the city as it began snaking through the streets towards Wimbledon. Surrounded by officers in full tactical gear, Scarlett and Frank struggled for balance while donning their borrowed kit in the sickly light of the windowless box.

DCI Griffiths hadn't needed much convincing to order the raid on the Wimbledon East Landfill and Recycling Site: the allure of closing a case of such magnitude was more than enticing – it was seductive. It made people operate on emotion, snubbing the usual bureaucratic back-and-forth in favour of decisive action, the promised glory outweighing the potential risk.

'Oh, shit!' gasped Frank, knowing he was going over as the driver swung them around some unseen obstruction. Catching him mid-fall, one of the officers helped him back into his seat like a pensioner at a care home. 'Thanks,' said Frank in embarrassment, shooting Scarlett an 'I'm too old for this' look before pulling the helmet down over his head.

Due to the scale of the operation – four armed teams, two dog units and a helicopter – and the media attention it would undoubtedly attract, the officer in charge had insisted everything be done by the book, including sourcing full kit for both of their Homicide tagalongs.

The radios clicked in unison, followed by the static hiss that always preceded a transmission: '...Approaching destination.'

The sirens cut out as they bounced over a speedbump... and then another... a final surge of acceleration before they came skidding to a stop. The doors burst open, blinding sunlight flooding in as Scarlett and Frank followed their team out through the back of the truck.

Disorientated, they both needed a moment to take in their surroundings.

SCO19 were doing what SCO19 did best: a whole lot of shouting – barking orders at the unfortunate local residents who now found themselves trapped on the premises, while rounding up all of the brightly dressed council workers. Scarlett spotted Dumpy Dave, the fallen king in his hardboard castle, mouth hanging open as three armed officers came to fetch him. And the handlers were holding items of Francesca Labelle's clothing up to their dogs' noses as the helicopter appeared in the sky above them, enjoying a God's-eye view of the pandemonium.

'Christ,' muttered Frank. 'This had better lead to something.'

Scarlett didn't reply, not wanting to admit, even to herself, just how much was riding on her instincts at that moment. 'Let's do a lap,' she suggested, keen to discover her fate either way. 'Meet back here.'

'Be careful,' Frank told her, the two of them heading off in opposite directions.

Dwarfed by massive metal containers on either side, Scarlett walked away from the main gate, passing one of the search dogs as its handler encouraged it into a gap he couldn't fit through himself. There was a separate lane for trade and large vehicles so she followed that, stopping to peer into a rusted skip, the garden of weeds inside suggesting it had been there some time.

She moved on, her radio clicking to life: 'All personnel accounted for.'

Feeling like a rat in a maze, she climbed the metal stairs scaling the container labelled *Glass* and gazed out over the predictable layout. A loop of tarmac followed the outer fence, the uniform containers giving way to an expansive open area sunk into the ground; from up high it looked like an amphitheatre for a far grander purpose than mere *Household and General Waste*. The helicopter still hovered overhead, but judging from their lack of input it hadn't spotted any more than the rest of them.

She climbed back down and continued walking, interest piqued on seeing a break in the thoroughfare leading to an area signposted *Staff Only*. Losing sight of her colleagues, she went to investigate, the tarmac deteriorating into dirt as she approached a set of cargo containers standing ominously apart from the rest of the site.

'Police!' she called. 'Anyone back here?!'

Only the breeze answered.

She proceeded slowly, pulling open the heavy door to the first container to find it empty bar a couple of mismatched stools, the mug of cigarette butts indicating it served as a break-time shelter on rainy days.

Sliding through the gap into the second container, she

discovered a classic car – its guts spilt across the floor, suggesting someone was attempting to rebuild it.

Anticlimactically, the third was clearly where the employees stashed their better finds: bikes that still looked perfectly rideable, board games stacked high, toys and sporting equipment. Feeling a little deflated, Scarlett pushed the door to and headed back out onto the main loop where the other dog handler was approaching from the opposite direction, the lead in his hands pulled taut as the German Shepherd tugged against its harness, directing him across the grass to the outer fence.

Scarlett quickened her pace, watching the animal sniff about and then bark loudly.

She realised she was sprinting now, the handler peering into the treeline beyond as the dog continued barking, still pacing the same area of fence.

'India 98 to Trojan 1. We may have something at the north-east corner of the site,' their colleagues in the sky updated them, the beat of the blades stuttering in the background.

Scarlett was about forty feet away when she spotted a way through – a small patch where the criss-crossing metal had curled away from the ground. Ditching her helmet, she pulled off the cumbersome tactical vest and hurried over, lying flat on her back to drag herself under. More of their colleagues were rushing to join them as she followed the fence round to where the agitated animal was pawing at the ground.

'Straight ahead,' the handler told her through the metal, Scarlett dashing into the thick undergrowth, heart beating faster as the hum of the rotor blades followed her out.

The ground was uneven and sloping away from her. Up ahead she could see a clearing in the trees... but then she felt her boot snag on something, pulling her feet out from under her. Unable to stop herself she fell head first, gaining momentum as she tumbled out onto an area of fresh dirt.

'*Shit*,' she complained, coughing up a lungful of dust.

Bruised and nauseated, she waited for the world to stop spinning before slowly getting up onto her hands and knees to see where she'd landed.

'Jesus!' she gasped, scrambling back from the pale hand protruding from the earth just a few feet away.

Still panting, she stared at the feminine fingers, extended as if waiting to drag an unsuspecting soul into the underworld. As she gradually brought her breathing under control, she frowned on noticing the foul smell on the air and then the buzz of a thousand flies, almost not wanting to look as she turned her head to peer down earthen walls into the bottom of a deep pit: partially submerged beneath the surface of mud and foetid water, the bodies of countless people had been piled on top of each other.

Scarlett gagged. Holding her hand over her nose and mouth, she crawled back towards the treeline, fumbling for her radio in a desperate search for clean air. 'Scarlett to Frank.' Her trembling fingers could barely hold the button down long enough to transmit, all sense of protocol and professionalism gone. 'Frank, are you there?!'

A static hiss and then Frank's concerned voice responded. 'Scarlett? Where are you?'

'Frank! I need you.'

THIRTY-TWO
A BRIEF CASE OF SUBMERSION

The carriage lights flickered.

Mysterious flashes out in the dark tunnel.

The rhythmic sound of wheels clacking along rickety rails pouring through the open windows.

It might just have been her current state of mind, but the District Line was beginning to feel like a tacky fairground ghost train; although it would have to do *a lot* better than that to shock her now, Scarlett confident she'd just witnessed the very worst that life could possibly throw at her.

She could still taste them in the air – the bloated bodies decomposing into a communal soup, the more recent of them bobbing about in the filth as if fighting to stay above the surface, even in death. She shuddered and forced her attention, for the umpteenth time, back to the colourful travel-insurance advertisement above the doors.

Naturally Frank had covered for her without even needing to be asked, assuming control of the scene as if he'd always intended to do so, and giving Scarlett an unspoken opportunity to sneak away while she still could. She felt awful for leaving him with it but knew she couldn't have stayed there a moment longer.

The train's brakes squealed as if they'd never been used before, Scarlett getting off and resurfacing at Westminster to make the short journey over to New Scotland Yard. But as she approached the oppressive grit-grey building, she paused, watching the famous revolving sign spin playfully, promising something far more entertaining awaiting her than vice-like pressure from above and below and a bombardment of questions that she was in no mood to answer relating to her grisly discovery.

Turning her back to it, she checked the time, took out her phone and dialled Mark's number.

'Hey you!' he greeted her after the third ring.

'You're on lunch, right?'

'Certainly am. Was meant to be running my Shakespeare in the Skate Park club, but no one turned up... again. So, I'm treating myself to an M&S duck and hoisin wrap. How's your day going?'

Perhaps she was just projecting her own issues onto him. Perhaps he hadn't picked up on the despondent tone in her four words, but it felt as though he didn't want to know... not really. It was no more than a pleasantry. And she was supposed to smile and say 'fine' and then they would talk about what they were going to have for dinner later. It was a cruel irony that at a time when she so desperately needed an element of normality in a life that was spiralling out of control, that normality only emphasised the ever-widening gap between the two of them.

She needed to talk to someone, feeling like there was something inside her that she needed to get out. Mark could never understand, and with Frank otherwise disposed, she could only think of one other person who would...

She took a deep breath and fixed a smile upon her face. 'My day's fine. Just wondering what we're doing for dinner.'

* * *

Following Henry's instructions to the letter, Scarlett had boarded the Thames Clipper at Westminster Pier at precisely 1:46 p.m.

From the water, she barely recognised the city that she knew perhaps a little too intimately, for the first time in a very long while feeling like a tourist in an exciting foreign capital. Iconic landmarks came and went, vying for attention amid a monochrome forest that had now outgrown them. The crowds, the traffic – usually so suffocating – suddenly seemed intoxicating, raucous and full of possibilities.

Sitting out in the sunshine on the rear deck, she watched the disturbed water in their wake gradually forget them, jealously wishing she could still her racing mind with such ease.

* * *

Henry watched the boat come in, the Tower of London looming behind him as the engines shut off and it glided in to dock. Dressed in uncharacteristically casual clothing, he'd worked up quite a sweat lugging the rucksack of tungsten around the entire eastern part of the city, even the climbing-grade carabiners dangling from bungee cords adding significantly to the weight. There were denser metals, of course, *but why waste gold or platinum when one could simply buy a bigger bag? Plus, he'd had some left over*.

He regarded the faces of those out on the deck and checked the time again to ensure he had the correct boat.

'Sir, are you getting on?' the young woman waiting at the gate asked him.

'...Yes,' he decided, stepping aboard and making his way through the cabin with the weighty bag as he headed for the rear deck.

'So sorry!' he apologised, colliding with someone the moment he stepped outside. Curiously, the man, who looked to be well into his sixties, had a briefcase handcuffed to his left wrist. 'Are you alright?' Henry asked, shooting him a winning smile as he slid the rucksack off his shoulder and dropped it over the side of the boat in one fluid motion.

The man's look of confusion never fully formed, the bungee cord pulling taut against the carabiner now fixed around the leather handle... ripping the briefcase out of his hand... the metal chain tightening before pulling him over the side with it.

With a quick glance around to ensure no one had noticed the seven-second interaction, Henry peered over, the murky water betraying nothing, having swallowed the bag, the case and his target whole. Whistling innocently, he made his way over to Scarlett.

'This seat taken?' he asked, sitting down beside her to take in the view. 'Hadn't heard from you in over two days. I was beginning to worry you'd found yourself another morally corrupt but effortlessly charming cold-blooded partner-in-crime,' he joked, Scarlett staring out over the water as if she hadn't heard a word he'd said. 'I hav—' But before he could even finish the thought, she had thrown her arms around him. 'Hey... Hey,' he said softly, embracing her. 'What is it? What's happened?'

They were making their way back upriver past the Docklands by the time Scarlett had got it all out of her system – the raid, the evidence recovered there, their suspected next victim, the glitzy event scheduled for Friday night and, last but not least, her gruesome find at the landfill site.

It had been a lot to take in all at once, and Henry had needed a couple of minutes to process it.

'So... How did you even find out about the landfill site?' he asked.

'Indentations in the ground behind Francesca Labelle's apartment block,' Scarlett explained, all trace of her morbid excitement and ruthless ambition long gone. 'One of the neighbours remembered a skip out there and tossing her toaster away in it. So, we found the toaster, and it came back with Francesca's DNA on it.'

It was the first time Henry had heard her refer to one of the victims by their Christian name only, and it wasn't a good sign. He sighed heavily. 'You're too smart for your own good. You know that?'

She smiled, a marked improvement in her mood. Neither of them spoke for a beat as they drew level with the entrance to St Katharine Docks.

'You know, you could still walk away from this,' Henry told her. 'You've already more than proved yourself.' For a moment, he actually thought she was going to agree... but then, predictably, she shook her head.

'I've come too far for that... or should I say *descended* too far,' she corrected herself.

'Far enough, perhaps?' he suggested.

'How much further could I go?'

'Six feet under.'

'Not when I've got you looking out for me,' she smiled, Henry shifting uncomfortably. 'I'm not walking away from this.'

'Then there's something I want you to have,' he said, removing a nine-millimetre pistol from his pocket and placing it in her lap. 'Just until it's over.'

Scarlett picked the gun up and turned it over in her hands before passing it back to him. 'Thanks but...'

He'd tried.

'How do you do it?' she asked him, the Tower of London

making a reappearance. 'All those people. All that death following you about.'

'It doesn't,' he answered, '...follow you about, I mean. It ends there and then in that moment and that's it.'

Scarlett looked at him, her expression equal parts revulsion and envy.

'I don't believe in God,' he continued, the non-sequitur clearly losing her. 'And I think I've seen the lights go out in enough people's eyes to have earned that opinion. It's always the same, the same sequence of emotions: fear, followed by hope, hope that something's coming that never is, and then a split-second of realisation before...'

'Before?' she prompted him.

'Nothing,' he told her, surprising himself with his raw honesty. 'You start to realise that these bodies we're in are just that. They're vessels. They're not *us*.' From the look on Scarlett's face, he wasn't explaining himself very well. 'I suppose what I'm trying to say is that those bodies you saw down in that pit today weren't people anymore; they were just the meat and bone they left behind. They don't care that they're down there. The only people who would are their loved ones, and something tells me they're never going to find out the more distressing details about how you found them.' Henry shook his head. 'I'm sorry. I don't feel like I'm helping at all.'

'Actually,' said Scarlett, 'in a weird way, you are.' They shared a smile before Henry was distracted by a familiar rucksack floating downriver. It looked to have ripped open. 'Can we talk about something else?' she asked him.

'Of course,' he said, trying to keep the concern off his face as a black leather briefcase bobbed past...

'I think I've had enough death for one day,' she explained.

...Closely followed by the outstretched arm of its drowned owner.

Giving her a slightly awkward second hug, Henry held

Scarlett until the corpse had disappeared with a thud beneath the boat.

They disembarked at Westminster Pier, Henry walking Scarlett back to her car as their conversation grew increasingly more ridiculous.

'Show me!' she demanded.

'What, here?'

'*Uh huh,* or I'll have no choice but to presume you're lying.'

'Fine,' he said, coming to an abrupt stop in the middle of the pavement. Untucking his shirt and unbuckling his belt, Henry attracted a number of strange looks as he pulled the waistband of his trousers down to reveal an old scar on his lower, lower, lower back.

'Bullet wound?' she asked, sounding suitably impressed.

'Arrow.'

She opened her mouth to ask a follow-up question but then decided to leave it. 'Oh yeah? Well, feast your eyes on this,' she said, pulling up her blouse to expose the deep set of scratches torn across her abdomen.

'Nasty,' winced Henry while re-dressing himself. 'Broken glass?'

'Vengeful cat,' she told him, unlocking the car. There was a heavy pause, neither of them wanting the conversation to end. 'I'm going to check out the event space. You're more than welcome to join me.'

'I'm afraid I can't,' he said genuinely. 'But I'm going to need you to get me in there Friday night.'

She nodded, tossing her bag onto the passenger seat before getting down on her hands and knees to check beneath the car, not seeing the look of realisation that had just dawned on Henry's face.

He gasped theatrically. 'Oh my God!'

'What?' she asked, getting back up and heading round to the driver's door.

'Your cat gave you those scars.'

'Yeah.'

'Because he has "issues."'

'Yeah.' She looked uncomfortable.

'...And only three legs!'

'...*Yeah?*'

'*You* ran him over!'

A beat.

'It was an accident!' she said defensively, seizing a gap in the traffic to climb in. With a huff, she wound down the window when Henry tapped on the glass. 'What?!' she asked him, starting up the engine.

'You never did tell me why you named him Alkie.'

She hesitated. '*Alkie*... as in *alcoholic*,' she said, switching on her indicators as she waited to pull out. 'You know – because he's... "legless,"' she explained guiltily before stamping on the accelerator.

'Oh, that is *dark*... And I thought *I* was meant to be the cold-hearted one!' Henry called after her, laughing to himself as he watched her speed away.

* * *

The crane lowered yet another bag to the ground, the twenty-first soul they had plucked from the earth. Frank waited for the forensic technician to log the DNA sample and then stick a barcode onto the outside of the body bag, scanning it as two others lifted it onto a gurney and wheeled past, as if it were a box of Crunchy Nut Cornflakes at a supermarket checkout.

His stomach rumbled, Frank realising that he'd completely missed lunch... and breakfast for that matter... and dinner the previous evening, come to think of it.

A trickle of foul liquid escaped from one corner of the bag, leaving a dark line in the dirt behind it, Frank making sure to hop over it as he took a deep breath and approached.

'Female, twenties-to-thirties. Head, as of now, unaccounted for,' the technician informed him, reading out the basic description provided by her colleague down in the pit.

'Let's prioritise that one then,' Frank told her, making a note before retreating back to the pile of stones that marked the spot where he could breathe again.

The crane powered up once more.

Something was troubling him: not only the sheer number of corpses in comparison to The Jackdaw's known body count but also the vast array of MOs used in dispatching them – both bullet and knife wounds, blunt-force trauma and broken necks.

Perhaps a killer experimenting... learning her trade... or perhaps, just perhaps, something else entirely.

* * *

It was incredible how a disused warehouse could be transformed into an 'event space' simply by erecting a sign to that effect.

Scarlett walked a lap of the cavernous main hall as people bustled about, setting up lights and speakers, rolling equipment around on trolleys and uncoiling thick black wires – metal connectors protruding from their ends like the fangs of a snake.

A hardwearing green carpet marked the boundaries of the presentation area, while numerous displays had been installed on sturdy metal frames, creating a maze of the controversial activist's most famous exploits. Scarlett wandered into the exhibit, pausing when she reached a double-spread account of the tragedy at the distribution centre earlier that year.

'OK!' she heard someone bellow, the overhead lighting shutting off with a bang as the mood-lit installation illuminated all around her. Standing in the glow of a screen set into the display, Scarlett watched the video begin to roll: various news reports cut together, photographs of the man who'd eventually been discovered inside, followed by footage of the fire raging out of control, her hair alive with the colours of flame and smoke.

It was mesmerising: as beautiful as it was terrible – a blazing testament to the collateral damage of good intentions.

'Looks good!' the same voice called as the house lights were restored, flooding every inch of the hall.

Scarlett remained where she was however, staring at her reflection in the blank screen, the fire gone but the crackle of its burning lingering in her ears.

THIRTY-THREE

THE GOOD, THE BY THIS STAGE MORALLY ON PRETTY THIN ICE AND THE INCREDIBLY HANDSOME

It was almost midnight by the time Frank stepped off the bus and began his six-minute trudge home.

For once, health and safety regulations had come to the rescue, forcing his superiors to find somebody to relieve him; otherwise he knew they would have happily left him there all night in that floodlit graveyard.

The more they dug, the more they found – thirty-three bodies and counting. *Christ knew how many more they'd have discovered by morning.*

Frank's little house stood dark and unassuming between two far grander homes. Although every property on the street had started out life the same way, like an underachieving sibling, somewhere between the decades, lavish extensions and landscaped gardens had left 62 Gainsborough Crescent behind. Truth be told, it was still far more than Frank needed and, given the choice, he'd gladly knock out at least one of the upstairs rooms – the cold, empty voids under his own roof only serving as a reminder of how alone he was.

He unlocked the front door, an unpleasant smell greeting

him the moment he stepped inside as a subdued Max watched from his dog bed.

'It's not your fault,' Frank told him, stooping down to scratch him behind the ears. 'It's mine. Come on. Let's get you some dinner.'

He knew, with his job, it was borderline cruel to keep a pet, the poor animal sentenced to the very life of solitude it was sparing him from. Frank had considered giving him up so many times but the thought never tended to stick for long. Walking into the kitchen, he opened a can of dog food into one bowl for Max and then a tin of meatballs in gravy into another for himself, the two dishes looking nigh-on identical.

With the mess on the mat not going anywhere in a hurry, he carried his microwaved meal through to the sitting room and switched on the television, chuffed to find that *The Good, the Bad and the Ugly* was the late-night film. He managed to make it a whole ten minutes in before having to close his eyes for a few seconds...

It was light outside. Max was asleep at his feet. On the television, some angry host was interviewing some angry guests in front of an audience of equally angry people. The camera flicked to a smug-looking reverend, which explained a lot; no one enjoyed a good shit-stir more than God and his lackeys.

'*Christ*,' blasphemed Frank as he sat up, feeling no more rested than when he'd shut his eyes, the hours doing nothing for his unappetising dinner which sat untouched, cold and congealed on his lap.

He showered, got dressed and cleaned up the hallway before taking Max for a long-overdue walk around the block. With a full Thermos of coffee in hand, he was just about to head out the door when he paused, gaze fixed on the oddly shaped cupboard under the stairs. He'd passed it on countless occasions without giving it a second thought but now felt drawn to it – that same sixth sense that had saved his life all those years earlier now resonating again.

Opening the flimsy door, he pulled out some boxes to reach the little black safe behind where he kept the firearm and ammunition that hadn't seen the light of day since his last re-certification. Letting out the straps on his shoulder holster, he pulled it across his chest, concealing the weapon beneath his jacket.

Regardless of whether he'd find himself in a situation where he'd need to use it, Frank suspected an eventful day awaited them all.

* * *

The office was heaving by the time Frank walked through the doors, his conspicuously the only unmanned desk in the entire department. He was heading for it when Scarlett came rushing over, looking flustered.

'Thank God! You're here,' she said, glancing behind her as though she were being followed. 'Fancy a coffee?' she asked, Frank raising his Thermos in answer, but she was already well on her way to the lifts. 'I need to get out of here for a few minutes.'

They stepped inside and Scarlett pushed the button for the lobby, the ground-floor café notoriously the only near-passable excuse for a hot drink in the building.

'Thirty-seven bodies,' she continued as they descended. 'Griffiths has put just about the whole department on it while we attempt to identify them. He's also fast-tracked all forensic requests, so it's pretty much Christmas up there right now.'

The doors parted and they crossed the atrium towards the counter. 'Extra shot flat white with an extra shot,' she ordered, turning to Frank. 'Want anything?'

He shook his head.

'So... is that an extra shot *on top* of the extra shot or just an extra shot plus the two regular shots?' the person in an apron asked uncertainly.

Scarlett looked puzzled. 'The first one... I think.'

'That'll be three pounds sixty, please.'

Reaching into thin air, she winced. 'I've left my bag upstairs. Can I owe you?'

Looking exasperated, Frank beeped his card on the reader and then shuffled along the counter with her.

'We've identified two... Possibly three,' continued Scarlett. 'One had his wallet on him – a lawyer, I think. From the sound of it, he was pretty unpopular... even by lawyer standards.' They inched towards the coffee landing area. 'Looks like only one or two of the staff at the landfill site were in on it, but they're not talking.'

'Quadruple-shot flat white!' the person standing two feet away broadcast to the entire building, Scarlett grabbing her coffee and making it as far as the sugar station.

'I've got people scouring their financials but so far it's looking like a cash-in-hand job.' She added three sugars and a lid to her drink before marching back over to the lifts, catching the doors when they tried to close on them. 'I checked out the event space yesterday afternoon,' she told the crowded metal box. 'Bugger-all point in trying to control anything right now. They're meant to be done setting up by 11 a.m. Friday morning though, at which point we'll move in. Better see if that tux still fits. ...*Oh!*' she gasped, looking very tempted to use the bald spot on the head of the little man standing between them as a coffee table as she reached for her phone. 'One of the bodies they dug up overnight was wearing a rather distinctive dress.'

She held up a particularly gruesome photograph for Frank (and several others) before flicking back to the uploaded image of Francesca Labelle's decapitated body, the same golden dress catching in the light.

'*Jesus Christ!*' someone complained.

'It's a police station not a Build-A-Bear Workshop. Get over it,' Scarlett told them before continuing. 'We think it's her. Just waiting for forensics to confirm.' They stepped out onto their floor and headed back into the office. 'It's being prioritised along with the three others you singled out.' She sounded out of breath and it occurred to Frank that he hadn't actually uttered a single word during the five-minute monologue. He opened his mouth but Scarlett cut him off. '...OK. Good chat,' she said, raising her takeaway cup in thanks before being swallowed up by the crowd loitering beside her desk.

Frank shook his head and was about to turn around when he spotted Fernandez in with the chief and another man he didn't recognise, the cut of his suit suggesting he wasn't involved in any form of constructive police work. Disconcertingly, all three of them were staring out at him, watching as he returned to his seat.

Frank instantly felt his heart beating faster. '*Shit.*'

* * *

The net around The Jackdaw was closing fast.

By 2 p.m. they'd identified four of the bodies excavated from the landfill site, one of which forensics had identified with 96.4 per cent certainty as Francesca Labelle. They were in the process of tracking down the five skip-carrying trucks flagged from the CCTV footage, and one of the workers had been in a heated discussion with his lawyer for over an hour regarding cutting a deal.

There was an excitement in the office, it having a re-energising effect on the team and they could all feel it – less a peek behind the curtain of an impossible killer's theatrics, more them tearing that curtain down upon her... That was until Newbury got off the phone and made his way over to Scarlett's desk. She thought her unofficial number two a little overfamiliar when he crouched down close to speak to her, but soon understood why.

'That was forensics,' he started, voice barely breaking a murmur. 'They just had a match on another of the bodies Detective Ash prioritised last night.'

'How's that even possible?' asked Scarlett. They'd already ruled out their other victims and had only been able to confirm Francesca Labelle so quickly because they already had her DNA for comparison.

Newbury shifted uncomfortably, the look not sitting right on the cocky young detective. 'You're not going to like it,' he warned her.

'Then just put me out of my misery.'

'It's Sun Jung Lin.'

She didn't even react. 'I'm sorry?'

'The body... that they say has been in the ground the best part of a week, probably dead twice as long... is Sun Jung Lin, our Jackdaw killer... or not, apparently.'

'That's not...' Scarlett lowered her voice. 'That's not possible. We've got her blood at one of the crime scenes. We've got a witness description from The Mountbatten Hotel from less than four days ago! They've made a mistake.' But even as she spoke the words, she could feel the investigation slipping away from her.

'That's what *I* said. But they haven't.' Newbury shrugged. 'I don't know what to tell you, boss. She's been dead two weeks, which means either your witness saw a ghost...'

'Or?' she asked, already knowing what he was about to say.

'*Or*... he was *lying* to you.'

* * *

Frank didn't notice Scarlett hurrying out of the office, too distracted by yet another email from DCI Griffiths, this time requesting a photocopy of his notebook from the night of Ameera Abdalla's murder at The Mountbatten.

He knew precisely what was going on – they were building their case against him, leaving a documentable record of every communication. Fernandez had seen him speaking to Henry in the aftermath of the heiress's shocking death, probably had photographic evidence to support that as well. The fact that he'd failed to mention their interaction in his notes was merely another nail in his coffin.

He closed the email, feeling unexpectedly calm about the end of his career as he returned to his work, having lost the previous day to the landfill site. The revelation that Francesca Labelle had received a text message at 12:53 a.m. had allowed him to focus his efforts on a particular time period. He'd been scrutinising each of the photographs from the party in turn, one even capturing the precise moment at which their victim had looked at her phone to read the one-word message: *Rooftop*.

The last photograph of Francesca Labelle alive was time-stamped 12:58 a.m. but the party had continued without her, losing none of its steam as he approached 1:29 a.m., Frank taking in the familiar faces, now knowing the names off by heart.

He moved on to the next, sitting up excitedly and leaning into the screen: the picture was almost identical to the last... almost, only this time Francesca Labelle's bedroom door stood very slightly ajar.

He scrolled through to the next photograph; judging from people's positions it had been taken only a few seconds later, the door now closed.

When his phone went off, he answered without taking his eyes off the screen. 'Frank Ash.'

'Frank, it's Griffiths. Could I ask you to join me in my office?'

'I'm just finishing something up,' said Frank. 'Can you give me a couple of minutes?'

'Of course.'

Putting the receiver down, he flicked between the photos repeatedly, the bedroom door opening and closing as if blowing in a digital wind, unable to see beyond the inebriated guests in the foreground.

He clicked the forward arrow... then again... then again... laughing bitterly and leaning back in his chair when his suspicions were finally confirmed. Zooming in on the image, Frank framed the killer's face centre screen, captured as they made their hasty exit from the festivities. Only one photograph out of the seven hundred taken of the night had caught them – one split-second misstep – but it was enough to seal their fate.

'Got you, you son of a bitch,' he muttered, printing out a copy of the pixelated face as he got to his feet.

On seeing that Scarlett was no longer at her desk, he knew he couldn't wait for her, so he shoved the assorted paperwork littering his workstation into an envelope, grabbed his keys and headed for the door, Fernandez rushing out of Griffiths' office after him.

'Hey, Frank! Frank!' he yelled across the room. 'You can't run away from this!' He was sprinting now as Frank stepped into the lift. 'Frank!'

'Go screw yourself, Alejandro!' Frank called back, giving the other man the finger as the metal doors glided closed between them.

THIRTY-FOUR

A LITTLE STANDOFFISH

'Come on. Pick up,' muttered Scarlett, pacing like a metronome outside New Scotland Yard's main entrance. 'Pick up.'

'The person you are trying to reach is unavailable...'

'*Shit*,' she spat, turning her back to the noisy road to leave a message, missing Frank as he exited the building behind her and hailed a taxi. 'Henry, it's Scarlett. I don't... Look, I *really* need to speak to you so call me as soon as you get this, OK? We need to talk.'

Ending the call just as Frank clambered into a black cab, she headed back inside.

'Hey! ...Hey!' she barked on returning to the office to find Fernandez rooting through Frank's things. 'What do you think you're doing?'

He glared up at her challengingly. 'You're more than welcome to take it up with the boss if you don't like it.'

Something about the confidence in his tone and the deafening lack of support from those around her told Scarlett to keep moving. After sitting back down at her workstation, she waved Newbury over. 'What the hell's going on?' She gestured toward Fernandez as he emptied a drawer over Frank's desk.

'Weren't you here for that?' he asked in surprise. 'Fernandez pretty much chased Detective Ash out of the office. Two minutes later, the boss comes storming out to tell us he's no longer involved in the investigation.'

'Did he say why?'

Newbury just shrugged. 'Mentioned to the chief yet how the suspect you said was one hundred per cent our Jackdaw and who he went public with is, in fact, one hundred per cent dead?'

'Not yet,' she replied.

'*Yeah.* I'd probably leave that till later.'

Scarlett's mobile was already out on her lap by the time Newbury headed back to his seat.

> Where are you???

Hitting *send* on the short text message, she slid her phone back into her pocket and stared down at the piles of paper in front of her in a futile attempt to concentrate on her work.

An hour and a half went by before Scarlett felt her phone buzz. Conscious that people would be watching her, she managed to unlock the screen without looking, glancing at the message from Frank beneath her desk:

> Francesca Labelle's. Come alone.

Retrieving her keys as subtly as she could, Scarlett got to her feet, purposely leaving her handbag out on show to suggest that she couldn't be going far. Feeling her colleagues' eyes on her back, she calmly headed out of the office and into the toilets.

'One ...Two ...Three,' she counted before pulling the door back open and crossing the corridor into the stairwell opposite.

* * *

'Thought you'd quit!' called Scarlett as she dodged the traffic outside Francesca Labelle's building.

'Which time?' joked Frank. He took one final drag then stamped the cigarette out on the pavement. 'You came.'

'Of course,' she replied a little sharply, offended by the insinuation there was ever any doubt.

'Come on then,' he said, already climbing the steps up to the lobby.

The doors opened out onto the familiar penthouse.

'Going to tell me what's going on between you, the boss and Fernandez?'

'Later perhaps,' Frank teased as he stepped out and paused dramatically. 'So... I did it.'

Scarlett looked blank. 'Did what?'

'I worked out how The Jackdaw killed Francesca Labelle... How they managed to make a body vanish from an effectively sealed room.'

'Show me,' said Scarlett excitedly.

She followed him through to the master bedroom, where a series of printouts littered the bed. Picking up the first, Frank handed it to her.

Scarlett gazed down at the regrettably familiar image uploaded from their victim's own phone: Francesca's decapitated body at sunrise, her distinctive tattoos assuming the role of mortuary toe tags, tiny explosions occurring where the gold sequins of her dress caught the light.

Frank handed her a second image, the photograph that Scarlett herself had taken at dawn the following day.

'The answer's been staring us in the face the whole time,' he said; although, bar the absence of a body in the latter photograph, Scarlett was none the wiser.

'Can I get a clue?' she asked him.

Moving a little closer to the window, Frank pressed his hands together and then began opening and closing his fingers in unison. Frowning, Scarlett was just about to ask whether he was having a stroke or some other age-related crisis, when she noticed the bird-like shape he was casting across the carpet... wings beating rhythmically as if brought to life.

'Look again,' he told her.

'The shadow!' she gasped, hurrying over to join him beside the window while holding the sheet of paper up to the building opposite. 'There's no television aerial in the uploaded picture!'

Frank nodded. 'Yet they were taken at the *exact* same time of day just twenty-four hours apart, which means—'

'Either the aerial was erected in between the two photos being taken...'

'Which it wasn't.'

'Or...' She hesitated. 'It's not the same room!' Frank gave her a knowing smile. 'How though?' she asked him. 'The picture was location stamped. The tech guys confirmed it.'

'I'll show you,' he said, grabbing the remaining printouts off the bed and heading into the main living area. 'The key to everything... the thing we never considered... was that Francesca Labelle already knew her killer.' He let that revelation settle before continuing. 'At 12:53 a.m. the party was still in full swing out here, but Francesca receives a text.' He handed Scarlett the next sheet of paper.

'"Rooftop,"' she read aloud, this the first she'd heard about the deleted message.

'She makes her excuses and heads off to bed.' Frank led the

way back into the bedroom, closing the door behind them for authenticity. 'She doesn't go to bed however. Instead, she goes straight over to this window,' – he turned the key and unhooked the latches to lift it open – 'and climbs out onto the fire escape for a secret rendezvous up on the roof terrace.'

Without the slightest hint of grace, Frank pulled himself out onto the rusted staircase, a strong breeze playing with what little hair he still had left.

'They share a drink,' he said as Scarlett reluctantly clambered out after him, looking down before she could remind herself not to. 'After which, our Jackdaw lures her back down the fire escape... past Francesca's open window and...' – he descended the stairs – '...into the apartment below.'

Somehow re-entering the building even more awkwardly than he'd left it, Frank hit the floor like a sack of potatoes, the vacant apartment a whitewashed twin of the penthouse above.

'But the room didn't look this way that night,' he explained. 'It had been meticulously made up as a carbon-copy reproduction of Francesca's bedroom, right down to the "carelessly" discarded pair of jeans on the floor and photographs lined up on the dressing table. And then it happens,' he said solemnly, 'the trademark silk scarf wrapping around her neck, pulling tighter and tighter until...' He stared down at the pristine white carpet as though she'd just fallen at his feet. 'The first photograph is taken. It's dark outside: the complete body, five scratches across her face. Then comes the decapitation, her killer keeping a little of her blood back for later.'

'Keeping it for what?' Scarlett asked him, but Frank proceeded as though she hadn't spoken.

'Armed with Francesca's severed head and a container of her blood, The Jackdaw climbs back up the fire escape and in through the open window, securing it behind them. The head, a pair of Francesca's jeans and a believable amount of blood are placed with precision. And then at 1:29 a.m. our killer simply

sneaks out of the bedroom under the cover of the festivities, no
one noticing them in the five seconds it takes to reach the front
door. Using the internal staircase they return to this room,
where they set about repainting that far wall, visible in the first
photo. There's no rush. They have hours to wait for their
perfect shot – the detail that makes it all so impossible – a
photograph of Francesca's headless body in what appears to be
her own bedroom at sunrise.

'At 5:27 a.m. the picture is taken and uploaded, at which
point the killer rolls up the body, painting materials and sheets
in the soiled grey carpet, lifts it onto the fire escape and drops it
into the skip below. Finally, they collect up the reproduced
photo frames, the bedding and the pair of jeans, bundle it all
into a bag and roll out the original carpet, leaving the actual
murder scene spotless before making their exit through the
window. Well, almost spotless.'

Prising up one edge of the white carpet, Frank began to pull
it back from the floor, exposing bit by bit the large, dark stain
that had seeped into the wood beneath.

Scarlett stared down at it, needing a few moments to catch
up. 'You said The Jackdaw left Francesca's room at 1:29 a.m.
How could you possibly know that?'

Frank hesitated but then removed a crumpled sheet of
paper from his pocket. 'I'm sorry, girl,' he said, handing it over.
'It's him. It's always been him.'

As she looked down at the blurred image of Henry in her
hands, she felt the bottom drop out of her world.

'There never was a Jackdaw,' Frank told her. 'He *invented* a
serial killer to cover a series of very high-profile assassinations,
to divert suspicion away from those who'd benefit the most from
their deaths: Francesca's father... Dame Edith's soon-to-be ex-
husband... Keeya Rose's former manager... Each and every one
of them had acquired powerful enemies, all of whom *just so
happened* to have rock-solid alibis for the nights in question.'

Scarlett was dumbstruck.

'I should've put it together sooner,' Frank laughed in exhaustion before continuing. 'Disfiguring the faces: Keeya Rose's manager accused her of spending the money she owed him on cosmetic surgery. There's a certain twisted poetry to undoing that as a final insult. And the dame's husband – he seemed to care more about retrieving his still-unaccounted-for family heirloom than about losing the house in the divorce. Oh, and guess what Ameera Abdalla's father contributed to over in Saudi Arabia: the public *beheading* of a rival, the rest of his body vanishing without a trace. *The scratches, the trinkets, the absent bodies...* coincidence?'

'I... I don't understand,' stammered Scarlett.

'These were all conditions of the kill,' explained Frank animatedly. 'In isolation, they're effectively smoking guns leading back to those responsible... but do the *same* to *all* of them and it becomes a fictional serial killer's MO.'

He rubbed his weary face. 'It's him, Scarlett. Think about it. How would he ever have got to Ameera Abdalla up in her rooftop fortress if you hadn't brought him in through the front door with you?'

Scarlett thought she might throw up, her imagination running wild: *Henry leaning over to place the explosive onto the outer glass of the infinity pool.*

One of his associates using a make-up brush to dust sodium powder over Ameera Abdalla's face earlier in the day.

The head of security's blood already staining Henry's hands as he 'discovered' the broken body out in the stairwell.

'The bracelet,' muttered Scarlett, the mystery of the heart-shaped treasure's miraculous reappearance now making sense.

Henry bravely holding onto Ameera Abdalla's wrist as she dangled over the city, The Jackdaw needing to replace the neck-lace they had so carelessly 'lost'.

'And what led us to her in the first place?' asked Frank, driving his point home.

Henry planting the wildly expensive neckpiece in the hidden void in Dame Edith's dressing room before he lifted the decapitated corpse off her.

'He's been directing us to *exactly* where he wanted us right from the very beginning.'

Henry pouring a vial of Sun Jung Lin's blood onto the pavement beside the stain that Keeya Rose had left behind.

His fabricated sighting of a dead woman through the glass wall of The Mountbatten Hotel.

Him tactically leaving the newspaper clipping concerning the famous activist next to the hacker's computer.

Henry on the phone to her while scaling the outer wall of a warehouse by the river... a warehouse like the event space currently being set up for Friday night's gala.

'He's been using you,' Frank finished as a slow applause emanated from the other room, Henry materialising in the bedroom doorway.

He appeared calm, but that didn't alter the fact that he had a gun with a silencer attachment tucked beneath his arm.

'Very impressive, Frank,' he smiled before turning to Scarlett. 'Detective Delaney.'

'You followed me?' she asked, voice laced with betrayal.

He shrugged. 'After you found the landfill site, it was only a matter of time before you discovered the... *inconsistencies* in my story about Sun Jung Lin. Judging from your voicemail message, you got there even quicker than I expected, so I thought it best we talk... away from the skyscraper of police officers, of course.'

'Who was she? Sun Jung Lin?'

'Just another job,' he replied, as a plumber would in reference to fixing a sink. 'Much like our flambéed Russian and the "bleedy man" you managed to sleep through.'

He took a step into the room, both Scarlett and Frank taking a step back.

Henry raised his hands. 'You have *absolutely* no reason to be afraid of me,' he assured her. 'I'm trying to protect you.'

'Protect her?' scoffed Frank, but Henry didn't break eye contact with Scarlett.

'Frank's right, of course,' he nodded sadly. 'I have been using you... because the *only* reason you're still breathing right now is because *I* convinced them that you're still of use. The *moment* you cease to be, they *will* kill you, and I'm not prepared to let that happen.'

'Bull... shit,' spat Frank, turning to her. 'He's trying to manipulate you! You can't trust a word that comes out of his mouth!' He addressed Henry once more: 'They won't be killing anyone when they're all in prison... Linus Bergman,' said Frank, Henry unable to keep the surprise off his face. 'The body-builder... The woman in the red dress... We know who you are and we're coming for you.'

Henry winced and rubbed his temple. 'Believe me, that's not going to end well for anybody. You're not making this easy. Look, I have a plan, and the best thing we can *all* do right now is just pretend this little conversation never happened and you get me into the event on Friday night as planned.'

Frank laughed out loud as Scarlett finally rediscovered her voice. 'You expect me to help you murder someone else?'

'I *expect* you to help me *save* you. You can't escape these people on your own. You have no idea what they're—'

'Drop the gun!' yelled Frank unexpectedly, a sharp click as he raised his own weapon to Henry's chest.

'Frank!' gasped Scarlett, the situation escalating.

'Sure you want to do that, Frank?' asked Henry as he held Scarlett's fearful gaze.

'Henry Devlin... or whatever your real name is, you are

under arrest. Drop the weapon!' With a protracted sigh, Henry raised his hands. 'I said put the gun down.'

'Alright,' said Henry evenly. 'Alright. I'm reaching for it now.' He carefully pulled the weapon from under his arm, the scene playing out as if in slow motion to Scarlett, the tension unbearable, like the calm before a storm.

'He's off limits,' she whispered, it sounding more like a plea than an instruction as Henry released his grip on the handle, the heavy weapon sinking into the thick carpet. 'You swore to me.'

But even as she uttered the words, Henry was reaching for a second weapon concealed in his waistband, spinning around to point the gun at Frank.

'No!' she cried, flinching against the anticipated gunshot... but it never came, both men still standing, each with a weapon trained on the other. Unable to even begin unravelling the tangle of emotions she was experiencing, Scarlett only knew that she needed to diffuse the situation by any means possible. 'Frank... perhaps we should hear him out.'

'You should listen to her, Frank,' Henry concurred.

He shook his head. 'You know I can't do that. This ends here and now.'

'Frank. Frank!' tried Scarlett, her words falling on deaf ears as he fixed his eyes on Henry. 'Henry?' she pleaded.

There was a beat, a moment's silence... and then the first deafening gunshot sounded, the mirror behind Frank's head shattering into a billion pieces as Henry made for the doorway, three bullets peppering the wall behind him as he tore out into the main living area, Frank hot on his heels.

'Wait! Frank, wait!' yelled Scarlett, running out after him, a lamp on the console table beside her exploding as she took cover.

* * *

'Sorry!' called Henry, his back to one of the metal pillars that supported the kitchen above their heads. He peered around it into the seemingly empty room. 'Frank!'

'What?!'

'Scarlett's out here! And I don't think *either* of us want bullets flying around with her about.'

'Toss your gun out then!'

'How about *you* toss *yours* out?'

'I will... once I see yours.'

Henry rolled his eyes. 'At the same time then?'

'Deal. On three?'

'On three.'

'One!'

'Two!'

'Three!'

...Nothing happened.

Henry glanced over at the open front door, beckoning to him across a sea of wooden flooring. He huffed. '*Frank?*'

'Yeah?'

'Are you going to do it this time?'

'Yeah.'

'Me too,' Henry told him while simultaneously checking his weapon and ammunition situation. 'On three!... One!'

'Two!'

'Three!'

Again, nothing happened.

'Well, that was predictable,' muttered Henry as the sound of slow footsteps started to approach.

* * *

'Scarlett!' hissed Frank, venturing as far as he dared from the wall to try to pull her back as she headed out into the middle of the room, positioning herself directly between the two of them.

'Henry?' she called.

'Still here... regrettably.'

'I'm out here. Please don't shoot. Same goes for you, Frank! I need you to put your guns down. *Both* of you.'

There was a pause before she heard a click, Henry's hand emerging from behind the pillar, the gun hanging between his thumb and forefinger. 'OK! I'm coming out.'

Feeling as though she were clawing back some semblance of control, Scarlett smiled when Henry stepped out into the open, Frank emerging from behind his wall, weapon still raised.

'He must not have heard you,' deadpanned Henry, nodding in the other man's direction.

'Put it away, Frank... Please.'

'Yes, come along, Frank. We both know you're not going to use it with Scarlett standing there,' chimed Henry as, uncon- cerned, he brushed bits off his black jumper. 'Well, this has been great, but I think I'm going to head off.' He frowned. 'No pun intended.' He managed two steps towards the open door before the sound of Frank's gun cocking brought him to a halt.

'I'm afraid I can't let you do that,' Frank told him.

'Frank!' said Scarlett imploringly. She knew he was in the right, of course, but also knew that Henry had no intention of going down quietly. Turning to talk some sense into him, she sensed Henry move, sprinting for the door as Frank fired repeat- edly, Scarlett caught in the crossfire. Dropping to her knees, hands covering her head, as if it made a difference, she watched Henry fire back wildly, the apartment's sparse furnishings going up in clouds of feather, plaster and dust, as he dived out through the door.

All was quiet.

Tentatively, Scarlett got back to her feet and had to double check that she'd survived the ordeal in one piece. The once immaculate living area looked as though a bomb had gone off as she sighed in relief and turned to Frank, the look on his face frightening her more than anything she had ever experienced before, the fear in his eyes telling her that something was very wrong before her gaze could even fall to the growing bloodstain soaking its way through his shirt like a flower blooming. He slumped back against the wall...

'Frank!'

...and slid down onto the floor as Scarlett rushed over to him.

'Frank! Oh my God!' she panicked, fumbling with her phone as she dialled 999, clamping it between her shoulder and ear. Ripping his shirt open, she was unable to even find the wound, there was so much blood. 'Hold on, Frank. Hold on!' she told him as the call was connected. 'Yes, hello. Ambulance please...' she managed before feeling him take her hand.

He wheezed hauntingly. 'You have to tell them... this was all me.'

'Don't talk, Frank. I'm getting help.'

He squeezed her hand tighter. 'Promise me.'

Scarlett hesitated.

'Do you promise me?'

'...Yes.'

'Say it.'

'I promise.'

The strength in his grip faded as quickly as it had come. And then, Scarlett could only watch helplessly as a look of realisation crossed his face... and the lights went out in his eyes.

She dropped the phone to the floor.

'Frank?' she whispered, giving him a shake. 'Frank?'

Unable to comprehend what had just happened, Scarlett just stared down at him, waiting for it to hit her.

'Scarlett?' a distant voice said softly. Slowly, she tore her eyes away from Frank. Henry had returned, looking sick as his gaze shifted from Frank's lifeless body to her covered in his blood. 'Scarlett, I... You've got to believe me, I didn't... I never meant to...'

And then it finally came – washing over her like a wave, overwhelming guilt and anger pouring in and stealing the breath from her lungs as she held her chest, panting staccato breaths as tears streamed down her face.

'Scarlett?' Henry took a step towards her.

Grabbing Frank's gun off the floor beside her, she pointed it up at Henry and pulled the trigger, the bullet tearing through his abdomen and dropping him to the floor, one long smear of blood charting his route as he dragged himself towards the door. A second shot splintered the wood beside his knee, a third exploding the door handle above his head as he pulled himself to safety.

With trembling hands, she kept the weapon trained on the empty doorway until she heard the heavy stairwell door swing shut and could be sure they were alone. Letting the gun drop to the floor, she could barely see through the tears as she held a bloody hand to Frank's face.

'I'm so sorry, Frank,' she cried. 'I'm so sorry.'

THIRTY-FIVE

DISHONOURING THE DEAD

'Detective Delaney? Detective Delaney?'

Blinking her eyes back into focus, Scarlett looked at DCI Griffiths.

'Are you sure you're up to this today?' he asked her.

She nodded and sat up in her chair, neither the insipid little office nor her boss doing much to hold her attention. 'Do you think I might be able to get that coffee, after all? I didn't get a lot of sleep last night.'

'Of course.' In some sort of well-meant gesture, Griffiths got to his feet to go and make it himself. 'How do you take it?'

'Milk and two, please,' she replied through a protracted yawn. 'On second thoughts, three sugars.'

With a smile, he headed out, leaving Scarlett to admire the view of the brick wall opposite, it serving as a welcome opportunity to go over her story one last time.

Griffiths had dropped her back home himself the previous afternoon, another colleague following up later that evening to take her statement. While Mark busied himself with some passive-aggressive washing-up during the intrusion, Scarlett had obediently carried out Frank's dying wish – blaming each and every one of her more damning indiscretions on the only father figure she'd ever known, tainting the memory of a man who cared about her so deeply, he was still protecting her – even in death.

A letter had been discovered. Sitting at the very top of a drawer in Frank's desk, addressed to Scarlett, Griffiths and Fernandez, it amounted to a full confession, Scarlett reluctantly corroborating how Frank had first introduced her to Henry, setting up the ill-fated meeting at The Mendeleev restaurant. She went on to say that she'd believed him to be a security consultant and had been greatly impressed by his input at both the Edith Donohue and Keeya Rose crime scenes and, as such, had no reason to question it when Frank told her that Henry would be attending the walkthrough of Ameera Abdalla's hotel residence in his stead.

It had been one hell of a performance.

She'd cursed herself for not running a full background check, for blindly trusting the word of 'a liar' – excusing herself for a few minutes to throw up immediately after uttering the words. Feeling both dirty and cowardly, she'd returned to conclude the interview, picking up from where the letter left off, revealing how Frank had asked her to meet him at Francesca Labelle's penthouse – presumably to confess. But she'd arrived to find him and Henry engaged in a heated argument. Shots were fired, during which Frank sustained a fatal chest wound, Scarlett discharging his weapon three times and striking Henry once before he could escape.

She'd never been quite so disgusted with herself.

Griffiths entered the office carrying two mugs. Setting one down in front of Scarlett, he returned to his seat.

'I needed this. Thank you,' she said, taking a sip.

'As I was saying – this whole thing has turned into an unprecedented mess, so we're keeping the story that we put out to the public simple: Henry Devlin is now the prime suspect in The Jackdaw investigation and is also wanted for the murder of Detective Sergeant Frank Ash.' He sighed. 'Look, I can't even begin to fathom what Frank's motivations were for getting involved with a man like this, but I'd known him almost as long as you had and *know* he was a good man at heart. I don't think either of us want to see his legacy tarnished by this final lapse of judgement.'

'No, sir.'

'Fernandez picked up on some of Frank's recent behaviour but feels the same way. Olsen came forward too... but he knows it's in his own best interests to keep his mouth shut. A further investigation *will* take place, but it will be conducted as sensitively as humanly possible.'

'I appreciate that, sir,' said Scarlett, finding it a relief to actually say something truthful for once.

'As for you... You broke protocols. You intentionally omitted vital information from your reports that could have prevented this tragedy. You let your ambition eclipse your sense of duty and behaved in a manner I consider far below what I would expect of one of my detectives.'

Scarlett nodded.

'But,' he continued, 'out of respect for Frank, and considering what you've just been through, I want this dealt with quietly... once Henry Devlin is in custody... and we *both* have had the chance to bury our friend. But make no mistake, it *will* be dealt with.'

'Yes, sir.'

'You will remain lead detective on the investigation in name only. Cooper will be stepping into Frank's role, and you are to obey his every command to the letter. Understood?'

'Understood.'

Lecture over, Griffiths' tone softened. 'Do you need a couple of days?'

'I'd rather be at work, sir... and the gala is tomorrow night.'

'Very well. I'll expect you at your desk in the morning then,' he said, dismissing her. Scarlett got to her feet and walked to the door. 'And Detective Delaney.' She paused to turn to him. 'I really am sorry about Frank.'

She smiled sadly: 'Me too.'

* * *

Hidden in plain sight among the private clinics, dentists and cosmetic surgeons on London's famous Harley Street stands an innocuous red door. Behind that door stands an armed guard, and behind that guard, a state-of-the-art hospital catering to a very select group of people, possessing both the means and need for such an exclusive establishment.

Nurse Jethro Vaughn completed his security check and made his way through to the lobby; as with all the neighbouring buildings, it felt more like a wealthy relative's home than a place of work. Wishing the receptionist a good morning, he climbed the stairs, noting the single drop of blood that the cleaning crew had missed, and entered through the lone door on the landing. He'd done it hundreds of times and yet the contrast never failed to surprise him, feeling as though he'd been transported across the city into the heart of a major hospital.

He got changed into his scrubs and Crocs and then headed out to the nurses' station in time for handover, his counterpart looking drained from her nightshift and already waiting for him.

'Bad night?' he asked.

'Steady,' she replied. 'The usual assortment of knife wounds and broken limbs in the clinic. One instance of poisoning that turned out to be a shellfish allergy.'

Jethro chuckled. 'Well, they tend to be a paranoid bunch. What about our overnight guests?'

'Oh!' she said, remembering something. 'We've got a samurai-sword wound in bay three. Ever seen one of those?'

'Not for a while.'

'Cut through him like butter. Bed four's on a transfusion after accidently sticking himself with an impressive amount of blood-thinner.' She laughed. 'If he got a paper cut right now, he'd probably turn into a puddle.'

Jethro shook his head and looked up at the board. 'Am I reading that correctly?'

'I was saving the best till last,' she told him. 'Because bed one is a real-life celebrity! Henry Devlin, man of the moment and all over this morning's news.'

'Aren't they saying he killed a police officer or something?'

'Fortunately, we're paid to leave our conscience at the door,' she told him, shutting that conversation down. 'Single bullet wound to his left lumbar region. Came out of surgery around six and is yet to come round.' Dropping the stack of clipboards into Jethro's hands, she smiled sweetly. 'Enjoy!'

* * *

Mark had been incredible.

He'd gone and collected Max in the middle of the night, even taking him out for a walk when they got back. He'd stayed up with Scarlett, called in sick for work, chauffeured her to and from her meeting, taken on the task of notifying the utility companies of Frank's passing and was now busy helping her pack up the house.

He and Frank had never been particularly close, but Mark had received the seal of approval back when he and Scarlett had first started dating. Much later on, she'd learned this had nothing to do with him as a person, but because Frank liked the fact she could probably 'take him down' if he ever got any 'fresh ideas'.

She smirked at the memory.

Moving into the living room, Scarlett placed the box she'd labelled *keep* and an overflowing bin bag in front of the mantelpiece. She collected up the photo frames in turn, packing them carefully before coming to the item she'd deliberately left until last. Taking the dusty presentation case in her hands, she knew exactly what Frank would say, having always maintained that he didn't deserve it. She had no idea how she was supposed to feel about it considering what it had been awarded for, but then read the tiny inscription etched across the medal's surface:

For outstanding bravery
over and above
the call of duty

She pictured him stealing the security footage from the restaurant on her behalf, snapping it in two and dropping it into the river. She thought back to Frank facing down a professional assassin in an attempt to finally free her of him once and for all. Her eyes glistened at the memory of him making her promise to drag his name through the mud to give her a chance at saving herself.

There were many different forms of duty. And whatever imagined debt Frank had believed he'd owed her, he'd paid it back a hundred times over.

Wiping the dust away, she carefully packed it up surrounded by pictures of the two of them together.

* * *

Henry had been drifting in and out of sleep for hours, the haze of the pain medication, conspiring with the melody of the beeping machines, too hard to resist. He opened his eyes, however, when someone entered the room.

'Sorry about this,' apologised the nurse who'd been tending to him, Henry peering down in confusion as his wrists were handcuffed to the sides of the bed.

Sitting up as far as he was able, he was just about to question the man on his curious behaviour when all became clear.

'Secure!' called the nurse.

The ominous click of high-heeled shoes preceded Rebecca's arrival. Effortlessly chic as ever, she was carrying a large bouquet of flowers and an unfortunate-looking cuddly toy.

'Henry, dear!' she greeted him before turning to the man still lingering in the corner. 'Get out.'

'Yes, ma'am,' he said, half-bowing as he backed out of the room, Rebecca taking a seat beside the bed.

'Tell me, how are you feeling, darling?'

Henry winced. 'Like I've been shot in the gut.'

'Well, that would make sense. Should I take it this little dance between yourself and Detective Delaney has finally come to an end?'

'What would give you that impression?'

'Speaking as a woman, when someone starts putting bullets in you, it's probably time to move on.'

Henry shrugged... which he realised was a mistake. With a groan, he changed position. 'She's a redhead. She has a temper,' he deadpanned before turning serious. 'What's the damage?'

'Oh, it's all fucked, darling. All of it. Your beautiful visage is everywhere I look, and I've got clients who paid us very handsomely currently sitting in custody suites. I was actually on the phone to Mr Donohue when they came knocking at his door.'

'Shit.'

'Indeed. He said he still wants his ring back.'

'Jumper pocket,' Henry told her, Rebecca getting up and crossing the room to where his clothing had been neatly folded.

Reaching inside the bloody garment, she produced the antique wedding band, chuckling to herself as she sat back down.

'I do feel for you,' she told Henry. 'What was it again – a water bungalow in Trinidad?'

'St Lucia,' he mumbled.

'Oh.' She frowned down at the toy she'd brought along. 'I don't suppose the red howler monkey means a lot to you then?'

'Afraid not,' he replied blankly.

Discarding it in the bin, she continued. 'Alas, you were so *very* close. You should be proud of yourself. You almost achieved the impossible: Donohue, Rose, Labelle, Abdalla – *no one* could have pulled off what you did. But as they say – "man plans and God laughs."'

'If being laughed at is the worst thing coming to me,' said Henry, 'I'll take it.'

Rebecca chuckled. 'Well, that's still to be determined, my dear. Unfortunately, these are not decisions even *I* can make in isolation. But just so we're all on the same page – I'm surprised they haven't already told me to put a bullet between your eyes. Nothing personal. You know that. But you're useless to them now.'

'I can still finish the job.'

'It's been released to the open market.'

'Everything's set up,' Henry insisted. 'I can do it, prove to them I'm still of use.'

Rebecca tapped her fingers on her knee as she considered it. 'I can't promise it will sway the board's decision.'

'But it might.'

'It might.'

'Then I may still need Detective Delaney.'

'Well, let's hope that's not the case because that *is* my decision to make. Detective Delaney will be taken care of this evening and, to spare you having to wrestle with your conscience, these handcuffs will remain in place and you will be sedated. ...*Heavily*.' She got up and placed the flowers on the chair. 'Now, get some rest. We'll expect you tomorrow night after the gala to receive the board's verdict. I suppose it's unnecessary to remind you that running would be futile.'

'It is.'

'Nurse!' she called, the anxious man hurrying back in. 'You have your instructions.'

Pulling against his restraints, Henry watched the man prepare a syringe. 'That's really not necessary!' He pulled harder, shaking the metal but only succeeding in cutting into his hand. 'Rebecca!' he called after her, unable to hide the desperation in his voice. 'Rebecca, I still need her! Rebe—'

The medication already circling his veins, the world faded to black.

THIRTY-SIX
MEDIUM-FIRM HOLD

Linus Bergman had been sitting in the dark car for over an hour, time enough to acclimatise to his surroundings – watching the comings and goings of those on the street: who'd arrived home, who'd gone out for the evening, making note of the intermittent streetlight six along, the security camera on number thirty-six's garage and the yappy dog next door which was set off by every passer-by.

Meticulous preparation – that was his mantra – *to expect the unexpected* – *reduce the number of variables, because variables were what got one killed.* Of course, even then, all the planning in the world couldn't account for every eventuality. He absent-mindedly raised a hand to the rough skin that claimed the entre left side of his face along with a considerable portion of his upper body, then brushed his hair back over to cover it.

He had parked a little way down the road from his destination: the pastel-blue townhouse with a white Fiat outside, a warm glow seeping from behind its closed curtains, steam escaping into the night sky from one of the upstairs windows.

Shifting in his seat to make himself a little more comfortable, he checked his watch and then reached down to retrieve the supper he'd brought with him, carefully laying out the cutlery and napkin, as if about to dine out at a fancy restaurant.

He had all night.

* * *

Henry's eyes fluttered open but, overcome with nausea, he was forced to shut them again. His head felt heavy and slow, the world ever so slightly out of focus – like trying on someone else's glasses.

He wondered what time it was... how long he'd been out... whether Scarlett was already lying dead in a ditch somewhere while he'd been sleeping.

Taking a steadying breath, he willed his eyelids back open, searching the windowless room for any indication of the time but finding nothing before having to close them once more.

* * *

A young woman wheeled a pram along the pavement.

She clearly hadn't noticed Linus sitting in the darkness when she came to a stop beside his passenger window. Remaining very still, he wrapped his fingers around the handle of the weapon stashed between the two front seats, watching out of the corner of his eye as she stooped down to pick up a plastic toy then continued on her way. Satisfied she'd moved on, he looked at his watch again, deciding he'd probably learned all that he was going to prior to entering the property.

So, pulling on a pair of gloves, he ensured the street was completely empty and then climbed out of the car.

* * *

For once, Scarlett had allowed Mark to fuss over her. Since returning from Frank's, she'd been treated to an hour's soak in the bath complete with candles and a gin and tonic. And, despite her insistence that she wasn't hungry, he'd prepared her a mini charcuterie board, which she was picking at while pretending to read on the bed. The book was for Mark's benefit; it made no difference to her whether she stared at a page or blankly into space but seemed to make him feel better.

He couldn't understand that no matter how hard he tried, there was no distracting from the guilt and sorrow she was feeling.

He'd gone for a shower to give her some peace and quiet, at least until his preposterously expensive 'ionic diffuser' hairdryer roared to life in the other room. Giving up on her book, Scarlett set it down, unable to even hear herself think, let alone the sound of glass shattering two floors below.

* * *

Henry was biding his time, feigning sleep, knowing he'd only get one chance.

The nurse was on the other side of the room and yet to notice the blood on the sheets from the laceration Henry had torn into his leg on a protruding edge of the metal handrail. It was minor but he'd made the most of it, dabbing the wound across every inch of white cotton within reach.

Footsteps approached the bed.

'Mr Devlin?' asked the man warily, even giving Henry a tentative poke when he didn't respond. 'Mr Devlin?'

Having confirmed Henry was still out cold, he moved a little closer, gently inspecting his patient's leg for the source of the bleeding...

...Like a coiled snake, Henry sprang from the bed, wrapping

his legs around the other man's throat and dragging him up onto the gurney while his limbs flailed about uselessly.

'Stop it! Stop!' Henry ordered, his captive gradually submitting. 'Do you know who I am?'

An indecipherable wheeze.

'Nod if you know who I am.'

He did.

'Then you know I could snap your neck like a twig and will have forgotten you ever existed by the time I reach the door?'

Again, the man nodded.

'Good. You have the handcuff keys on your person?'

When he took too long to answer, Henry increased the pressure, the red-faced man reaching into his pocket and retrieving the key.

'Unlock them.' Fumbling about blindly, the nurse eventually got both the locks open. 'What's your name?' Henry asked, slackening his hold just enough for him to answer.

'...Jethro.'

'Jethro, I'm going to release you now but remember you're still sharing a *very* small room with a *very* agitated professional killer.' Coughing and spluttering, Jethro slid down onto the floor. 'Now, would you be good enough to get my things for me?' As Henry took his first unsteady steps off the bed, the terrified man hurried over with his box of possessions. '*Shit*,' hissed Henry on seeing the time. He quickly unlocked his phone and called Scarlett's number; it rang off and went to voicemail. '*Shit!*'

Jethro flinched.

Henry deliberated for a moment, his mind still lagging behind: *she'd be relatively safe at work, the nature of her job making her commute unpredictable.* Coming to a decision, he dialled another number: 'Police, please... 47 Alton Road, Clapham. I've just seen an armed man firing shots at people from the windows... Send everyone.' Hanging up, he turned back to Jethro. 'You're going to handcuff yourself to the bed now,' he said, quickly getting himself dressed as the nurse did as instructed. 'Do you have a car?'

'No... Well, not here.'

'Does the hospital?'

'Only the ambulance.'

'Even better.'

* * *

Trying not to disturb Alkie, Scarlett got up off the bed and collected her empty gin glass along with the remnants of her dinner, the knife still planted in a particularly pungent blue cheese she hadn't thought much of. Carrying it out onto the landing, she tried to shout over the racket of Mark drying his hair. 'Do you want any of this before I take it down?!'

Receiving no reply, she shrugged and carefully descended into the dark. Her hands were too full to even contemplate switching on a light as she edged through the pitch-black hall-way, the bucket by the door sounding worryingly full after both a bath and shower. She reached the top of the second staircase, the warm light of their basement kitchen illuminating the way, when she heard her phone buzzing nearby. But as she turned towards the bluish glow emitting from her coat pocket, a shape separated from the surrounding darkness and charged at her.

She instinctively stepped back, missing the first stair entirely and tumbling down the staircase in a mess of limbs, glass and left-over food, head hitting the brick wall at the bottom, leaving her dazed as the shape followed her down. Scarlett didn't recognise the blond-haired man as he moved a little further into the light with each subsequent step.

'I had other plans for you,' he started, in what sounded like a Scandinavian accent. 'But a broken neck should suffice.'

Scarlett simply gazed up at him, the tinnitus in her ears so distracting, something tickling her skin as it dripped down her back. He knelt beside her and brushed the hair away from her forehead, savouring the moment as Scarlett's eyes drifted from the deformed skin of his face to the black gloves he was touching her with.

'I wish we had a little more time together,' he told her regretfully. 'But orders are orders.' He got back up. 'Could you lean forward for me? That's it,' he said. In her confused state, Scarlett allowed him to position her so that he could step behind. He placed one gloved hand across the top of her head, the other beneath her jaw. 'Everything's going to be alright,' he lied just as Scarlett's senses came rushing back to her. She started pulling against his hand in desperation. '*Shhhh. Shhhh.*'

Glancing from the upturned cheese board on the step beside her to the broken gin glass lying well out of reach, she ran her hand across the floor, finding the handle of the cheese knife... and driving it into her attacker's leg. A howl of pain – and the hands around her head fell away, Scarlett scrambling back up the stairs while Max went berserk behind the utility-room door.

'Mark!' she screamed as the heavy footfalls chased her up, the roar of the hairdryer the only response as she tore along the hallway, skidded around the bannister and began to climb. 'Mark!' she cried again, landing heavily on the stairs when her pursuer grabbed hold of her foot.

Kicking out viciously, she scaled the staircase before falling head first into the spare room, slamming the door behind her and blocking it with her weight.

'Mark?' she asked despairingly on realising the room was empty, the noisy appliance still billowing out hot air where it lay discarded on the carpet.

Then came the sound of a struggle out on the landing, a serrated hunting knife piercing the flimsy wood just above her head.

'Mark!' gasped Scarlett, scrabbling to her feet and throwing the door open to find him taking on the intruder alone, forcing the weapon in one hand away as the blond man reached for the knife embedded in his leg with the other.

Before she could even shout a warning, he'd pulled it from his own flesh and lashed out at Mark, slicing a deep gash across his forearm.

Sure it was over, she started towards them, refusing to go down without a fight; however, her conflict-adverse boyfriend didn't let go of the hunting knife, didn't recoil in shock, didn't do any of the things she was ashamed to say she'd expected of him. Instead, he cried out – not in pain but in fury, forcing the other man backwards into the bathroom, the mirror cracking as they collided with the wall before tumbling into the empty bathtub, taking the collection of flickering candles with them.

As Scarlett rushed to help, the sleeve of the intruder's jumper caught light, the look of unbridled fear in his eyes – the panic painted on his face as he stared into the flame – unmistakable as he seemed to forget about Mark altogether. And then, with a guttural scream, he fell out of the bathtub, now a raging ball of fire as he picked himself up off the floor and staggered down the stairs, setting off the smoke alarms, the orange glow he cast against the wall fading with every step.

Scarlett was still standing open-mouthed when Mark crawled out onto the bathroom floor.

'Oh God, Mark!' she gasped, running over and embracing him so tightly his back cracked, Max still barking incessantly over the noise – another smash downstairs followed by the sound of the back door swinging closed. 'Are you OK?'

'Never been stabbed before,' he said, looking a little pale as he regarded the impressive wound to his arm. It was more of a cut, but Scarlett let him have it. 'Is he gone?'

'He's gone,' she said, tears of relief gathering at the corners of her eyes. 'You were so brave!' she told him, embracing him again. 'So brave!' She shook her head in disbelief. 'I can't believe he went up like that.'

Mark looked a little guilty. 'Well, my first move *might* have *maybe, possibly*, been to try to mace him with hairspray.'

She really tried not to smirk.

'Suppose we'd better call the police then,' he said, reaching for a flannel to stem the bleeding. But no sooner had he said it than the sound of sirens and skidding tyres filled the street outside.

Scarlett stared into the hypnotic light strobing against the bedroom window and felt sick as it dawned on her what an attempt on her life would mean in her present precarious position. She'd be taken off the investigation for starters, but then would come the questions – the ones that Frank had tried so hard to protect her from, the ones that all the lies in the world couldn't cover.

'What is it?' asked Mark.

'Just...' she started, running her fingers through her matted hair as she got to her feet. 'Just stay here.'

'Scarlett?'

'Don't move!' she called back to him as she hurried down the stairs, wincing as she passed beneath the piercing alarm. She was standing in a puddle of water. Noting the upturned bucket by the front door, she pulled her coat over her bloody pyjamas, the hood up over her head and retrieved her ID from the pocket as she stepped outside.

'Police! Stop where you are!' bellowed one of the seven officers, training a gun on her.

'DC Scarlett Delaney!' she called back, ID on display. 'What's going on?'

There was a change in tone when he answered, his assertiveness replaced with doubt. 'We had reports of an individual discharging a firearm from the windows of your property.'

The look of confusion on Scarlett's face was genuine, at least. She'd presumed one of the neighbours had overhead their ordeal, but this made no sense whatsoever. With a groan, she shook her head. 'Bloody kids. I'm so sorry. Some of the local delinquents found out I'm a police officer and have been making a nuisance of themselves ever since: prank calls, posting things through our letterbox... but this is a *whole* other level.'

Lowering his weapon, the officer stepped out from behind his vehicle and approached, eyes studying Scarlett. 'Is that your alarm going off?' he asked, the suspicion in his voice clear as he peered beyond her into the hallway.

'Yes. I'm afraid that happens a lot when I'm cooking,' she joked, the man stony-faced as his eyes returned to her.

'Are you sure you're alright?'

'I'm fine,' she replied, folding her arms defensively, which did not go unnoticed by the armed man.

'It's just... your make-up is a little smudged.'

'I had a bath. I wasn't expecting company.'

'*Uh huh*. And do you live alone?'

Scarlett hesitated, seeing where his current train of thought was heading. 'No. With my boyfriend... and cat... and a dog at the moment.'

'Everything OK between you?'

'Well, the cat hasn't taken kindly to the dog's arrival, and the boyfriend's been jealous of the cat for years. But I'm sure they'll sort it ou—'

'Between you and your boyfriend,' he interrupted her.

'Yes. Everything's fine.'

'Mind if I come in for a moment? Say *hello*.'

There was no way she could refuse him, just as there was no way he wouldn't see the carnage and know she'd been lying the moment he stepped through the door, let alone after speaking to Mark.

She maintained an impassive expression. 'Of course.'

But as she turned to lead the way, the alarm abruptly cut out, Mark emerging from the house wielding a dishcloth and wearing a dressing gown and smile. 'Friends of yours?' he asked Scarlett casually before introducing himself to the officer, barely letting it show when he used his injured arm to shake the other man's hand.

'Actually, I don't believe Detective Delaney and myself have crossed paths before,' the officer answered on Scarlett's behalf when she failed to respond. He huffed then spoke into his radio. 'All units stand down. Stand down.'

On noticing the trickle of blood running down Mark's fingers, she gave him a glare. Quickly wiping it away with the dishcloth, he asked: 'Is there anything that can be done about these kids? They're making our lives miserable.'

As the assorted vehicles began to clear out, the officer and Mark continued their conversation, Scarlett distracted when the ambulance rolling past came to the briefest of stops, the silhouette in the driver's seat looking right at her before following the rest of the convoy up the narrow road.

She was still watching it turn the corner when the armed man headed back to his car.

'Detective Delaney,' he nodded, Scarlett and Mark waving him off like a departing house guest as he pulled away.

'I'm losing quite a lot of blood,' mumbled Mark through a forced smile.

'I'll take care of it,' replied Scarlett, her ventriloquism skills wasted in the Metropolitan Police.

'I think...' Mark dropped the act and turned to her, 'it's about time you told me what's going on.'

THIRTY-SEVEN

A PALATABLE VERSION OF SOME OF THE TRUTH

'We're leaving.'

'Let's not make any rash decis— *Oh*, OK,' said Scarlett, moving out of the way as Mark pulled a suitcase down off the top of the wardrobe, almost flattening Alkie, who hadn't moved from his spot on the bed throughout the entire conversation... nor the attempted murder beforehand.

'I'm not making a "rash decision,"' he bit back, boxer shorts taking to the air before he moved on to his sock drawer. 'You yourself said that *just yesterday* Frank was murdered by a professional killer. Less than an *hour* ago, a man broke into our home and stabbed me—'

'Slashed.'

'What?'

'It's just, he more... *slashed* you.' From the look on Mark's face, Scarlett wasn't helping the situation. 'Sorry. Go on.'

'Because he was here to murder *you!*' He was shouting now. 'I lied to a street full of armed police on your behalf, when they could've been out looking for this man! My arm is Gorilla Glue'd together! The *entire* house smells like burnt hair which at least is diffusing out through the broken window and door that we won't be able to claim on the insurance because, apparently, none of this ever even happened!'

Scarlett had shared what she'd believed to be a palatable version of some of the truth in the hope that Mark wouldn't freak out, but as she watched him partially move them out of their home, she was relieved that she'd only touched on the bad stuff... and steered clear of the *really* bad stuff altogether.

'Feeling better?' she asked.

He nodded. 'A little. But we're still leaving. We can't stay here with these people out there.' Scarlett showed no sign of moving. 'Please.'

Rolling her eyes, she picked up a crumpled blouse from under the bed and tossed it into the case.

'Thank you,' he said in relief, appreciating the gesture... before passing the garment back to her. 'But find your own case. This one's mine.'

Within half an hour they were all packed up: the two of them, two cases and two animals, all crammed into Scarlett's little Fiat.

'This is *ridiculous*,' she complained.

'This is us taking a sensible precaution,' Mark corrected her. 'So, we'll drop Alkie and Max off with my brother... *then* I'll tell you where we're going,' he added mysteriously.

'Holiday Inn?' Scarlett guessed, sounding unenthused.

'Not necessarily.'

She sighed and started up the engine. 'It's *definitely* the Holiday Inn.'

* * *

It had only been a short walk from the Holiday Inn to New Scotland Yard that morning, where Scarlett had been summoned for a 'get to know one another' chat ahead of the day, with the new lead detective on the case.

DI Richard Cooper had been everything she'd been expecting from the wide berth everybody tended to give him – a rigid, emotionless, mid-fifties robot of a man, sporting his ex-army buzz-cut like a badge of honour, and built like a brick shit-house. In no uncertain terms he'd instructed Scarlett to smile and nod along to anything and everything he said, to follow his every instruction to the letter, and had reiterated on several occasions that he could have her removed from the investigation with a click of his fingers. Fighting her better instincts she'd smiled and nodded accordingly, reminding herself that she was very fortunate to still have a job at all.

The team briefing had been a dry affair. All set-up crew were to be off the premises by 11:30 a.m., at which point the police would take over, securing all points of 'ingress' and 'egress' and installing additional security measures. Every inch of the event space was to be searched in collaboration with the dog unit, with the team breaking off in shifts from 5 p.m. to get some food and change into their evening attire.

One of Scarlett's few suggestions to have survived the change of leadership had been for surveillance officers to study all available photographs and video clips of the elusive activist. Face always covered, these rare moments caught on camera could at least give them an idea of her gait, posture and manner-isms – anything that might help identify her among the likely hundreds of guests. The idea: they could get her out of the building and to safety before she even came forward.

When the meeting adjourned, Newbury loitered behind to speak to Scarlett, an uncharacteristically serious expression on his face. 'I *errm...* I'm really sorry about Detective Ash,' he started, Scarlett nodding her thanks while gathering up the presentation materials. 'So, we finally got to the bottom of the silk-scarf mystery. That Edgar Crews crumpled like a house of cards the moment we got him in the interview room. He says it belonged to his late wife, and she was wearing it the day she died. The sick bastard actually *asked* them to use it on Francesca – some bollocks about her "going to join her mother."'

He shrugged and checked his notes. '...*Yadda, yadda, yadda*. "Didn't want her to suffer." Hey, did you know that poor man's barely been sleeping since having his own daughter killed?' he asked facetiously. 'He says he had no idea whatsoever Devlin was going to take her head off *or* put the pictures up online. Go figure.'

'Good work,' said Scarlett, sounding a little flat.

Flipping his notebook shut, Newbury gestured toward Cooper as he marched past the windows. 'I notice you got yourself a Terminator,' he joked.

'*Not* my decision,' she told him.

'So... we're taking orders from him now?'

'The team certainly are,' she replied, a smirk curling at the corners of her mouth. 'But *you're* not. You can still take your orders from me.'

* * *

The final lighting technician was practically chased out of the doors at 11:34 a.m., the only personnel left on site being the police and an extensively background-checked caretaker to provide access to whatever they needed.

Although devoid of all atmosphere in the cold light of day, there was an electricity in the air of the event space, a nervous excitement at the glitzy gala dinner to come, the grand unveiling of the celebrity activist's true identity, and the impending arrest of the person responsible for The Jackdaw murders... a man who had killed one of their own – all in front of a worldwide audience.

While Cooper accompanied the caretaker on a quest to check every door and large cupboard in the building, Scarlett wandered the main room. The gallery exhibit, stage and carpeted area looked much as they had the other day, but the entire rear half of the room was now laid out with large round tables, white cloths and was dinner-ready. Frustratingly, the secretive numbered place settings had prevented them gaining any insight into the guest list.

Scarlett closed her eyes and took a deep breath, wanting to see the space as if for the very first time.

'Think like Henry,' she whispered to herself. 'Think like Henry.'

Opening them again, she ambled between the tables.

She knew that she'd called him while he was scaling the outside of a warehouse... and that he'd dropped something into the river. Taking out her phone, she opened up the map and walked a circle, trying to get her bearings. Eyes glued to the screen, she approached the wall bordering the river before gazing up at the numerous lead-lined windows filled with clear blue skies, most opening into thin air from where the warehouse had been converted, but some at the very top within reach of the wooden rafters.

'Newbury!' she called, her number two breaking off his conversation and making his way over.

'Boss?'

'I need you to find the caretaker. He's probably still with Cooper. Ask him if any of the windows in here have been damaged recently and if there's any way to gain access' to the roof space.'

With a nod, he headed out, Scarlett continuing her tour of the room while muttering to herself. 'He was just going to walk in through the main doors but can't do that now.' Again, she stared up at the intersecting beams spanning the width of the enormous room. 'Need to know if there's a way down.'

The hard floor gave way to soft carpet as she passed the entrance to the meandering gallery.

'He would've wanted to be close when it happened... within view at least, to avoid suspicion... and he would have accounted for the police presence.'

She frowned and continued along the green carpet.

'He has no idea who his target is either,' she reasoned. 'Of course he hasn't, yet whatever he's planned is already set up.' She rubbed her temples, trying to force her thoughts into some sort of order. 'Like Newbury said, he can't plan for a specific person, but he *can* plan for a specific *place*.'

Behind her, Newbury cleared his throat, having returned with news. 'Finally lost your shit, boss?' he asked.

'The microphone!' she exclaimed, she and Newbury turning in unison to look at the stage. 'He doesn't know who she is any more than we do, but he does know the *one* place she is guaranteed to be standing at the very moment the whole world is watching. It's the microphone,' she said decisively, gazing back up at the rafters directly above their heads. 'What did the caretaker say?'

'Knows nothing about any damaged windows but says there's a door at the far end of the hall that leads up there and safety equipment in a box by the stairs,' he informed her, before realising she was looking at him expectantly. 'Boss?'

'How's your head for heights?'

* * *

'So, this is how I die,' muttered Newbury as he stepped out onto the first beam, disconnected one rope, moved it onto the next beam along and then repeated the action with the second.

It was the same principle employed at the treetop assault course he'd somehow survived while still partially drunk on a stag weekend: one rope connected at all times, the worst that could happen a monumental wedgie from the harness strapped around his legs.

'Hurry it up!' Scarlett heckled him.

'That's very helpful! Thank you!' he called back down, a growing crowd of spectators gathering below as he shuffled cautiously along the wood.

Before he knew it, he was already halfway across, the point of no return, his legs trembling as he looked back at how far he'd ventured from the doorway.

* * *

'Shit! Cooper's coming! Cooper's coming!' someone hissed, the audience dispersing just as the intimidating detective inspector marched into the hall, Scarlett smiling innocently as he came to a stop directly beneath where Newbury was clinging to a beam for dear life.

'Detective Delaney,' he greeted her. 'Update?'

'The dog has been through – nothing suspicious. The metal detectors have been installed at the main entrance. The surveillance team are all set up, and I'm in the process of working out his intended MO, which I'll bring to you just as soon as it's coherent.'

He made a show of checking his watch. 'Don't think on it too long.'

She smiled and nodded, knowing he'd like that. 'I've got an officer following it up as we speak,' she told him, cringing at her unfortunate turn of phrase as she glanced up at her colleague. Without another word, Cooper turned on his heel and headed out, Scarlett waiting until he'd disappeared round the corner before giving Newbury the all-clear. 'OK! I think we're good!'

* * *

The sun blazed in through the windows, throwing shadows across Newbury's tightrope of wooden beams as he edged towards his destination. Even from five metres away, he knew he was in the right place.

'We've got a broken window pane up here!' he called down, his confidence growing as he moved directly above the stage.

'Anything else?!' Scarlett shouted back.

'Hang on!' he told her, negotiating the vertical strut blocking his path to discover a simple pulley system crudely installed into the wood. He followed the thin strand of wire from the spool down under his own feet and then along the rafter to a set of three identical rucksacks precariously positioned against the window. 'There's a pulley... and bags.'

'What's in the bags?'

'Don't know yet!' he called, frowning at the coil of lethal-looking razor wire lying beside a handful of single-use light-sticks, while dangling electrical wiring escaped one of the huge industrial lights. 'Looks like he's been doing a bit of rewiring!'

'Probably don't touch that!' advised Scarlett.

'We need to know what it does!'

'OK. But I'm moving! Be careful!'

Giving Scarlett a chance to vacate the stage area, Newbury reached for the hanging wires, wincing as he tentatively brought them together... There was a loud bang somewhere in the building as every light in the hall went out, throwing them into a pleasant natural daylight.

'*Huh*,' shrugged Newbury. 'And now we know.'

* * *

'I need a piss!' Newbury shouted down, having been stranded up there while Scarlett attempted to piece together Henry's plan.

At least the lights had come back on, it taking the bad-tempered caretaker almost a quarter of an hour to locate the fuse box and restore power.

'Five more minutes!' she promised, scribbling over what she'd just drawn and trying again... her eyes growing wide with excitement as she checked and then rechecked her sketch. 'I've got it! I've got it!' she exclaimed, jumping to her feet. 'Just... wait there!' she told Newbury, already running for the door.

* * *

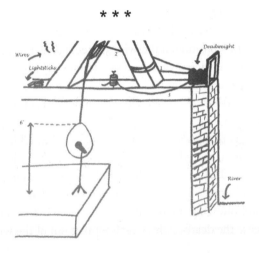

Cooper frowned at Scarlett's sketch ...and then at her. 'What is this?'

'This is what's above us,' she explained, holding up her phone as Newbury streamed his view from the rafters. 'We have three rucksacks secured together and filled with some sort of metal. This is the deadweight. Attached to this deadweight are three lengths of wire.' She handed him an offcut Newbury had tossed down beforehand. 'Incredibly strong and so thin it's damn-near undetectable.'

Giving it a doubtful tug, Cooper passed it to one of the other officers listening in as Scarlett continued. 'Wire 1 is secured to a rafter and has the simple job of holding the dead-weight in place. Wire 2 runs from the deadweight, through the pulley system and down to a large noose above the stage.'

Again, Cooper looked sceptical. That was until Scarlett removed the silk scarf she'd subconsciously chosen to wear and tossed it at the microphone, where it hung as if suspended in mid-air. Intrigued, he moved a little closer, the wire glinting in the sunlight: '*Ah*. I see it now.'

'Hen— Devlin,' she corrected herself, 'will have studied the footage as we have. He knows his target is no taller than five foot eight so he's positioned the wire six feet above the stage, a wide loop hanging down and loosely attached to the microphone, ensuring she'll step into it.'

'And Wire 3?' asked Cooper, looking back down at her picture.

'I'll get to that. So, with the whole world watching, our guest of honour takes to the stage, finally revealing her identity while, above us, Devlin snaps a lightstick in preparation. Once he's ready, he brings the two electrical wires together, blowing the fuse and plunging the room into darkness. He then cuts Wire 1 to release the deadweight, which topples out of the window and pulls the noose tight around her neck, lifting his victim into the air.'

Reaching over, she turned the page to where she had scribbled a second drawing.

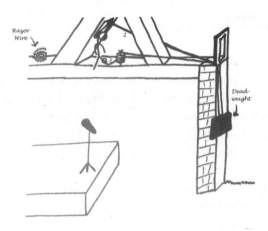

'The deadweight jerks to a stop as her body is pulled against the pulley, either breaking her neck or asphyxiating her. Working by the glow of the lightstick, Devlin then attaches Wire 3 around one of the victim's limbs. He gives her the calling-card facial scratches, perhaps even some fibres from the silk scarf, before performing the decapitation with razor wire. The *moment* the head is separated, it drops back to the stage, freeing Wire 2 and the deadweight, which free-falls into the river, taking Wire 3 and the rest of the body with it.

'The room still dark, he collects up his equipment and drops it into the water. He secures the window from the inside and carefully makes his way back along the rafters to the stairwell, rejoining the audience just in time to look appropriately appalled when the lights come back up. In a matter of minutes, a woman decapitated in front of a roomful of people, her body inexplicably vanished – another successful kill by The Jackdaw.'

Applause broke out from up in the rafters but failed to spread as Cooper looked from the rough sketches to the stage, apparently still unconvinced. 'Seems convoluted.'

'Impossible murders tend to,' reasoned Scarlett.

'You're sure about this?'

'I am.'

He nodded. 'I can't argue with your track record, so we'll go with it. I want the surveillance team to install an additional camera up there. I'll liaise with the Marine Unit about getting a boat out on the water in case he should attempt to escape via that route. Is there a way to make this pulley system safe without immediately alerting him to it?'

'A single cut to Wire 2 should do it,' replied Scarlett.

'Do it. I'll discuss the wiring with the caretaker. We may need to get somebody in. Good work, Detective.'

Not one to waste time, Cooper immediately set to work, a forgotten voice calling from above: '...Can I get down now, please?'

* * *

At 6:55 p.m. Scarlett passed through the security check, the warehouse utterly transformed from how it had looked only an hour earlier. The tatty white rags hanging from the entrance-hall ceiling were now great sails bathed in pinks and blues, the buzz of conversation accompanying the background music as a small army of hired help put the finishing touches to their respective areas while they awaited their guests – not to mention the scores of paparazzi laying siege to the street outside.

The celebrity activist's plan had created the media frenzy she'd no doubt been hoping for, various celebrities and note-worthy people taking to social media to announce their eleventh-hour invitations and 'dilemmas' over what to wear.

The oxblood dress Scarlett had got changed into back at the hotel was one of her go-to favourites yet still a far cry from the Viktor & Rolf masterpiece now residing somewhere within the Hilton's refuse area. She cringed, still feeling awful about it...

and then her thoughts inevitably strayed to Frank – him discovering her bag at the bottom of Francesca Labelle's wardrobe, covering her tracks as usual. *He should've been there, standing at her side as always.*

Interrupting, and looking a little uncomfortable in an ill-fitting suit, Newbury headed over. 'Boss,' he nodded in greeting, handing her an earpiece, which she put into place under her hair.

'Anything to report?' she asked.

He sniffed the arm of his jacket. 'Only the unsolved case of whoever died in this suit.'

She sniggered. 'Clear on the plan?'

'The official plan or the... *less* official plan?'

'Both.'

'Clear on the plan,' he confirmed as they both turned their attention to the main doors, where the flash of camera bulbs lit up the glass like lightning as the first guests began to arrive.

Scarlett composed herself with a deep breath. 'Here we go.'

THIRTY-EIGHT

BLACK TIES/WHITE LIES

7:24 p.m. Wine glass of lemonade in hand, Scarlett weaved a path through the mingling guests, scanning the faces belonging to the bow ties and lavish dresses, catching snippets of a hundred different conversations in search of any clue to the celebrity activist's true identity... in search of Henry.

The entrance hall had been generously rebranded a *Reception Suite* for the purposes of the evening, the doors to the main event space remaining sealed while welcome drinks and canapés were served to the distinguished attendees packed together like tuxedoed cattle.

Scarlett stopped walking when her radio hissed in her ear.

'Surveillance to Cooper. Over.'

'Receiving.'

'One-hundred-and-sixty-two guests now on site. One-hundred-and-eighty place settings. Six public "unable to attends". Including their plus-ones, that leaves six still unaccounted for.'

'Copied. Out.'

. . .

7:44 p.m. The roar of conversation had built to an uncomfortable level, fuelled by drink and stoked by the high walls and natural acoustics when, without warning, the doors to the event space were opened up. Overheating guests began pouring into the main room while Scarlett and a couple of others lingered behind to keep an eye on the stragglers still waiting for drinks at the bar or for partners to return from the bathrooms.

Taking her phone out of her bag, Scarlett faked a call, holding a finger to the transmitter in her ear. 'Delaney to Harris and Norton – carry on through to the hall. I'll stay out here.'

Without showing any outward sign of acknowledgement, both men casually picked up their drinks and moved on.

8 p.m. As one of the handful of police personnel to be posing as a guest rather than staff, Scarlett found an empty space and took a seat, the flipside to the activist's last-minute invitation that, inevitably, some had been unable to make arrangements in time. She wasn't hungry in the least, the knot in her stomach pulling tighter with every minute that passed, but she knew it would look suspicious if she didn't join the other diners.

Staring up at the shadowy rafters above the stage, she was at least somewhat comforted by the knowledge that she wasn't the only one watching them as the waiting staff erupted from the kitchens and, with the efficiency of a well-oiled machine, placed plates in front of entire tables of guests at a time.

'And who might you be?' asked the red-faced gentleman to her left, extending a hand.

'Scarlett... Ash,' she replied with a smile, her background story at the ready as she was dragged into conversation.

. . .

8:28 p.m. It turned out that Scarlett *had* been hungry, devouring both the starter and main of the Thai-themed vegan menu. Ear buzzing away with non-information throughout, her foot was tapping anxiously as she looked around the room and then back up into the roof space, having hoped it would all have been over by this point.

'Wine?'

'I'm sorry?' she asked, turning back to the man teasing an expensive bottle of red over her glass. She automatically went to refuse but then noticed she'd scratched a hole through the table-cloth without even realising; she needed something to calm her nerves. 'Yes ...please.'

8:48 p.m. The first guests to finish their desserts were already making a beeline for the bar and gallery exhibit. Scarlett watched people she vaguely recognised from the television getting up from their seats as she wondered where the hell Henry was, the main event clearly not far off. Convinced she must have missed something, she excused herself from the table before subtly touching a finger to her ear.

'Delaney to Surveillance.'

'Go ahead.'

'Any possible leads for me on the activist?' she asked, an edge of frustration to her voice.

'That's a negative. We came up with over *twenty* possible candidates from the reception suite, and they've all been sat around eating ever since.'

'So, keep looking!' she snapped, not concentrating on where she was going as she rounded the corner and walked straight into someone. 'I'm so sor—' She stopped, mouth falling open as she stared up at Henry making no effort whatsoever to keep a low profile in a striking midnight-blue tux.

'Detective Delaney,' he smiled.

Taking a step back in surprise, she reached for her ear, Henry grabbing her arms before she could do so. '*No. No. No,*' he said, forcing her back against a pillar, the two of them standing chest to chest as he pinned her hands behind her back. 'What would you want to do something like that for?' he asked as she struggled against him. 'Calm down. I'm not going to hurt you.'

Giving up, Scarlett ceased fighting and scowled up at him, feeling his breath against her forehead as they shared the air between them – the familiar hints of whisky and sandalwood.

'How did you get in?' she asked.

'Well, as the saying goes, "this ain't my first rodeo."'

'It's not going to work,' she announced with some relish. 'We found your pulley system, the bags... the noose.'

'*We* found?' he asked sceptically.

'*I* found.'

He smiled. 'I don't doubt you did.'

'It's over.'

'It was already over,' he said wearily, the response disarming her as they remained undetected in their darkened corner of the room. 'I'm not here for her.'

A group of inebriated women approached, presumably en route to the bathrooms, Scarlett and Henry staying silent, pressed together in the shadows as they passed by.

'You could have shouted for help,' he said once they were out of earshot.

'I want some answers. Then I will.'

'*Nah,*' he said. 'I think we're still friends.'

'Have you forgotten the part where I shot you?'

'Forgiven, not forgotten.'

'You can keep your forgiveness,' she said while attempting to squirm out of his hold.

Henry leaned back to regard her. 'You look beautiful.'

'And you look a little chunky,' she fired back at him.

'That'll be the bandages.'

She looked away from Henry, towards the stage area, where people were beginning to congregate. 'What were the stipulations for killing this one?'

Henry looked blank.

'The trinkets/the ring. The scratches/the surgery,' she elaborated. 'So, which of The Jackdaw's many "traits" was this supposed to be?'

'The audience,' answered Henry. 'As big an audience as possible – a message to any other "tree-hugging terrorist out there with ideas above their station." The client's words, not mine.'

'And if you're not here for her then what *are* you here for?'

'You,' he replied simply. 'To say goodbye.'

'Goodbye?' she asked despite herself, hearing the hint of despair in her voice.

He nodded, his brow furrowing. 'I've got one last thing to do. For both of us. And then... if there is a *then*, I won't be coming back.' He looked at her sadly. 'I am truly sorry about Frank.' He tightened his grip as she made yet another attempt to fight him off. 'You *know* it was an accident. I know you know that. I could have killed him ten times over, but I didn't. I was just trying to get out.'

A mascara-blackened tear snaked down her face as she turned away from him.

'I know you know it,' he reiterated, glancing towards the stage, a communal sense of anticipation drawing the crowd together. 'That was all I came here to say. That, and to let you know they released the job onto the open market. It's going to be pandemonium, and I suggest you distance yourself from it immediately.' When she looked confused, he nodded towards the waiting staff clearing the tables. 'This whole place is crawling with assassins. Long grey hair in a ponytail – see him?'

'*Uh huh.*'

'And the big guy in the burgundy tux?'

'I see him.'

'That sasquatch once drove me off a bridge in Scotland.'

At that moment, one of the scantily-clad cocktail waitresses sauntered by with a tray of drinks in hand. On spotting Henry, she nodded in cautious greeting: 'Henry.'

'Kriztina,' he replied, ensuring that she'd continued walking before turning back to Scarlett. 'See what I mean?!' He sighed. 'I'm going to let you go now. OK?'

'The second you do, I'm going to bring my entire team down on you.'

Henry smiled. 'No, you won't.' He regarded her intently and then, very slowly, moved in closer, closing his eyes, lips parting, Scarlett breathing heavily as, at the last beat, he paused and planted a gentle kiss on her forehead. 'Take care of yourself, Detective Delaney.'

Releasing her arms, he took a step back, Scarlett reaching for her earpiece but then hesitating, her hand trembling with indecision as the crack of a gunshot filled the hall. There were screams, shouting, echoing into a cacophony as the floor rumbled with the footfalls of panicking guests.

Henry rolled his eyes. 'Bloody amateurs,' he tutted just as the stampeding crowd swallowed him up as it moved as one toward the main doors, Scarlett rushing to where he'd just been standing but losing him in the sea of people.

'Detective Delaney!'

Pressing her hand over her ear before realising the voice wasn't coming from the radio, she pushed her way through to the young officer. 'What happened?'

'One dead female and a male in custody.'

'Show me.'

She followed the flustered officer through the crowd to the area of green carpet, where the man in the burgundy tuxedo had been pinned to the floor as a small group of do-gooders stood around the body of a cocktail waitress, still beautiful where she'd bled out onto the floor. Cooper was barking orders over the radio, but Scarlett removed her earpiece to better hear Frank's voice in her head: *Rule nineteen – if somebody tells you someone's deceased – ignore them, and check the bastard's dead yourself.*

She walked over and knelt beside the body to press two fingers against the stagnant artery. A single bullet wound had penetrated her skull directly between the eyes, Scarlett recognising her as the same woman who'd passed by only a minute earlier.

'It's her,' said one of the tearful bystanders.

'She was *such* an inspiration,' concurred her friend in a sparkly blue dress.

Scarlett had T-shirts that were longer.

'I'm sorry, do you know this woman?' she asked them from the floor.

'Not personally. But it's her: E.W.'

'Yeah,' another man piped up as he consoled his wife. 'I heard that too. It's her.'

Now even more confused, Scarlett patted down the body, discovering the steak knife tucked into the deceased woman's waistband. 'And who did you hear this from?' she asked, suspecting she already knew the answer.

'Handsome guy. Dark-blue suit,' the man replied.

'Yeah. Same here,' nodded the tearful woman.

'Me too,' said another.

Looking back down at the dead assassin at her feet, Scarlett struggled to keep the inappropriate smile from her face.

* * *

Newbury flicked his cigarette away as he watched the entire gala empty out onto the road, his earpiece a confusion of overlapping communications as the crowd surged towards the waiting journalists, who'd just struck tabloid gold.

Unofficially posted across the street for the duration of the event, he couldn't know for certain what had occurred inside, but then spotted a lone figure moving calmly in the opposite direction to the others. Mirroring the man's footsteps as a convoy of speeding police vehicles passed between them, he needed to confirm an identity before straying too far.

'Come on, you bastard. Look over,' he muttered under his breath, glancing anxiously at the chaos he was leaving behind. 'Come on.'

And then, for no more than a split second, Henry looked back.

But it had been enough, Newbury crossing the street and keeping his distance as he followed his target round the corner and up a cobbled footpath towards the city centre.

THIRTY-NINE

THE SHOOTING GALLERY

Cooper had asked Scarlett whether she wanted to address the team alongside him: *after all, it had been her operation too.*

She'd told him *no.*

It was a curious thing, the magnanimity of captains of sinking ships. He was going to drown, and she was going to smile and nod as she watched him go under.

While they awaited forensics, the dead cocktail waitress remained where she'd fallen, the exhibition's metal frames repurposed to obscure her from view. No one but Scarlett knew that the body growing cold on the warehouse floor didn't, in fact, belong to the renowned activist at all, and she was in no hurry to ease her replacement's suffering.

Cutting a lonely silhouette as he stepped up to the stage, Cooper looked out over his assembled subordinates and sighed, Scarlett wondering for a moment whether his spine would hold out – whether he would accept his failings and face the music or attempt to deflect the blame elsewhere.

'Well, *that* was an unprecedented clusterfuck!' he began, Scarlett hearing all she needed to as her phone started to buzz and she stepped out of the crowd.

'Newbury?' she answered anxiously.

'Trafalgar Square. The National Gallery.'

She was already halfway to the door. 'I'll be there in ten minutes.'

* * *

An enormous moon hung over the city like a spotlight, an evacuated Trafalgar Square its stage, as Scarlett ducked beneath the cordon and crossed the vast expanse of paving stones while Horatio Nelson observed all from atop his solitary pedestal.

Approaching the figure pacing laps of the fountain, she watched another set of blue lights roll up silently to join the others beyond the cordoned area.

'Where are we at?' she greeted Newbury.

'He's still inside. No one else has come in or out,' replied her second-in-command, who'd done an admirable job of closing down a major London thoroughfare in such a short space of time. 'Armed response are round the side of the building. Team leader's name is Fields.'

'We've met,' she told him unenthusiastically.

'Channel two,' he said, handing her a radio along with a well-worn pair of Converse All-Stars. 'Helicopter is in the air and on standby in case we need it.'

'Thanks,' she said, kicking off her heels and slipping into her comfy trainers. 'Nobody moves until I have visual confirmation of who he's meeting.'

'Meeting?' asked Newbury, lagging a little behind on Scarlett's ever-fluid plans.

'OK,' she said, puffing out her cheeks as she regarded the grand entranceway. 'I'm going in.'

* * *

Henry negotiated the National Gallery's web of corridors alone, missing the respectful hush that roared through its halls during the daytime – the silence thick, church-like, gauntlets of dead faces lining every ornate wall.

On reaching the second floor, he made his way towards the estate's largest room, where Linus was already in the doorway awaiting his arrival.

'Bad night?' asked Henry conversationally on seeing the fresh burns to his face. He raised his arms to allow the other man to search him. 'Looks painful. But on the plus side, they say symmetrical faces are meant to be the most beautiful.'

Unamused, Linus finished patting him down and led him inside.

'I'm going to enjoy this,' he whispered, assuming his post by the door as Henry continued on without him.

More palace than gallery, Room 32's sumptuous red walls burned against the starry sky above, gold-framed masterpieces stretching into the distance as he slowly approached the bench on which Rebecca was sitting. With Sofia loitering in the exit to his left and Felix guarding the far end of the hall, he hesitated, expecting her to get to her feet... But she didn't move, didn't even register his presence as, unsurely, he sat down beside her. And then, for a couple of minutes, they just sat in silence in appreciation of their lavish surroundings.

'Another fine lesson in subtlety,' she said at last. 'It's all over the news.'

'Nothing to do with me,' he told her. 'I wouldn't make a mess like that.'

Finally tearing herself away from the artwork, Rebecca gave him a knowing look.

'OK,' he backtracked. 'I'd make a *different* kind of mess.'

* * *

The hum of voices carried effortlessly down the labyrinthine corridors. Scarlett, already on the main staircase, continuing her climb.

* * *

'Not that it would have made a jot of difference anyway,' Rebecca told him sadly, reaching over to place her hand upon his. 'The board's minds were already made up.' She frowned when Henry showed no reaction whatsoever to the death sentence she'd just dealt him. 'You don't seem surprised.'

'The painting sort of gave it away,' he smiled, gazing up at the fitting image she'd chosen to sit beside – beheaded and beautiful. 'Caravaggio: *Salome with the Head of John the Baptist*. I take it you're the reluctant king in this analogy?'

Rebecca nodded. 'Destined to carry out Salome's will, no matter how repellent.'

'Whose own wishes were dictated *to* her by one even more powerful.'

'Quite,' she sighed. 'They have demanded your head on a platter, my dear boy. ...Metaphorically speaking, of course. But still... not overly great for you.'

* * *

Scarlett crept ever nearer to the modest crescendo, recognising Henry's voice anywhere; the other voice was female with the diction and vocabulary of another time, when such things carried the weight of an arsenal at one's disposal.

* * *

'Are you ready?' asked Rebecca, the handsome woman giving her undisputed favourite a reassuring smile. 'You know, a part of me had hoped you wouldn't show tonight. We would have found you, of course, but...' She trailed off. 'Alas, I knew you *would*, and here you *are*. For someone so full of surprises, you can be painfully predictable at times.'

'Speaking of being predicable...' started Henry, finishing the thought by throwing himself to the floor and ripping free the shotgun he'd taped to the underside of the bench. Swinging the long barrel in Felix's direction, he pulled the trigger...

* * *

Scarlett was caught out in the open when the first gunshot sounded. Before she had time to react, one of the largest men she'd ever seen stumbled out of the next doorway along, arm bloodied as he looked up to see her standing there.

'Oh, *shit*,' she muttered.

He raised his weapon.

Darting along the corridor to her left, she held down the *transmit* button on her radio: 'All units. All units. Shots fired! Move in!'

* * *

Rebecca dashed towards the nearest exit as Henry fired again, blowing a no-doubt-priceless masterpiece to shreds before scrambling back to the bench to retrieve the handgun and knife he'd also stashed there, large splinters of wood showering over him as he was assaulted from all sides.

'The girl!' he heard Felix shout over the noise. He sounded hurt. 'The detective!' he continued as the shooting subsided. 'She's in the building!'

The news hit Henry like a physical blow.

'Well, get after her then!' ordered Rebecca from somewhere out of view, the onslaught resuming, trapping Henry behind his disintegrating bench as the wounded Latvian disappeared from his doorway.

Feeling helpless, Henry noticed a spark in the night sky, the glass roof masking the chug of rotor blades as a helicopter drifted overhead, flooding the room in artificial light.

Seizing his opportunity, he made for the doorway, bullets peppering the floor around his feet as he fired back blindly, colliding with the wall and falling out into the adjacent corridor. Eyes still adjusting, he checked himself over to find that he'd ripped his stitches, but otherwise made it out unscathed, before picking up his weapon and taking off in pursuit of Felix.

* * *

The gunfire had ceased.

Having run straight into a dead end, Scarlett edged round the corner as the enormous man entered the room she'd just vacated, the trickle of blood against the wooden flooring audible over the silence.

Through the crack in the doorframe, she watched him deliberate and then move into one of the other galleries, Scarlett stepping out and creeping back across the hall she'd just come from. With his vast back to her, she hurried past, returning to the main corridor, the staircase now within reach.

Spotting a well-dressed woman at a distant doorway, Scarlett locked eyes with her for the briefest of moments before another, blonde-haired and beautiful, staggered out between them. With the handle of a large blade protruding from her side, she slumped against a wall and slid to the ground, the doorway beyond now standing empty.

In shock, Scarlett sensed something behind her too late, turning to see her muscular pursuer tearing towards her at full pelt.

Closing her eyes, she braced herself for the impact... but it never came, Henry intercepting the massive man and sending them both tumbling down the stone staircase.

'Scarlett, run!' he called as they grappled part-way down, blocking her way, Scarlett choosing her moment to vault over them and continue to ground level, not daring to look back as she followed the signage towards the main entrance.

* * *

Henry knew he could never overpower Felix in a fist-fight, every blow feeling like he'd been struck with a baseball bat. Sensing the inevitable end drawing near he reached out in desperation, sinking his fingers into the larger man's fresh wounds, distracting him as he wrapped his arms around the thick neck and launched himself over the bannister, both men falling through the air and landing in a lifeless heap on the marble floor below.

* * *

The entrance hall was in sight, Scarlett able to hear her backup searching the ground floor all around her. With a sigh of relief, she paused to catch her breath... but then gasped when a gloved hand covered her nose and mouth, her scream muffled as she was dragged into a dark alcove.

'Shhhh. Shhhh,' someone hissed in her ear, the same unsettling voice she remembered from her basement kitchen the previous evening.

When an armed officer passed by, no more than a few metres away, she tried to call out, to kick free, the disfigured man's grip only tightening the harder she fought, Scarlett watching helplessly as her only hope of survival moved away. 'Shhhh,' he whispered soothingly. 'It's OK.'

Feet scrabbling uselessly against the floor, she caught the

glint of a blade in his other hand and forced herself to supress her panic, to think pragmatically...

Against her natural instincts, she suddenly stopped fighting, throwing the man off balance as he struggled to support her weight. And then, planting both feet against the wall, she propelled herself backwards, her attacker's grip loosening as she broke free of him and sprinted for the entrance hall, heavy footfalls bearing down on her, gaining with every step as she burst across the threshold to a cacophony of gunfire.

* * *

Henry groaned, the crack of gunshots echoing endlessly around the building as he rolled off Felix's body and staggered to his feet.

'Scarlett!' he wheezed, severely winded, arm more than likely broken. 'Scarlett!' he tried again, hurrying unsteadily towards the source of the sound.

Finding it frustratingly slow progress picking a route through the roaming police officers, he finally reached the entrance hall to discover Linus's ruined body lying in a crimson puddle of his own making. Hobbling over to ensure that he was dead-dead, he caught something out of the corner of his eye, turning in horror to see Scarlett slumped against a set of railings, blood smeared across the floor beneath her.

'Scarlett!' he gasped, rushing over and attempting to shake her awake, her drowsy eyes eventually finding him.

* * *

'Henry,' she said, raising a bloody hand to his face.

'What happened? Where are you hurt?' he asked, searching her body for a wound.

There were calls nearby as the armed officers closed in.

'Put your arms around me,' he told her. 'I'm going to get you out of here.'

She smiled up at him weakly. 'You should go.'

The breeze on her face teasing through the open doors combined with the glass dome above them made it feel as though they'd already made it out together.

'I'm not going anywhere without you.' He went to scoop her up, one useless arm, the pain in his side and Scarlett's dead weight thwarting his efforts. 'You've got to help me here, Scarlett,' he said desperately. 'Come on.'

Gently taking his hand in hers, she met his eye. 'Do you remember what we said to each other that first night we met?' Her voice was growing noticeably weaker with every word.

'No. What did we say?' he asked distractedly as the breeze returned, this time laced with the hum of a helicopter as its searchlights wandered the iconic square beyond the doors.

'We said...' She clicked the handcuff into place around his wrist. '...Best... deceit... wins.'

Henry stared down in confusion at the metal chain now binding him to the railings, his expression only intensifying as he watched Scarlett get to her feet.

'For Frank,' she told him, Henry chuckling as she raised her radio to her lips. 'Delaney to Fields – suspect in custody – main entrance hall. Come get him.' Straightening up her ruined dress, she looked down at her bloody hands. 'Not mine,' she explained with a glance over at the deceased Swede before turning back to Henry. 'So, I suppose this is it.'

'I suppose it is.'

'I'd be lying if I said it's not been... *interesting*.'

'That it has,' he agreed, still smiling proudly. 'Tell me something: if she'd been real and *if* we'd caught her back at The Mountbatten... would you have gone through with it? Our arrangement?' he asked in genuine interest.

Scarlett considered her answer but then simply shrugged.

'Goodbye, Mr Devlin,' she said emotionlessly.

'Goodbye... Detective Delaney,' he replied, watching as she turned away from him and headed out into the night without looking back.

EPILOGUE

PART 1

It had taken Armed Response Officer Stuart Reid no more than ninety seconds to get back to the cerulean-blue walls of the entrance hall. The enormous glass dome overhead was still admiring the heavens. The broken body was still lying in a puddle of blood as its soul descended to hell. But there was no trace of the prisoner supposedly awaiting extraction – only a set of empty handcuffs hanging from a metal railing... still swaying in the breeze.

EPILOGUE

PART 2

Scarlett sat down at her workstation, realising for the first time in a long while she was actually craving a little normality. The morning sunshine pouring through the windows hit the tower of paperwork in her post tray, casting a long shadow across the office floor. Her eyes followed it all the way to Frank's empty desk, Griffiths' minions having already picked it clean in their haste to build a case against a man who wasn't even in the ground yet.

Not wanting to think about it, she spun in her chair as she deliberated where to start.

News of the ongoing manhunt, the removal of two dead bodies from the gallery and the catastrophic damage caused to a number of the nation's greatest treasures had made at least half of the morning's front pages, the rest focussing instead on images of dinner-suited celebrities fleeing the ill-fated gala event.

They'd been spoilt for choice.

Under the circumstances, the anonymous activist had been left with no other option but to come forward with far less pageantry than she was accustomed to, walking into Charing

Cross Police Station at 11 p.m. on a Friday night and announcing her big reveal to the assembly of drunks and the exhausted night staff on the front desk. News of her overdue arrest for the death of the homeless squatter had been relegated to pages three or four on what had been an unusually eventful night.

Scarlett had been only mildly surprised, at best, to learn of Henry's miraculous escape, security footage from the entrance hall corroborating her version of events.

She'd done her job.

She had put the man responsible for Frank's death in cuffs... and yet, a confusing part of her couldn't help but smile at the thought of him still out there somewhere.

Conversely, in an unfortunate turn of events, all of the cameras on the second floor of the gallery had been down for the evening to carry out 'routine maintenance', a twist that had failed to surprise her in the slightest.

Focussing on the job at hand, she reached for the topmost folder, hoping for a nice boring spreadsheet or similar to ease her back in... her heart skipping a beat on seeing Frank's clumsy handwriting straddling the lines, an internal mail label stapled to the front. It had caught her off-guard, feeling like a message from beyond the grave. Scarlett frowned as she looked back over at his empty desk, wondering what he might have sent her that he couldn't simply have walked across the room with himself.

Hands trembling, she opened it up, tears stinging her eyes on finding the last note he would ever write to her waiting at the front:

That post guy's a dick, isn't he?

She laughed out loud.

The boss is onto me. Didn't want them finding this.
Bin it. Burn it. Use it. It's up to you. It's
yours.
Frank.

She wiped her eyes and placed the note to one side as she flicked through the wedge of paperwork contained within: photographs, financial records, on the very first page a scribbled list of Henry's known associates:

Henry Devlin
Linus Bergman   *Boss*
Muscular Male (6'7"+/Eastern European)
Attractive Female (20's-30's/Blonde)

Amazed at the amount of information her mentor had managed to acquire in secret, she grabbed a pen to add her own annotations to this unexpected final case together:

Henry Devlin
Linus Bergman   *Boss* ←——— *Who is she???*
Muscular Male (6'7"+/Eastern European) *(Woman)*   *How high up does this go???*
Attractive Female (20's-30's/Blonde) *(Well-dressed/50's)*

And then, settling back into her seat, she picked up the rest of Frank's assorted documents and started to read...

EPILOGUE

PART 3

Less than half a mile away, deep within the musty halls of the Houses of Parliament, the First Secretary of State had just got off the phone with the Prime Minister when his assistant entered carrying a tray.

'Your nine o'clock is here, sir,' she said, her overworked superior still signing documents even as she swapped the tea tray for the armfuls of paperwork. 'Do you need a few minutes, sir?' she asked.

'No. No. Please send them in.' He huffed, moving on to another task in his spare thirty seconds.

'He'll see you now,' he heard her say as he picked up a two-hundred-page report that he almost certainly wasn't going to read, the door closing as his guest entered and took a seat.

'Ah, Alastair, you remembered,' said his visitor, pouring a cup of tea while he finished up.

'An eventful few days you've had,' he commented distractedly.

'Isn't it always?' – the clink of metal on china as the person across from him waited patiently.

'And this fiasco at the National Gallery?'

'We lost a few good people, but they have been replaced. All is in hand.'

'What about this activist situation?' he asked, sliding the sheaf of paperwork to one side to finally give his visitor his full attention. 'I trust you have a plan?'

'As I said, darling,' said the impeccably dressed woman as she took a sip of her drink. Setting the teacup back down on the saucer, Rebecca smiled at him: 'All is in hand.'

A LETTER FROM THE AUTHOR

Dear reader,

Firstly, a huge thanks for reading *Jackdaw*. I hope you loved spending time with Scarlett and Henry as much as I did while writing it. If you'd like to join other readers in hearing all about my new releases and bonus content, you can sign up for my newsletter:

www.stormpublishing.co/daniel-cole

If you enjoyed *Jackdaw* and could spare a few moments to leave a review, that would be hugely appreciated. Even the shortest review can make all the difference in encouraging a new reader to discover my work for the first time. Thanks in advance!

Jackdaw was my lockdown book – written as much for my own sanity as other's enjoyment. I wanted it to be a joyful slice of irreverent escapism (but with dead bodies) and I feel it's probably needed as much now as it was back when I wrote it. If you've made it this far then you'll probably be pleased to hear that I started work on the second *Jackdaw* book the moment I finished the first – more on that in due course...

So, thanks again for being part of this journey with me, and I hope you'll stay in touch – more news very soon!

Daniel Cole

ACKNOWLEDGMENTS

Considering that writing a book is a solitary endeavour, publishing a book takes a great amount of hard work from a considerable amount of great people.

As always, I'd like to thank my family – Sarah & Belles, Ma & Ossie, Melo, B, Roo & Cam and Bob, KP & Archie. My very good friend Rob Parsons also deserves a mention for his unwavering enthusiasm and support.

At C&W: probably the best agent in the business, Susan Armstrong, along with Kate Burton, César Castañeda Gámez, Matilda Ayris, Alexander Cochran and never forgetting Tracy England and Dorcas Rogers (my favourite person in the world to receive post from).

At Storm Publishing: a huge thank you to my new editor Kathryn Taussig for believing in this book, as well as Oliver Rhodes, Melissa Boyce-Hurd, Anna McKerrow, Alexandra Holmes, Laurence Cole and Rachel Rowlands.

Internationally, my friend and sounding board Tom Harmsen and the whole team at L.S. Amsterdam have been incredible from the very beginning of my career, and the exact same can be said of Glenn Tavennec and Camille Racine at Robert-Laffont.

Finally, and most importantly, a huge thanks to all the readers. I've been told on numerous occasions that 'there is no reader loyalty in crime fiction' but that's not what I've found from those of you I've had the pleasure of meeting – geeking out with me about the tangled timeline of the *Ragdoll* trilogy, the hidden meanings in the short story at the start of *Mimic*. Without you, I wouldn't be able to do this anymore – so thank you.

– Daniel Cole